Ship's log, stardate ████ ██.█, First Officer William T. Riker reporting . . .

Captain Picard remains missing, transported away by Q, who alone knows when and if the captain will return to the Enterprise. *In his absence, I have barely managed to preserve both the ship and the crew, despite the best efforts of the gaseous life-form known as the Calamarain.*

Our situation remains grave. To escape the Calamarain, we have taken refuge within the outer fringes of the galactic barrier. Although our shields, modified to absorb psychokinetic energy from the barrier itself, protect us from the worst of its effects, we cannot remain immune to the destructive force of the barrier indefinitely. Already the more telepathically sensitive members of the crew are experiencing discomfort and even pain from the excess of psychic energy composing the barrier and now surrounding the ship.

Due to damage inflicted by both the Calamarain and the barrier, our warp engines are inoperative, and we have lost artificial gravity in large portions of the saucer section, including the bridge. I can only hope that we can complete the most needed repairs before we are forced to exit the barrier and reenter our galaxy, perhaps to face the Calamarain again. . . .

STAR TREK
THE NEXT GENERATION®

THE
Q
CONTINUUM

BOOK THREE OF THREE

Q-STRIKE

GREG COX

POCKET BOOKS
New York   London   Toronto   Sydney   Tokyo   Singapore

This book is a work of fiction. Names, characters, places and incidents are products of the author's imagination or are used fictitiously. Any resemblance to actual events or locales or persons, living or dead, is entirely coincidental.

An *Original* Publication of POCKET BOOKS

POCKET BOOKS, a division of Simon & Schuster Inc.
1230 Avenue of the Americas, New York, NY 10020

STAR TREK is a Registered Trademark of Paramount Pictures.

A VIACOM COMPANY

This book is published by Pocket Books, a division of Simon & Schuster Inc., under exclusive license from Paramount Pictures.

ISBN: 0-671-01922-8

First Pocket Books printing September 1998

10 9 8 7 6 5 4 3 2 1

POCKET and colophon are registered trademarks of Simon & Schuster Inc.

Printed in the U.S.A.

ACKNOWLEDGMENTS

A voyage this long, three books in length, doesn't get traveled alone. I want to thank John Ordover for encouraging me to commit my first trilogy, then waiting patiently for the result. Also deserving of credit is Carol Greenburg, for carefully and fruitfully editing all three volumes.

Most of all, though, thanks to Karen Palinko for being the work's first and most rigorous reader, as well as for penning the various sinister ditties that became so much a part of 0's character. *The Q Continuum* is a lot more of a collaboration than it says on the cover.

Q-STRIKE

Prologue

LET THE ENDING BEGIN. Begin the end of eternity. . . .

It was finally happening. After endless, empty aeons of exile, his liberation was at hand. Balls were rolling. Gears were turning. A shiny, silver key had inserted itself into the eternal lock and now awaited only a flick of the wrist to open wide the gate and let him back into that vast array of suns and planets and moons and swirling nebulae from which he had so long been barred.

Turn the key. Set me free. Free me, me, me!

Time, too much time, had taken its toll on the orderly procession of his thoughts, but not his infamous ingenuity and enthusiasm. He could scarcely wait to make his mark on the galaxy once more, teach it the true meaning of terror and torment. He'd pick up right where he left off—before Q spoiled everything.

All due to Q, and Q and Q, too.

Already a tiny portion of himself, the merest sliver of his soul, had slipped into a crack in the wall, merging with one of the crude and contemptible creatures there, peering out through its obsolete ocular apparatus, while the rest of him snapped and scratched impatiently at the primordial partition that had defied him for longer than his scattered mind could begin to encompass, but not for very much longer. *He is the key. The key is me. The key to set me free.* He had seen things through the primitive eyes of his avatar within the wall, seen the child of Q and Q, the child of the future.

My future. Mine! he roared at the silent wall, while spider legs of extended thought capered and clawed and craved release. *Hear me Q? Hear me here . . . and now.* He probed for further cracks in the wall, shouted into the flickering fissures.

Now the end has begun. Begin the end of Q. . . .

Chapter One

Ship's log, stardate 500146.3, First Officer William T. Riker reporting.

Captain Picard remains missing, transported away by Q, who alone knows when and if the captain will return to the Enterprise. In his absence, I have barely managed to preserve both the ship and the crew, despite the best efforts of the gaseous life-form known as the Calamarain.

Our situation remains grave. To escape the Calamarain, we have taken refuge within the outer fringes of the galactic barrier. Although our shields, modified to absorb psychokinetic energy from the barrier itself, protect us from the worst of its effects, we cannot remain immune to the destructive force of the barrier indefinitely. Already the more telepathically sensitive members of the crew are experiencing discomfort and even pain from the excess of psychic energy composing the barrier and now surrounding the ship.

Due to damage inflicted by both the Calamarain and the barrier, our warp engines are inoperative, and we have lost artificial gravity in large portions of the saucer section, including the bridge. I can only hope that we can complete the most needed repairs before we are forced to exit the barrier and reenter our galaxy, perhaps to face the Calamarain again.

LIEUTENANT BAETA LEYORO's pain-racked cry echoed throughout the bridge. If not for the lack of gravity, she would have surely collapsed to the hard duranium floor; instead the stricken security officer levitated in midair, her body doubled over in agony as the psychic flux of the barrier set her synapses on fire. A plait of black hair rose from her scalp, swaying like a cobra about to strike. A heart-wrenching whimper escaped her lips, squeezing out from between tightly clenched teeth.

Riker blamed himself. *I should have sent her to sickbay immediately, the moment I realized that her augmented nervous system made her uniquely vulnerable to the barrier.* Instead he had waited until it was too late, with the result that she had succumbed to her seizure halfway between her post and the turbolift. But now was no time to second-guess himself. "Beam

4

her directly to sickbay," he ordered, then slapped the comm badge on his chest. "Riker to Dr. Crusher. Lieutenant Leyoro requires emergency care. Expect her at once."

Even as he warned Beverly of the incoming patient, a shimmering silver glow enveloped the floating, fetal form of Leyoro. *Thank heavens the transporters are still working,* Riker thought, relieved that Leyoro could benefit from that technology at least, even if their jury-rigged deflectors, experimentally altered by Lieutenant Barclay and Data, had not been enough to protect her. The scintillating twinkle of the transporter effect shone even brighter amid the dimly lit bridge, where only flashing red-alert signals provided any illumination at all. Even the blue tracking lights that routinely ran along the floor of the bridge had been snuffed out by the abuse the *Enterprise* had sustained over the last several hours.

Riker's own head throbbed in sympathy with Leyoro; he suspected that his long-standing telepathic bond with Deanna had increased his sensitivity as well, weakening his brain's defenses against the psychic barrage. Swollen veins pounded beneath his temples and brow, although the ache was not yet fierce enough to make him abandon his post. *My brain will have to explode first,* he vowed defiantly, his jaw set squarely beneath his black beard. He nodded grimly as Leyoro vanished in a cascade of sparks that swiftly evaporated before his eyes.

"Got her," Beverly's voice confirmed via his comm badge. "Crusher out."

Convinced that Leyoro's fate now rested in the capable hands of the ship's medical officer, Riker leaned forward in the captain's chair and turned his attention to other pressing matters. A brilliant violet glow emanated from the forward viewscreen, catching his eye. Overloaded by the immeasurable radiance of the galactic barrier, the screen had initially gone dead upon their entry into the mysterious wall of energy. Now the screen flared back to life, but only to show a brighter form of blankness, filled from top to bottom by an undifferentiated display of pure luminosity. The glare from the screen pierced his eyes. "Someone dim the main viewer," he instructed gruffly.

"Affirmative, Commander," Data responded. Seated at Ops, the gold-skinned android manipulated the controls at his station. Scorch marks along the console's polished metal casing testified to the rigors of their recent battle against the Calamarain, as did numerous other scars all around the bridge. A fragment of torn polyduranide sheeting drifted past Riker's face, free from the downward pull of gravity, and he batted it away with a wave of his hand. On the screen, the phosphorescent effulgence of the galactic barrier faded to a more subdued but equally uninformative gleam. "Is that acceptable, Commander?" Data inquired calmly.

"That will do, Mr. Data," Riker said. The sooner they put the barrier behind them, the better. He tapped his comm badge again. "Riker to La Forge. What's our warp status?"

Geordi's voice answered him from Engineering,

sounding more than a little harried. "We've patched up the plasma-injection system, but the warp-field coils in the starboard nacelle still need a lot of work. We're talking another hour at least."

"Understood," Riker acknowledged. There was no need to urge La Forge to hurry; the engineering chief knew full well how shaky their shields were compared with the awesome power of the barrier. *The devil of it is,* Riker thought, *we don't even know* why *the Calamarain attacked us in the first place, even though it obviously had something to do with the barrier.* Were the gaseous entities still waiting for the *Enterprise* outside the wall? Riker didn't want to find out until he knew the ship could make a quick escape at warp speed. *With any luck, the Calamarain will have given us up for dead the moment we flew into the barrier.*

"I certainly hope you're not planning to sit here forever," said a voice to his left, belonging to a tall, auburn-haired woman who had usurped Deanna's seat in the command area. Her tone could be described as patronizing at best, contemptuous at worst. "As impressive and mystifying as our surroundings must appear to creatures of your ilk, I'm afraid I grew accustomed to such spectacles several millennia ago." She raised an impeccably manicured hand to her mouth in an only partially successful attempt to stifle a yawn. "Can't you *do* something just to liven things up a bit?"

The woman in question, balancing a sleepy toddler upon her knee, was reportedly Q's wife and the mother of his child, two propositions that frankly boggled Riker's mind whenever he cared to think of them, which definitely wasn't now. "If we're not sufficiently entertaining for you, you're more than welcome to leave," he informed her. Ever since she had refused to use her Q-like omnipotence to rescue the *Enterprise* from its current predicament, let alone enlighten him as to what Q had done with Captain Picard, he had resolved not to let either her or her child distract him from his duty.

"Don't be ridiculous," she said haughtily. The pips on the collar of her fake Starfleet uniform identified her (inaccurately) as a five-star admiral. *Typical,* Riker thought; from what he had seen so far, the female Q's ego was easily a match for her husband's. "I told you before, I intend to find out what precisely my esteemed spouse and partner finds so intriguing about this primitive vessel, no matter how excruciatingly tedious that task proves to be. Besides," she added, smiling indulgently at her small son, clad in equally counterfeit Starfleet attire, "little q enjoys your aboriginal antics."

"Ant-ticks!" q burbled happily. He waved a pudgy little hand, and a parade of tiny insects suddenly appeared on the floor of the command area, marching single file past the elevated captain's chair and across the top of Riker's gravity boots. Despite his determination to ignore Q's visiting relations as much as possible, the first officer had to suppress a shudder at this reminder of the seemingly harmless infant's abilities. Such amazing power in the hands of a child was enough to send a chill down a Vulcan's spine. *Like the original Q isn't immature enough,* he thought.

Naturally, q's mother was charmed by her offspring's naive misunderstanding. "Oh, isn't that adorable?" she said. Propelled by the motion of their miniature limbs, the insects began to lift off from the floor, adding to the ash and debris in the air. Fortunately, the female Q scooped up the floating bugs with a net she materialized from nowhere, then consigned both the net and its chittering contents to oblivion. "I'm sorry, dearest," she explained to the child, patting him on the head, "but our present surroundings are barbaric enough without any additional infestations."

Baby q objected strenuously to the sudden disappearance of his playthings. He scrunched up his face and let out an earsplitting squall while simultaneously kicking his little legs. His tantrum shook the entire bridge, which lurched from side to side, nearly throwing Riker out of his chair. Behind him, he heard Ensign Sondra Berglund, who had replaced Leyoro at tactical, stumble awkwardly in her heavy magnetic boots. "That's enough," he barked at the female Q. "He's your child. Do something about him."

To his surprise, the woman actually looked abashed, as if she feared the child's behavior reflected poorly on her parenting skills. "Now, now," she cooed to q in a soothing tone, "you can play with your funny arthropods another time." Accompanied by a brief flash of white light, an enticing *jumja* treat appeared in q's balled-up fist. Not surprisingly, the delectable glop-on-a-stick successfully distracted q, who abandoned his uproar in favor of sucking energetically on the sugary confection. "There," his mother said approvingly. "Isn't that better?"

Although the candy calmed the child, it also made something of a mess. Riker already spotted sticky handprints all over Troi's customary seat. Deanna herself was currently in sickbay, under the care of Dr. Crusher. He allowed himself a moment of concern regarding Deanna's safety, praying that the doctor's efforts had protected Deanna, with her empathic sensitivity, from the barrier. *Be well,* imzadi, he thought.

Deanna's Betazoid gifts rendered her unusually susceptible to the concentrated psionic energy surrounding the ship, as were their civilian passengers: Professor Lem Faal of Betazed, and his two children. As full telepaths, the Faal family were probably more at risk than anyone else aboard the *Enterprise.* For that reason, he had ordered all three Betazoids, along with Deanna, to sickbay before they even entered the barrier. He'd hoped that precaution would be enough to keep their guests safe, but, insanely, Faal had caused a disturbance in sickbay, attacking Deanna and escaping with his son. Even now, security was searching for the missing patients.

I knew Faal was upset about his experiment being called off due to the unexpected attack of the Calamarain, but I never expected him to resort to violence. Thank heavens, Deanna wasn't seriously harmed,

10

Riker thought, *or I'd be tempted to beam him to the Calamarain myself.*

At tactical, Ensign Berglund had regained her footing. "Shield strength is fluctuating, Commander," she reported, "by variances of twenty percent and more." Her eyes never left the display panel. "I'm doing my best to stabilize the deflectors, but it's not working."

Riker glanced quickly at Lieutenant Reginald Barclay, now positioned at the secondary aft science station. It had been Barclay's idea to divert telekinetic energy from the barrier to the ship's shields by way of the organic bio-neural gel packs in the *Enterprise*'s computer system, a hastily improvised tactic that had proven successful . . . so far.

"The gel packs are still absorbing energy from the barrier," Barclay assured Riker, gulping nervously, "but it's hard to quantify. I had to reroute the monitoring program to science two after the engineering station exploded." He cast a wary look at the charred remains of the main engineering console, only a few stations away. "The gel packs were never intended to serve as batteries for psychic energy, so there are no established parameters to judge their efficiency."

"This is correct, Commander," Data confirmed. He had carefully evaluated Barclay's preliminary findings earlier, as had Geordi La Forge. "Prolonged exposure to the barrier is causing a significant percentage of bio-neural circuitry to incinerate. At present, energy absorption exceeds extinction by a rate of approximately forty-seven-point-three-four percent, averaged over the duration of our stay in the barrier, but at any given moment the quantity of energy available to the deflector array can vary dramatically, just as Ensign Berglund reports."

Riker nodded. "Let me know the instant the scale tips the other way. Ensign Clarze," he instructed the young Deltan crewman at the conn, "set a course that takes us straight out of the barrier in the shortest possible time. When we go, I want to leave here in a hurry."

"Yes, sir," Clarze said. Riker had been impressed by the way the inexperienced ensign had kept his cool during this crisis, coping with both the hostile activities of the Calamarain as well as the always unsettling caprices of Q and his kin. He resolved to make a note of this the next time he and Deanna completed their personnel evaluation reports, assuming any of them came out of this alive. He gazed at the lambent glow of the main viewer. Somewhere beyond that incandescent haze, the Milky Way waited for them, as did, perhaps, an angry and homicidal mass of sentient plasma.

Where are the Calamarain? Riker brooded. *And, just as importantly, where is Captain Picard?*

Chapter Two

Six hundred thousand years ago:

"WHAT HAVE YOU DONE??"

The booming voice came without warning, reverberating through space-time and startling five celestial figures, in addition to two more who looked on anonymously from a slightly different phase of reality. Jean-Luc Picard, late of the *Starship Enterprise,* stood amid the starry vastness of space, accompanied by Q, his self-appointed guide on this forced excursion through galactic prehistory, and watched, as through a one-way mirror, as Q's younger self faced the consequences of his fateful alliance with the malicious cosmic entity who called himself 0, as well as with 0's trio of malevolent cronies.

Like 0 and the others, Picard presently existed on a sublimely magnified scale, such that stars and planets were no more than ball-sized spheres of matter and burning gas in comparison. His gaze encompassed parsecs of open space, and yet that stern and unforgiving voice seemed even larger than himself. Picard cast a speculative glance at Q, then lifted his eyes heavenward. "The Q Continuum, I presume?"

"Just so," Q affirmed. Clad in the latest Starfleet uniform, he gestured toward his younger self, standing a few light-years away. More than a hint of melancholy tinged his ordinarily sarcastic voice. "In truth, I wasn't too surprised, even then. I could hardly expect the Continuum to overlook the small matter of a premature supernova, not to mention the total destruction of a major spacefaring civilization."

Still saddened by the tragedy, Picard looked back over his shoulder at the lifeless void that was all that remained of the mighty Tkon Empire, destroyed by 0 in a fit of pique after his underlings failed to subvert its civilization. Where once a sophisticated and admirable people, numbering in the trillions, had spread their culture throughout their solar system and beyond, achieving heights of technological wizardry exceeding those of the Federation, the detonation of their sun, brought on abruptly by 0's supernatural puissance, had extinguished nearly every trace of their existence, leaving only a few scattered ruins on distant outposts to mark their passing. Picard could still feel the relentless tug of the black hole the Tkon's sun had become. Invisible to his naked eye, even in this transfigured state, the dense gravitational vortex pulled on him like an undertow, so that Picard found himself leaning forward to counter its attractive force. *What was done to the Tkon,* he mused, *was a crime of interplanetary proportions.*

Now, it seemed, as detective Dixon Hill might put it, the time had come to face the music. . . .

"I'm s-sorry," the younger Q stammered, staring up at the source of the bodiless voice. His fine attire, which had resembled that of an eighteenth-century European dandy, several hundred millennia ahead of its time, transformed at once into a coarse and uncomfortable sackcloth robe. "I never meant for this to happen."

In fact, Picard recalled, the young Q had played little part in the annihilation of the Tkon, had even attempted to stop 0 once he realized what the other was up to, but to no avail. At worst, he had been only an unwilling accessory to genocide, not that this seemed to have spared Q's conscience much. After all, if not for Q's recklessness and gullibility, 0 and his unholy associates would have never gained entry to this reality in the first place. Q had promised to take responsibility for 0 when he rescued the mysterious wayfarer from some extradimensional wasteland. 0 in turn had welcomed three lesser entities into Q's reality, making Q responsible by extension for the depredations of these sinister beings, who now faced judgment beside Q and their ruthless sponsor. Picard wondered how much the other Q would hold the young Q to his original promise.

"WHAT HAS BEEN DONE CANNOT BE UN-DONE."

Young Q flinched beneath every syllable, just as his older counterpart winced in sympathy. The mature Q was clearly troubled by this peek at his ignominious youth, but made no effort to intervene in what transpired. Even the Q, Picard observed with a certain relief, drew the line when it came to tampering with the past; not even the gods could erase yesterday, no matter how much they might want to. *Q obviously survived this occasion,* he inferred, *or else he would have never been able to torment me in the future.* He shook his head. *Lucky me.*

"It all started out as a game," young Q tried to explain, pleading for understanding with outstretched hands, "a simple test of their resourcefulness. . . ."

"That's enough, boy," 0 interrupted harshly. Unlike Q, he saw no need to discard his anachronistic finery. His stylish velvet suit, olive green in hue, looked even more elegant and ostentatious next to Q's penitent gray robe. The buckles on his polished black shoes shone like silver, while one ruffled sleeve, Picard noted, was scorched from when he had thrust his merciless hand into the heart of the Tkon's murdered sun. "We've no need to justify ourselves to their sort."

"But it's the Continuum," Q pointed out, while his older self mouthed the very same words. This incident was obviously imprinted deeply in the later Q's memory. "They've come for us. They know what we've done."

"Stiffen your spine, I say, and shut your mouth." 0 limped across the vacuum and rested a meaty hand upon Q's shoulder. His three henchmen, whom Q knew as Gorgan, (*), and The One, clustered behind him, letting their leader face the judgment of the Continuum. "We're all in this together, Q. There's no backing out now."

"YOU," the stentorian voice targeted 0, sounding not unlike Picard's own resonant timbre. "YOU AND YOUR FAMILIARS DO NOT BELONG HERE. YOU MUST BE CAST OUT FOR ALL TIME."

"I've heard that before," 0 said with a chuckle, then glared at the sky with icy blue eyes. He placed his hands on his hips and thrust out his wide chin. His raspy voice held not a note of regret or repentance. "How dare you judge any of us, you pontificating pests? What do you know of the noble art of testing developing species, forcing them to prove their potential and worthiness to survive? Of the guile and glory of pushing lesser life-forms to their ultimate limits and beyond? What have you ever done that can match what we have accomplished, you cautious Continuum? We're better than the lot of you!"

"0!" young Q whispered frantically to his former role model and mentor. Once 0's insolent disregard for the authority of the Continuum had thrilled and delighted the callow superbeing, but that was before 0 had gotten him into real trouble. Before Tkon. Picard could only imagine how tempted the elder Q must have been to warn his younger self of impending events.

"Don't hide behind these sonorous sound effects,"

0 challenged the bodiless voice. "Face us in person, preternatural deity to preternatural deity, if you've got the guts and gumption."

"YOU ARE NOT WORTHY TO LOOK UPON THE Q. YOU SHALL BE BANISHED FROM THIS REALM."

"Do your worst," 0 dared the Continuum. Taking a deep breath, he seemed to call upon his full strength, just as he had when he froze the Coulalakritous into a solid mass. A flickering aura formed around his humanoid guise, along with a vague impression of another, less substantial form superimposed upon his anthropomorphic persona.

Once before, another half a million years in the past, Picard had beheld this shadowy other aspect of 0. As then, the images were indistinct and almost subliminal in nature, and all the more ominous for their tantalizing and suggestive elusiveness. Try though he did to discern the actual shape of 0's alter ego, Picard caught only transitory glimpses of whipping tendrils that extended beyond the boundaries of 0's human form like the unfurled wings of some alien raptor. *That which is only half-seen is all the more troubling to the imagination,* he reflected; although Picard had often conversed comfortably with alien beings who varied dramatically from the humanoid model, what he spied of 0's other form sent a chill through his body. *Or maybe it is just the implication of deliberate deception that is so unnerving.* What other secrets might 0 be hiding?

Whatever his shape or origins, 0 remained a force

to be reckoned with. Even separated from the scene by one degree of existence, Picard felt the power radiating from 0, stinging his exposed face and hands like a freezing wind. "Stand fast," he called out to Q and the others, his gravelly voice rising to a thunderous roar. "These censorious charlatans don't know whom they're dealing with! If we stick together, we can withstand any foe."

But the cumulative force of the Continuum struck like disruptor fire from a Romulan warbird, dispersing 0's ectoplasmic tentacles and sending him staggering backward into Gorgan and The One. Gorgan's voluminous robes and flowing white locks, suffused as ever by a faint greenish aura, flapped like hung laundry in a hurricane while The One's gleaming metal armor protected him only slightly better. His stern and bearded visage blinked in the face of the attack, the flesh of his face pulled tightly against the skull beneath. Hovering above their heads, the glowing crimson sphere that was (*) was stretched into a faint, translucent oval by the concussive force directed against them. "Do your worst!" 0 bellowed, ribbons of smoke rising from his scared garments. "I'll not surrender, never again!" Pressing forward, dragging his lame left leg behind him, he clenched his fists and hurled blasts of pyrotechnic energy at his unseen foes. Blazing fireballs arced like meteors across the heavens, exploding into scarlet bursts of light and heat so bright that Picard was forced to look away.

"Here," the Q beside him said, thrusting a tinted

eyepiece, similar in style to Geordi La Forge's old VISOR, into Picard's open hand. "I wouldn't want you to miss anything."

Picard took the lenses without comment. Not for the first time, he wondered what Q's purpose was in showing all this to him. *What have these fantastically ancient events to do with my own life and times?*

If 0's fiery assault had any effect on the Continuum, Picard saw no sign of it. 0 was powerful, no doubt, but he was only one where the Continuum represented the collective might of who knew how many. Of his lackeys, only The One rose to his defense. "Bow not to false gods!" He declared, flinging one thunderbolt after another after 0's fireballs. His austere, patriarchal features could've been carved from the hardest Cardassian granite; even His long, forbidding beard was stiff and unyielding. "Feel the sting of My Righteous Fury."

Despite the aid of The One, 0 began to lose ground. Battered by the irresistible force of the Continuum, the murderer of the Tkon Empire was forced to retreat once more, spewing a trail of blinding conflagrations behind him. Young Q felt the wrath of the Continuum as well. He tumbled head over heels, nearly rolling away from 0 and the others before 0 reached out and grabbed on to Q's forearm, digging his fingers into Q's metaphysical flesh. "I'll never yield, never I say," the stranger gasped, squinting his eyes against the impact of the Continuum's offensive, "but even the most courageous combatant knows when to retreat. Time to flee to fight again, Q. Get us away from here!"

"What?" The beleaguered young godling looked uncertain. Wringing his hands nervously, he looked back and forth between 0 and the direction from which the Q's attack emerged. *Can he see his fellow Q?* Picard wondered. *Does he know too well how angry they must be?* The Continuum had punished Q before, he recalled, for follies far less consequential than this. "I don't know what to do," the youth said. "I'm not sure."

"Don't run, you fool," the later Q whispered to his young self, who, alas, could not hear the voice of experience speaking. "You're only making it worse."

"Run!" 0 urged him. He tossed away his stylish brown wig, exposing his own reddish hair, tied in the back. His black silk cravat had come undone, dangling loosely around his neck. "We have to flee, Q, now. Or are you prepared to take the blame for what happened to the late, lamented Tkon Empire?" His crippled leg dragged behind him, reminding Picard that 0 was unable to travel faster than light without Q's assistance. "Are you ready to pay for my crimes?"

"But it wasn't my fault," Q whimpered. His face was contorted by fear and distress. Tears leaked from his eyes. "Not all of it, not really."

"Are you so sure of that?" 0 asked, showing him no mercy. "Are you certain that the high-and-mighty Q Continuum will see things the same way? From what I've seen so far, they're not the forgiving type." A devilish grin stretched across his broad, ruddy face. "They'll deal with you most harshly of all, I'll wager."

"YOU CANNOT OVERCOME US," the voice of the Continuum intoned. "SUBMIT TO BANISHMENT OR RISK DESTRUCTION."

"Don't do it," the older Q said, shaking his head mournfully.

"Now's the time," 0 spat through clenched teeth. "I can't hold them off any longer."

He's going to panic, Picard realized, only a heartbeat before the young Q let out an inarticulate howl and swept he, 0, and the rest of their infamous party away in a flash of white light. Picard found himself alone in deep space except for the continuing presence of the Q he was accustomed to. The rest of the Continuum remained invisible to his senses.

"You don't need to say anything, Picard," his companion said. "I know when I've made an ass of myself."

> *"Got a fine young maid,*
> *Her dowry's paid,*
> *My fortunes made,*
> *My plans are laid,*
> *I'll sit awhile in shade. . . ."*

Young Q shook his head in disbelief. 0 sounded altogether too pleased with himself for someone who had called down the judgment of the Continuum upon them all. How could he sing at a time like this?

I'm a fugitive, he realized, *and an immortal one. My life is over and it won't ever end.*

Dejected, he sat upon the ground, his knees drawn up beneath his chin. The ground itself consisted of solid dilithium, its crystalline surface worn smooth by the ceaseless passage of the dense metallic liquid that enveloped Q and his partners in crime. The metallic sea, which covered the entire surface of the polished, planet-sized mass of dilithium, extended for hundreds of thousands of kilometers overhead before eventually segueing into an even vaster expanse of swirling helium and hydrogen vapors blown by hurricane-force winds exceeding five hundred kilometers an hour. The buried core of this gas giant, upon which they now resided, located in what would someday be called the Detrian system, had been one of his favorite hiding places when he was a child; it was like being on the yolk of an enormous eye, shielded from prying eyes by several layers of liquid and gaseous shell. He had told no one about it, not even 0, but never had he dreamed that he would someday use it to hide out from justice. *This isn't the way it was supposed to happen,* he grieved.

"Maybe we should turn ourselves in," he suggested, looking up from the polished surface of the core. He could no longer bear to stare at his own guilty reflection. "Perhaps the Continuum will show mercy if we surrender freely."

0 did not respond to his suggestion, but instead kept on skating and singing, missing only a beat or two in the melody, as the lyrics took a peculiar turn:

Greg Cox

"Woe to those who are afraid,
I've never looked kindly upon being betrayed. . . ."

Why is he looking at me? Q thought nervously. 0 was just singing, that's all. "You don't know the Continuum like I do," he insisted. "They can actually be quite reasonable on occasion. I'm sure if we explain ourselves, show them how matters simply got out of hand, we could expect some leniency."

"I venture I'd be quite dismayed. . . ."

Several meters away, skating blithely over the slick crystal plane, 0 laughed out loud at the end of his song. He retied his unfurled cravat as he coasted over the solid dilithium. "You've a lot to learn about being a rebel, my naive young friend. Rule Number One: Never surrender. Isn't that right, fellows?"

The other entities clustered nearby. The One had formed Himself an impressive-looking dilithium throne in which He sat rather too regally, Q thought, for One who had so recently been forced to flee for His liberty. Gorgan looked significantly more agitated, pacing back and forth behind The One's throne, the hem of his amethyst robe brushing the ground. His immaterial form shimmered, looking slightly less solid than a hologram. Silent as ever, (*) hovered in the flowing currents of the metal sea, casting a bloodred radiance over the entire scene.

"Isn't that right?" 0 repeated loudly, a dangerous edge in his voice. Bubbles streamed from his lips,

24

ascending toward the gaseous atmosphere far, far above.

"Oh yes, certainly," Gorgan piped up unctuously. As always, his voice had a peculiarly unnatural echo, as if it was generated artificially by a being whose lips and lungs were merely simulcra of the real things. "No surrender at all," he insisted.

The One sat immobile upon His throne, His upper limbs resting upon sculpted armrests. His golden plate armor, medieval in style, showed no sign of rust or corrosion, despite the liquid nature of this undersea hiding place. "The final battle is not yet fought. My Might will endure unto the last."

"That's more like it," 0 said gruffly, sliding toward 0. "An occasional reversal is to be expected when you're living boldly. I warned you there'd be danger, Q. That's the price you pay for taking chances."

They were not entirely alone. Eyeless, segmented, cylindrical life-forms, evolved to survive the incredible pressure of the gas giant's lower depths, swam through the molten dilithium, instinctively giving 0 and the others a wide berth. *They're smarter than I was,* Q thought, envying the primitive creatures. "Is that what we're doing?" he asked. "Living boldly? Being rebels?" He stared glumly at the horizon, where the solid dilithium met the aqueous sky, refusing to look at 0. "So why do I feel like some wretched criminal on the run?"

0 glared down at him. "All right then, let's have this out here and now. What are you so morose about? The Tkon? Ephemeral creatures whom the universe

will never miss. A million years from now? They'll be completely forgotten, while we go on forever. They should be thankful they attracted our attention. At least we'll remember the fine sport they provided. That's a better legacy than most such mortals can expect."

"Sport?" Q jumped to his feet, practically shouting in 0's face. Blind eels, their sinuous bodies covered by iridescent scales, swam away in alarm. "They didn't stand a chance. It wasn't fair."

"What does fair have to do with it?" 0 held his ground. "Of course the outcome is always the same. They're just animals after all. Crude, corporeal creations fit only to provide us with a bit of diversion. It's the *style* with which such savage species are dispatched that matters, Q. You have to learn to appreciate the elegance of extinction, the deft and delicate dance of destruction."

"You blew up their sun! You call that delicate?" The angry words came gushing out of him in a flood of bubbles. He couldn't have held the accusations back if he wanted to. "I saw you, 0. I was there. You weren't concerned with style. You were just angry at the Tkon because they beat Gorgan and the others at their own morbid little games. They beat *you*—and you killed them for it."

"They were creatures!" 0 spat angrily. "Why can't you understand that? Creatures like that *can't* beat beings like us. It's impossible by definition." He sneered scornfully at Q. "Don't waste my time crying over the poor, unfortunate Tkon. I know what your real problem is. You're afraid. For the first time in your puerile, immature existence, you've stepped outside the boundaries set by that hidebound Continuum of yours, and now you want to go scurrying back in search of forgiveness." He made a clucking sound with his tongue. "I thought you were braver than that, but maybe you're just another timid little Q after all."

"That's not true," Q shot back, but with less certainty than with which he had spoken for the Tkon.

"Isn't it?" 0 asked. "Where's the Q who pulled me through the Guardian of Forever, and the devil with the consequences? I thought you wanted to be different from your conservative brethren. I thought you wanted to make your mark on the multiverse, maybe even give the rest of the Continuum a much-needed jolt or two. I thought you wanted adventure and excitement and glory."

"I did. I do. I . . . I . . ." He didn't know what he wanted anymore.

"That's not what it looks like to me. One little scolding from the other Q and suddenly all your revolutionary zeal and ambition collapses like a chronal wave in a transtemporal field." Without warning, 0 shoved Q hard enough to knock the younger entity off his feet. Q landed with a bump onto the ground, his flailing limbs churning up the viscous fluid surrounding him, creating short-lived eddies in the flowing dilithium. "See," his assailant taunted, "a little pressure and you fall right over. You can't even stand up for your own convictions."

Is that true? Q wondered, sprawled upon the glossy surface of the core. *Am I merely afraid of getting caught?* He was afraid of what the Continuum might do certainly, and with good reason, but was that all he felt at this moment? Maybe 0 was right and wrong at the same time, at least where Q was concerned. *This is absurd,* he thought angrily, too disgusted by himself and this entire situation to even bother climbing to his feet again. *I'm a Q. I know all there is to know. So how come I can't even figure myself out?*

"What I didn't realize, in the greenness of my youth," the later Q said from a few meters (and one plane of reality) away, "was that I had far more options than simply 0 or the Continuum. There were an infinite number of ways I could amuse myself, and scandalize my fellow Q, without throwing my lot in with 0 and his motley band." A deep-dwelling eel, taking a long detour around the five fugitives, passed through the older Q's torso as though he wasn't there. "As you must have noticed, *mon capitaine,* I've hardly required assistance to make your humdrum life more interesting."

Picard decided to let that remark pass. He'd exchanged enough repartee with Q to last him a lifetime. He was rather more interested in finding out what happened next to the younger version of Q, who seemed to be digging himself a deeper and deeper hole with each new development. Although there was little love lost between himself and the usual Q, Picard could not help sympathizing with the star-crossed youth at 0's feet. He knew too well how easily an inexperienced, impetuous novice could get in over his head, wincing inwardly as he recalled that long ago incident at the Academy when his headstrong folly had nearly cost him his Starfleet career before it had truly begun. *Too bad there's no Boothby to counsel young Q at this crucial crossroads,* he reflected, *only 0 and his unsavory compatriots.*

"You're looking unusually pensive, Jean-Luc, even for you." Q plucked a couple of unsuspecting eels from the adjacent reality and began tying them into knots, much like a traditional children's performer turning balloons into animals. An instant later, he presented Picard with a tangle of alien organisms twisted into a miniature replica of the *Enterprise.* "Hit a nerve, have we?"

Picard scowled, unhappy to be reminded that his ship was facing danger without him. The Calamarain had only just come within range of Data's sensors when Q snatched him away from the bridge. Although he had complete confidence in Will Riker to command the *Enterprise* in his absence, he found it deeply disturbing not to know how his ship was faring several hundred thousand years from now. "Are you quite sure that you are the more mature Q?" he said acidly as he took the quivering memento from his guide. As gently as possible, Picard tried to extricate the abused eels from their forced contortions. It was like trying to untangle a plate of writhing *gagh.*

"Touché, Jean-Luc," Q said, looking pleased to have provoked a response from Picard, "but do not confuse adult whimsy and irreverence with juvenile misbehavior." He gestured toward his younger incarnation, awash in difficulties and confusion. *"I* would never get into such an embarrassing fix."

"Except you did," Picard pointed out. Successfully liberating the knotted eels from each other, he released them to swim away as quickly as their long, segmented bodies could carry them. He wondered if they would ever find their way to back to their own phase of existence. "That troubled boy is you."

"Please!" Q rolled his eyes in exasperation. "Is an oak tree the same as an acorn? Is a silicon nodule no different than a Mother Horta? He is then. I am now." He shrugged his shoulders. "Granted, at the moment now *is* then, but that's another matter altogether."

Picard endured a familiar frustration. *Why do I even try conversing with him?* He contemplated the younger Q once more. If anything, Q had gotten even more vexing and impossible to deal with over the intervening aeons.

Intent upon their own ongoing drama, neither young Q, nor the bad company into which he had fallen, had noticed the abrupt disappearance of two eels from the murky ocean enclosing the planet's solid core. Instead 0 focused all his formidable personality upon the fallen form of Q. "Well?" he demanded. "What's it going to be? Are you going sit there, stewing in childish self-pity and remorse, or are you ready to take on the Continuum and anyone else who tries to stop you from fulfilling your true potential?

Think carefully, Q. Your destiny depends on what you do next."

Before the young entity could answer, an intense white flare illuminated the metal sea, overpowering (*)'s incarnadine glow. For an instant, the nocturnal depths of the gas giant were suffused with the brightness of a sunny afternoon. "It's the Continuum!" Q shouted, his voice torn between alarm and relief. "They've found us!"

Chapter Three

THE READINGS ON HER MEDICAL TRICORDER shocked Dr. Beverly Crusher. As she scanned Lieutenant Leyoro's brain with the handheld peripheral sensor, the display screen on the tricorder reported alarming levels of bio-neural energy. The stricken security officer's cerebral cortex was being drowned in neurotransmitters, accelerating her synaptic activity at a dangerous rate. *She can't survive much more of this,* Crusher realized.

Leyoro's unconscious body had been beamed directly onto the primary biobed from the bridge. A surgical support frame was clamped over her torso to provide cardiovascular support and even emergency defibrillation if necessary. Crusher kept a close eye on her patient's vital signs and basic metabolic functions, as reported on the monitor mounted above the bed. To her distress, the heightened electrical activity within Leyoro's brain was causing inflammation and spasms all along her artificially augmented nervous system. Leyoro's limbs twitched uncontrollably until Crusher programmed the SSF to provide a steady intravenous infusion of benzocyatzine to inhibit the muscular contractions. Thankfully, the equipment did not require gravity to function effectively. The muscular relaxant merely took care of one symptom, though; treating the root cause of her condition was going to be a lot trickier.

I'm dealing with too many unknowns here, Crusher thought, frustrated. There was little reliable documentation on the telepathic shock sometimes induced by the galactic barrier, primarily because all attempts to cross the barrier had been explicitly banned for close to a century because of that very danger. Furthermore, there was too much she didn't know about the specific neurological modifications the Angosian military scientists had performed on Leyoro during the Tarsian War. Leyoro's medical records were on file, as were the examinations Crusher had performed years ago on Roga Danar, another victim of Angosian biochemical tampering, but that hardly prepared her to treat this unexpected interaction between the barrier's psychic energies and Leyoro's heightened neurology. This was a one-of-a-kind medical emergency.

Fortunately, sickbay had calmed some now that the battle with the Calamarain was over for the time being. Most of the casualties from that conflict had been treated and discharged already, except for a few of the more serious cases which were currently under the watchful care of the EMH. Crusher shook her head in disbelief; she never thought she'd be grateful for having that supercilious hologram around. Maybe he had his uses after all, even if his bedside manner still left a lot to be desired. Too bad, though, that Selar had transferred to the *Excalibur*. Vulcans were supposed to be immune to the barrier's effects.

She glanced over quickly at the adjacent biobed, where Deanna Troi rested in an artificially induced coma, a set of cortical stimulators blinking upon the Betazoid officer's forehead. Crusher had placed Troi in a coma herself, lowering her brain activity, in hopes of protecting the empathic counselor from the same telepathic overload that was killing Leyoro. So far, judging from the display above Troi's biobed, it seemed to be working; Deanna's synaptic levels were well within the acceptable range for an adult Betazoid of her age and telepathic ability, even though her metabolism was only gradually recovering from the overdose of polyadrenaline she had received from Lem Faal's hypospray.

I'm still shocked by what he did, she thought, remembering the scientist's startling attack on Deanna. *I knew he was agitated about his experiment, not to mention his terminal disease, but I never thought he'd go so far as to assault a crew member rather than abandon his project.* She had not seen Faal since he fled the sickbay after injecting Troi with the polyadrenaline, nor did she know what had happened to

Faal's young son, Milo, who had taken off after his father. As Betazoids and full telepaths, both Faal and the boy were also in severe danger from the psychic effects of the barrier. She had sent a security officer in search of them, and informed the bridge of the disturbance, but so far security had not returned either Lem Faal or Milo. *For all I know, they could be worse off than Leyoro right now.*

The security chief's neurotransmitters continued to rise. An agonized moan escaped her lips. Crusher knew she had to try something—anything—before Leyoro suffered permanent brain damage or worse. It was too late to use a cortical stimulator to induce a coma the way she had with Deanna; Leyoro's condition had to be stabilized before Crusher could even attempt to shut her brain down in that fashion. Tapping on the touch-sensitive controls of the surgical clamshell, she added four hundred milligrams of triclenidil to the intravenous infusion. It was a dangerous ploy; the triclenidil would enhance Leyoro's natural defenses, but might also enhance the psionic sensitivity that had rendered her vulnerable in the first place. She wished she could risk an analgesic as well, maybe hyrocortilene or metacetamine. The poor woman sounded like she was in agony, but Crusher couldn't take the chance that further medication might produce a dangerous counterreaction to the chemicals she had already administered to Leyoro.

Thank goodness the little girl is safe at least. Alyssa Ogawa was watching over Lem Faal's youngest child,

Kinya, over in the emergency pediatric unit, where the Betazoid child slept in a coma similar to Deanna's. Crusher knew the nurse would call her instantly if Kinya showed any symptoms at all of neurological distress.

Crusher's gripped the steel supports of the SSF as she watched for the slightest improvement in Leyoro's brain chemistry. *Come on, Baeta,* she silently urged her patient. *Help me here.* Overhead the sensor cluster hummed quietly as it scanned Leyoro with a full array of diagnostic tools. Crusher's heart leaped as she saw the production of neurotransmitters within Leyoro's cerebral cortex begin to level off. "Yes!" she whispered. The triclenidil was working! Leyoro was a long ways from out of the woods yet, but at least she had a chance. Crusher cautiously administered another hundred milligrams and crossed her fingers.

The entrance to sickbay slid open and three more crew members rushed in, carrying the unconscious bodies of Lem and Milo Faal. She recognized Ensign Daniels, the security officer she sent in search of the missing patients, along with Ensign Gomez from Engineering and Lieutenant Sumi Lee from Science. "Dr. Crusher, over here," the EMH called out. The holographic MD was already helping Ensign Daniels get Lem Faal's limp body onto the nearest empty biobed. For once, Crusher was thankful that the gravity was out; it had to make transporting the two bodies easier.

"Keep an eye on Lieutenant Leyoro at Bed One," she instructed the EMH, racing toward the new arrivals. The heavy magnetic boots made her feel slow and clumsy. "Let me know if her brain activity increases by any factor."

"Understood," he said, without any of his usual sarcasm or grousing. Apparently even a hologram knew when there was no time for a bad attitude. He headed straight for Leyoro, his image flickering only for a second during a brief but worrisome power fluctuation. The lack of gravity did not slow him at all.

"I found him by a turbolift, sprawled on the floor," Ensign Daniels informed Crusher as she checked Lem Faal's vital signs. He was still alive, thank heavens, but unresponsive. He seemed to be whispering, having a feverish conversation with himself, but she strained to make out what he was saying.

"The wall . . . the wormhole . . . must bring down the wall. . . ."

To her slight surprise, his breathing sounded fine; the last time she had seen Faal he had been gasping for breath, his weakened lungs succumbing to the wasting effects of Iverson's disease.

"The boy was with me," Ensign Gomez explained as Crusher shifted her attention to the supine eleven-year-old form of Milo Faal, whom Gomez and Lee had lowered onto the next biobed. "He had gotten lost somehow, and I was escorting him back to sickbay when he suddenly clutched his head and collapsed."

The memory brought on a shudder. "It was very strange. There was some sort of bizarre optical effect, maybe an X-ray discharge. For just a second, he looked like a photo-negative version of himself; then, in a flash, he looked normal again. I tried to wake him, but he was out cold. Then Lieutenant Lee found us."

The science officer nodded. "Lieutenant Commander Data had sent me to investigate a pocket of concentrated psionic energy he had detected from the bridge."

Crusher didn't like the sound of that. "Did you find the source of that energy?"

"Yes." Lee waved a standard tricorder in the direction of both Lem Faal and his son. "It's them."

"What do you mean?" Crusher asked. Milo's vital signs were encouraging, too. Neither of the Betazoids appeared to have been affected as severely, or in precisely the same way, as Baeta Leyoro.

Lee hesitated before answering, double-checking the display on her tricorder. "I can't be sure. Ensign Breslin is still scanning the corridors for any residual traces, but it seems like these two people have each absorbed a portion of the barrier's energy."

Is that even possible? Crusher wondered. *And what sort of effect could it have on them?* This was different from what had happened to Leyoro; that had been a severe neurological shock, potentially fatal, but still subject to medical understanding and treatment. But this . . . science couldn't even explain what the barrier was, let alone how that mysterious energy could sustain itself within an ordinary humanoid brain. She initiated a full diagnostic scan of both patients' brains, while placing Professor Faal under restraint, just in case he awoke on his own. She didn't want another violent episode like before.

The results of the scans were puzzling. The monitors above both father and son reported accelerated brain activity, but without the adverse side effects that had endangered Leyoro. It was as if their respective cerebellums were rapidly evolving and adapting to accommodate the greater demands being placed on them by the explosion of synaptic activity. The very structures of their brains were being reconfigured before her eyes. Even stranger, the sensors recorded *two* distinct sets of brain waves coexisting within Lem Faal's mind, as though one personality had been superimposed upon another. *Like during a Vulcan mind-meld,* she thought, remembering a similar dual pattern in a recent study from the Vulcan Science Academy.

Some form of psychic possession? Crusher speculated. She'd seen stranger things during her years aboard the *Enterprise,* and it might explain a lot about the scientist's increasingly erratic behavior. But who or what could be possessing Faal? The Calamarain or something else entirely? There was always Q, of course, but somehow this didn't feel like his style.

Taking a more hands-on approach to the examination, she gently reached out and raised one of Lem

Faal's eyelids, wanting to check on his pupils. She let out a gasp, startling the three other crew members, as she was met by an unexpected sight. Faal's once-brown eye now glowed with an eerie white light that stared up her, suffused with what had to be the energy of the galactic barrier itself.

"Oh my God," she whispered.

Chapter Four

THE BRIGHTNESS FADED and the fugitives, as well as Picard and the elder Q, were surrounded by four new individuals, clad in the intimidating armor of Roman legionnaires. Picard recognized the female Q, significantly younger than she had appeared upon the *Enterprise*, not to mention a stern-looking humanoid who bore an uncomfortable resemblance to himself. *One of Q's little jokes,* Picard theorized, recalling that the true appearances of the Q had been translated into images his human mind could comprehend. *Should I be flattered or insulted that Q keeps casting me as the heavy hand of authority?* He suspected the latter.

The remaining new arrivals were unfamiliar to him. One was a pale-skinned male, holding his crested bronze helmet against his breastplate, who looked about the same age as the young Q, with straight blond hair combed back away from his brow. He appeared nervous, looking back and forth among his fellow Q for support. The fourth newcomer, somewhat older than the others, had sad eyes, accented by mournful pouches, and a philosophic manner. "Good old Quinn," the original Q said beside Picard. "May he rest in peace."

The Q quartet raised their arms at their sides and coruscating beams of blue-white energy leaped from their fingertips, connecting with the outstretched hands of their associates to form an incandescent fence around 0 and the other malefactors, or, more accurately, a living quincunx with the young Q at its center. The brilliant beams crackled with unleashed power. Picard could not help feeling trapped, even though he knew that the hunters were not even aware of his presence.

The archaic armor donned by the Q only made them look more formidable. The scintillation of their discharged energy reflected off polished bronze helmets, cuirasses, and greaves. Crescent-shaped plumes of thick horsehair crested the Corinthian-style helmets that partially obscured their deceptively human features. Short, double-edged swords hung on their right hips, held on by a leather belt or baldric. While realizing that the historical costuming was largely an illusion created by Q, Picard had to admit that the ancient armor seemed more appropriate to this primeval conflict than, say, the plum-colored Starfleet uniforms he and Q now wore.

"You cannot hide from the Continuum," said the Q who could have been the captain's twin. Picard recognized his double's voice as that which had boomed from the heavens earlier. Apparently the spokesman for the Continuum had deigned to make a personal appearance after all. "Do not resist our judgment."

No, Picard thought, rethinking the matter. Not a spokesman, but a judge. A imperial Roman judge. A quaestor.

"Yes, Q," his future mate urged, resembling an Amazon in her martial regalia, "give up this lunacy before it's too late. You've gone too far this time."

"It's for the best, Q," said Quinn, more in sorrow than in anger. "I know you meant well."

"That's right," the blond Q added, attempting a not terribly convincing smile. Picard guessed he was a friend and contemporary of Q's. "Hey, I misplaced the entire Deltived Asteroid Belt once, but it all turned out okay in the end."

Unlike the rest of the tribunal, who seemed to have Q's best interests at heart, the quaestor had no patience with the erring youth and his dubious acquaintances. His Picardian expression was deadly serious. "Q is our problem and will be dealt with accordingly. The rest must be banished forthwith."

Penned in by the power of his peers, young Q rose to his feet. His simulated Adam's apple bobbed sheepishly as he opened his mouth to speak. *What course will he take now?* Picard wondered. Would he surrender without a fight?

0 made the decision for him. "Never!" he cried, firing a blast of searing energy from his hands at the immense dilithium crystal beneath them and triggering a matter-antimatter explosion that flung them all, through countless layers of liquid and vapor, out of the gas giant's majestic atmosphere into the icy vacuum of space. Picard felt himself being propelled at incredible speeds, like a quantum torpedo fresh from its launcher tube. Agonizing g-forces yanked the flesh of his face tightly against his skull as he achieved escape velocity from the gravitational sway of the Brobdingnagian planet. He was unable to halt or even control his headlong flight through the Detrian system. *Blast you, Q,* he cursed as he rocketed helplessly. *You could have warned me.*

Finally, after several endless moments, some sort of metaphysical friction, or perhaps the cushioning effect of numerous quantum filaments, curbed his momentum and brought him to a stop somewhere outside the solar system he had just been forcibly expelled from. To his annoyance, he found Q waiting for him, looking none the worse for wear. "My, I had forgotten how exhilarating that was," he observed. "Hope you enjoyed the ride, Jean-Luc."

Picard gave Q a withering look. "Never mind me," he said darkly. "What happened to 0 and the others?"

"Look behind you." Q shook his head glumly and

affected a pained expression. "I'm afraid it's turned into something of a free-for-all."

The battle was fought on a cosmic scale. As Picard looked on from what he prayed was a safe distance, colossal figures strode the stars, hurling entire planets and suns at each other. Millennia passed in what felt like seconds as the war against 0 wreaked havoc on what Starfleet would later name the Alpha Quadrant. Picard tried to take it all in, but it was impossible to do more than glimpse fragmentary snapshots of the unthinkable devastation:

The gleaming plate armor of The One, more appropriate to the Age of Chivalry, clashes anachronistically with the Roman war gear of the blond Q, who has reluctantly hidden his face behind his plumed helmet. Determined to resist capture, He saps the energy of a nearby star, turning it against His foe. On the third planet orbiting that sun, the days grow ever colder, forcing an unsuspecting people to cope with the incidental consequences of a conflict beyond their understanding. . . .

The android Ruk stood upon a snow-covered hilltop on Exo III, watching as massive drilling machines carved a cavern into the face of a granite cliff. Many such caverns were being dug these days, as his Creators sought to escape the freezing conditions upon the surface by seeking shelter deep beneath the planet's crust. He and his fellow androids would join the Creators underground, serving the Creators as they always had. There would be many changes in the days to come, as both androids and the Creators adapted to their new subterranean existence, but Ruk was confident that he would continue to function effectively regardless of any unexpected alterations in the parameters of his existence. Had not the Creators programmed him to adapt and survive?

An icy wind blew flakes of frozen moisture against the angular planes of his face. His dermal sensors recorded that the external temperature was several units below the freezing point, but he did not feel the cold as a Creator might. His massive body was immune to pain or discomfort. His heavy feet sank deep into packed layers of snow and permafrost that would never ever thaw.

No one knew, not even the finest minds among the Creators, why the sun had grown steadily colder year after year. None knew how to reverse the process. All the Creators could do was burrow toward the planet's core in search of the warmth they needed to survive. Ruk admired their resolute determination to outlive the fading sun. The Creators were teaching him an important lesson.

Nothing was more important than survival.

(*) thrives on war, so war it incites, feeding on the chaos it created to find the strength it needed to fend off the scholarly Q with the sad eyes, whose metaphorical spears rain on (*) without cease. On yet another world, caught unbeknownst in the midst of the celestial war, it

*discovers a people whose mental gifts, and towering
ambitions, leave them ideally suited to its purposes. . . .*

"But, Sargon, are you absolutely sure this is necessary?" Thalassa asked. "Isn't there some other way?"

Sargon considered his wife's plaintive entreaty. It
was indeed a lot he was asking of her, of all of them,
but they had no choice. His eyes swept over the
austere lines of the hastily constructed vault. Row
upon row of steel niches ran along the opposite,
stretching the entire length of the futuristic catacomb,
each niche holding a single translucent globe. All but
two of the spheres glowed from within, holding the
psychic essences of valiant comrades. One of the
remaining globes awaited Thalassa.

"It is the only solution," he said solemnly. "According to my calculations, the forces unleashed by
the war will soon rip away the entire atmosphere,
rendering our world uninhabitable. Only by storing
our minds in these receptacles can we hope to preserve some vestige of our population and culture."

"But to live without bodies of our own? And for
how long?" She stared in anguish at her own hands,
memorizing the fragile complexity of the flesh and
bone she soon must sacrifice forever. "It's horrible."

Sargon nodded. "Perhaps it is price we must pay for
our terrible arrogance." *The coming cataclysm is no
one's fault but our own,* he thought. *We dared to think
of ourselves as gods and look what has become of us.*

"Speak for yourself, Sargon," a sardonic voice
requested. Henoch strolled toward the elderly scien-

47

tist and his wife, smiling. The representative from the Northern Coalition smiled more than any man Sargon had ever met; it was one of the reasons he distrusted him. "I take no responsibility for the precarious position we now find ourselves in. Perhaps you should have said as much to your own generals, before they challenged our claim to the borderlands."

Sargon frowned, resisting the temptation to strike out at the foreigner with the power of his mind. "You are here as a gesture of peace," he reminded Henoch, "in hopes of future harmony among our people. Do not abuse our generosity by baiting me with your self-serving propaganda."

Henoch shrugged. "I suppose it is rather too late to argue politics at this point. If I did not think the war unwinnable by either side, I would not have joined you here today." He scratched his chin speculatively. "Funny, though, how quickly the conflict escalated, almost as if powers beyond our ken were somehow pulling our strings, setting us against each other."

You seek to blame anyone but yourself, Sargon thought, wondering once more whether it was wise to include Henoch and a handful of his followers among those whose consciousness would be stored in the receptacles, against the far-off day when they might live again. He did not care for Henoch, whose affable charm barely concealed a scheming nature, but he and his people were part of the society Sargon had worked so hard to preserve. To exclude them from this final chance for salvation would be an act of selfishness and paranoia comparable to those that had doomed their world. *For better or for worse, he is one of us.*

An explosion upon the surface, several miles overhead, shook the vault despite its reinforced steel walls. The war was drawing nearer and growing more intense. "It is time, my love," he told his wife.

"I am ready," she said bravely and approached one of the dormant spheres, securely tucked away in its recess. For the last time, save in memory, Sargon gazed upon the physical form of his lifelong mate and partner, savoring the elegant arch of her eyebrows, the delicate tips of her pointed ears. Then she laid her palms upon the curved shell of the receptacle and closed her eyes in concentration. "Until we live again," she said.

A bluish glow flared within the sphere only an instant before a bright red nimbus spread over her body. Sargon wanted to look away, but could not, standing by passively as the scarlet energy consumed every trace of Thalassa's corporeal remains, leaving not an atom behind. Only when her body had been completely disintegrated, her life force transferred to the interior of the globe, did he lower his face into his hands and sob.

From a technical standpoint, it was not necessary to destroy the body while transferring the mind, but practically there was no better alternative, lest the underground vault become a charnel house. Judging from the sound of the battle being waged above, soon there would be no one left to dispose of the bodies of those whose thoughts and memories now resided within the receptacles. *Forgive me,* he thought to the glowing globe that held his wife's spirit. *Forgive us all.*

"So you actually went through with it," Henoch observed, inspecting Thalassa's receptacle before wandering over to the last empty sphere visible within the catacomb. "I insisted upon being the last to go, just in case there was trickery afoot, but seeing that you were genuinely willing to sacrifice your own wife to this far-fetched scheme, I suppose I might as well trust you one crucial step further." He ran a finger over the empty globe, inspecting it for dust. "So how long do you expect we will wait in this underground mausoleum before some wayfaring space travelers drop by to say hello?"

Sargon wished he knew. "Perhaps only a few hundred years. Perhaps forever. The receptacles will preserve our essences for half a million years, maybe longer. Time enough, I hope, for interplanetary explorers to stumble onto the ruins of our civilization, perhaps providing us with new bodies with which to greet tomorrow." If only there had been time to construct android bodies for their dispossessed souls, to provide them with mobility after the turmoil on the surface died out, but the war had come upon them too quickly. Indeed, it was a small miracle that he had succeeded in preparing this vault and these few receptacles before the inevitable catastrophe rendered organic life impossible on this planet for all time to come. "It seems probable that other species will explore the stars, just as our own ancestors did. We can only pray that our alien successors will possess the curiosity and the compassion to free us from our long imprisonment."

"You pray, old man," Henoch responded. "For myself, I just hope that our future bodies, if any, won't be too unappealing in appearance." He laid his hands upon the final dormant sphere, then glanced back over his shoulder, a mocking smile upon his face as always. "Let me guess, it won't hurt a bit."

A moment later, nothing was left of Henoch except a constant glow at the center of his chosen orb. Sargon could not say he missed him. *If I don't hear his voice again for half a million years, then that might be a blessing of sorts.*

Now it was his turn. With a mental command, he extinguished the lights in the catacomb, so that only the collected life force of his fellow refugees illuminated the chamber as he left it behind and entered an adjacent compartment only half the size of the depository he had departed. There a solitary globe, as yet unlighted, rested atop a central podium linked to the most advanced sensor apparatus Sargon could assemble in the face of the mounting hostilities above. Here was where his consciousness would wait out eternity, searching the heavens for the instruments of their deliverance. Unlike Henoch and Thalassa and the rest, whose minds would dwell in dreamless slumber until they were awakened once more, a portion of his psyche would remain aware throughout the centuries, probing the empty corridors of space and sending out an urgent plea for assistance to whatever enterprising beings might someday pass this way.

As he placed his palms against the cool, inanimate surface of the receptacle, and felt his mind flowing out of his body and into the motionless sphere, he wondered how long he would truly have to wait.

The female Q has Gorgan on the run. His seraphic features melt into a hideous mask of bestial fury, only partially obscured by his verdant aura, as he snarls back at his relentless pursuer. Sensing a convenient wormhole, he dives toward that tantalizing means of egress, but some unknown presence within the wormhole blocks his entrance long enough for the Q to catch up with him. She cuts off his retreat with a searing blast of fifth-dimensional fire and he retaliates in kind. . . .

Brightly colored lights streaked the night sky above the western hemisphere of Bajor. Upon a balcony at the top of highest tower in the temple, the kai watched a burst of chartreuse flame erupt in the heavens, then sputter and die as it traced its way above the horizon. More eruptions filled the sky in its wake, obscuring ancient constellations and outshining the stars. It was as though the Celestial Temple itself was on fire.

"What is it, Holiness?" asked Vedek Kuros fearfully, tugging on the kai's silken sleeve to draw her attention down from the inexplicable stellar pyrotechnics. "Is it the Reckoning?"

The kai shook her head thoughtfully, causing the ornate silver chain dangling from her ear to sway back and forth. "I think not," she said. "The Sacred Texts are very clear that the Reckoning shall not occur until after the Coming of the Emissary." She gave him a playful smile. "You haven't, by any chance, neglected to inform me of the Emissary's arrival, have you?"

"Oh no, Holiness!" the vedek insisted. "How could I? I wouldn't dream of it."

"Calm yourself, Kuros, I was only joking." She reached out to cup his ear and sensed that his *pagh* was deeply troubled by the curious lights in the sky. "The Reckoning is not yet upon us. This is something far different, I think."

The vedek was not alone in his fears, she knew. From her lofty perch high above the sacred city of B'hala, she could see the people gathered in the great square below, their eyes turned upward in awe and terror. Hundreds of Bajorans, from every clan and *D'jarra,* surrounded the monumental stone *bantaca* in the center of the city, perplexed and unnerved by the violent heavenly display, but unable to look away. The vivid colors of the celestial explosions cast a shifting spectrum of shadows upon the faces and rooftops beneath her. It was as beautiful as it was mysterious.

I must issue some manner of statement, the kai realized, knowing it was her duty to comfort her people in this time of turmoil, *but what can I tell them?* Nothing in the Sacred Texts spoke of such tumult amid the firmament nor hinted when the unnatural phenomenon might cease. In her heart of hearts, she knew that the dazzling portents lighting up the night were not the work of the Prophets, nor even the unholy mischief of the dreaded *Pah*-wraiths. Those powerful beings, both the good and the wicked, were of Bajor. These disturbances, she sensed deep within her own *pagh,* were something different, something alien to them all, but no less dangerous to all who lived.

The strange lights shone on for a thousand days. . . .

The furious struggle between the Q and the forces of 0 attract the interest of other transcendent beings. Some such entities come to investigate. . . .

"Q," Picard asked. "Who are those beings over there?" He gestured toward a quartet of humanoid figures standing silently at the perimeter of the war, looking on with pained expressions upon their faces. Unlike the combatants, they had not assumed the garb of Earth's ancient warriors, wearing instead simple Grecian chitons made of what looked like common wool. Their faces were youthful and unmarked by time. They clasped their hands together before their chests in a meditative pose. Picard was struck by the aura of peace and dignity the beings projected, which reminded him somewhat of the sadly departed Sarak of Vulcan.

"Oh, *them,*" Q said disdainfully. "Those are the Organians. Relative youngsters compared to the Continuum, but still reasonably evolved at this point in galactic history."

The Organians, Picard thought, wide-eyed and astounded. They were semi-mythical beings in his own time, legendary for their historic role in averting a bloody war between the Federation and the Klingon Empire decades before Picard's birth. The Organians had largely kept to themselves since then; Picard had never thought that he might actually see one in person.

Q was considerably less awestruck. "A bunch of upstart, idealistic kids, really. Slackers and layabouts, all of them. Compared to their childish doctrine of pacifism and noninterference, your Prime Directive is practically an incitement to riot."

Picard took Q's assessment of the early Organians with a grain of salt; small wonder Q dismissed a people who practiced the virtues of forbearance and restraint. The Federation of his own time owed a lot to the reluctant peacemaking of these people or their descendants. Still, he could not deny that the Organians of this era seemed content to stay on the sidelines during the Continuum's heated struggle to subdue 0. As he watched the cosmic battle develop, his doppelgänger among the Q plucked a steel-tipped lance from the ether and hurled it at 0 himself, who materialized a disk-shaped shield just in time to block the spear. Deflected, the weapon ricocheted toward the assembled Organians, who merely shook their heads sadly at its approach. The spear vanished only seconds before it would have struck the placid spectators, followed a heartbeat later by the Organians themselves. The four figures dissolved into the emptiness of space, having apparently seen enough of the barbaric melee.

"And good riddance," Q commented derisively. "You know what they say, Jean-Luc, if you're not part of the solution, you're part of the whole godawful mess."

"Is that so?" Picard asked. "Your younger self doesn't appear to be contributing much to the situation, one way or another."

It was true. The young Q cowered in a desolate corner of space, apart from the others, looking distinctly miserable and conflicted. He squatted in the vacuum, rocking back and forth on his heels, as he peered at the furious hostilities through his fingers as he held both hands over his face. It was a far cry from the preening arrogance Q would display in the future. "It's all my fault," he whispered, although no one but Picard and his older self was listening. "What have I done?"

"Q!" 0 cried, besieged by the leader of the Q, who seemed to have an inexhaustible supply of spears. "Cease your babbling and help me, friend. We're under attack here!"

"Don't listen to him, Q." Always a tall woman, the female Q was nothing short of imposing in her armor. She thrust at Gorgan with her short sword while shouting at Q. The deceptively angelic entity pounded his fists atop each other, invoking his power, but the sword kept cutting closer and closer to his emerald aura. "He's not your friend. You don't owe him anything."

"She's just jealous," 0 insisted, parrying another

assault from his grim opponent. His iron shield transformed into a rubber trampoline that bounced the other Q's spear back at him. The quaestor ducked promptly, but the rebounding lance sliced the crest off his helmet. A gigantic crescent of horsehair flew off into a nearby nebula where it would later confound generations of Iconian explorers. "They're all jealous. They envy our vitality, our courage and freedom. They can't stand that we actually have the guts to enjoy our omnipotence as we see fit, that we want to shake things thing up instead of simply maintaining the status quo. They want to destroy us because we prove how weak and impotent the rest of them really are." Seizing the offensive, he fired at his foe with a crossbow that hadn't existed a second before. "Do you want to be destroyed, Q?"

"No one will be destroyed," the quaestor promised, "if you surrender now." The bolt from the crossbow spontaneously combusted before it could strike home. The young Q looked up hopefully at the quaestor's words, a reaction that did not go unnoticed by 0.

"You might as well annihilate us all," he bellowed as he loaded another quarrel into the crossbow. "What's the alternative? Submitting to the will of the Continuum, condemned to an eternal half-life of dull conformity and anonymity? No, I'd rather take my chances here, and if you're smart, Q, you'll do the same!"

The young Q reacted by throwing his hands over his ears to keep the sound of the debate away from him. He squeezed his eyes shut and let out a mournful howl that could be heard even above the clang of armor and weaponry. *Not the most mature response,* Picard noted, *but strangely in character. Only Q could think that the universe and all its dilemmas would go away if he just ignored them.*

"I didn't know what to do," the later Q recalled. "I felt like unbridgeable chasms had cut me off from both 0 and the Continuum, but that neither side would let me alone. I was lost and alone in the middle of a war."

Like I was, Picard thought with a start, *after Locutus was captured from the Borg, but before Beverly restored my humanity.* He had been isolated, too, neither of humanity nor of the Collective, but an exile from each. *That was not at all the same thing,* he reminded himself hastily; unlike Q, he had not brought that hellish limbo upon himself. Still, he found himself identifying with the young Q more than he liked.

"Where are the other Q?" he asked, eager to change the subject. It dawned on him that he had no idea how many individuals comprised the entire Continuum. Were these four pseudo-legionnaires the sole extent of Q's peers? That seemed unlikely; he had always gotten the impression that the Q's population was as infinite as their abilities.

"Putting out fires, mostly," Q answered. "In case you haven't noticed, this particular donnybrook is producing no end of collateral damage on various planes of existence. A battle between beings of our exalted nature does more than break a few windows, Jean-Luc; why, during a recent civil war among the Q, in your own far-off century, there were supernovas going off all over the Delta Quadrant." He shuddered at the memory. "To be honest, those fractures in the galactic barrier, the ones that your Federation scientists are so keen on, are actually a regrettable after-effect of that nasty little war."

Now he tells me, Picard thought, although he still wasn't sure what the barrier had to do with 0 and this hard-fought conflict in the distant past. *Why am I here?*

"Anyway," Q continued, "the majority of the Continuum are occupied with patching up the most grievous wounds in the fabric of reality, leaving a few close friends and associates to deal with me personally. In their own inimitable fashion, of course."

Q's explanation sounded plausible enough. Now that he knew to look for them, Picard thought he glimpsed phantom figures scurrying about in the background. They were like shadows, insubstantial silhouettes moving almost too fast to be seen, going about their mysterious errands like stagehands at work behind the scenes of some massive theatrical production. *Are they always there,* Picard mused, spying them only out of the corner of his eye, *or only during a crisis of this magnitude?* Despite all he had witnessed, there was still so much he did not understand about the metaphysical realm the Q inhabited.

"So I see," he said, turning his thoughts to less

ineffable matters. "And just how long did this personal matter go on, Q? Strange as this may seem to you, I am anxious to return to my own life at some point."

"If you must know," Q said, "this ugly altercation lasted a mere one hundred thousand years as you reckon time." He nodded toward the celestial battle-field. "Look, the tide is already starting to turn."

His face a twisted mass of lumpen flesh, his shim-mering robes reduced to smoking, blackened rags, Gorgan was the first to abandon the fight. His insub-stantial form wavered in the void like a mirage above the desert. Turning his back on the female Q and her slashing sword, he fled through space with the ar-mored woman in hot pursuit. Desperate to escape her, he raced back to the very site of the Tkon Empire's destruction, diving into the gaping black hole that had once been their sun, apparently choos-ing to risk the unknown perils beyond the event horizon rather than face the wrath of the Q. "Cow-ard!" the female Q called out. "Don't let me see you showing your hideous face in this multiverse again."

Emboldened by its comrade's escape, (*) retreated from the fray as well. Quinn lowered his sword arm, showing little interest in chasing after the evil entity now that it had been routed. He heaved a heavy sigh, gratefully removing his helmet, as (*) disappeared down the black hole after Gorgan. The hungry gravi-tational vortex swallowed up every last flicker of (*)'s bloodthirsty light.

"They're just letting them get away?" Picard asked.

He knew that neither entity had truly been destroyed. If Q was to be believed, both Gorgan and (*) would later bedevil James T. Kirk in the twenty-third century.

"Without 0, they're petty nuisances at best," Q said with a shrug. "From now on, they'll be forced to lurk furtively in the most obscure recesses of the galaxy, preying like highwaymen on the occasional unwary starship. Nothing the Q need worry about, in other words."

"Your concern for the rest of us is overwhelming," Picard pointed out dryly.

"It's all a matter of scale, Jean-Luc. Haven't you figured that out yet?" Q grabbed Picard by the shoulders and forcibly turned his view away from the insatiable black hole and back toward the sector of space where 0 and The One continued to contend against the Continuum with every weapon at their disposal, apparently undaunted by the desertion of two of their allies. "Now, that pair posed rather more of a problem."

Disdaining symbolic weaponry, The One unleashed lightning bolts from his fingertips. The scent of ozone wafted through the vacuum as the electrical barrage held Q's friend at bay. "Heathen! Infidel!" The One raged, the luster of his golden armor undimmed. Overlapping metal plates covered The One's entire body from the neck down; only his forbidding visage remained uncovered. "Feel the power of My Holy Anger. Quake in terror, O foolish one, as My Mighty Hand strikes you down."

"That remains to be seen," the Q shot back, his blond locks concealed beneath his helmet. His superior tone resembled Q's, although not quite as scathing in its sarcasm. "The Q do not quake."

He ducked his head beneath the upper edge of a bronze, rectangular shield. His cautious stance, crouched behind his protective shield, testified to the intensity of The One's thunderbolts. Although Q had said that the battle was turning against 0 and his allies, Picard saw no sign of imminent defeat where The One was concerned; if anything, the monotheistic monster had the advantage against the opposing Q. Even His burnished plate armor, worthy of a medieval knight, appeared superior to the primitive Bronze Age gear of the Q warriors.

"Curb thy mocking tongue," He declared, advancing on the Q, His fulsome beard framing His stern features like the mane of a roaring lion. "The time of thy chastisement is at hand."

"Not if I have anything to say about it," the Q retorted from behind his shield, whose gleaming surface was now dented and scorched in places. He backed away from The One, holding up his shield all the while. Sparks flew from the battered shield as The One's relentless pace consumed the distance between Himself and His intended victim. "Q! Oh, Q!" the overwhelmed Q called out to his compatriots. "Help me out over here! Better sooner than later!"

Picard had no way of knowing exactly which Q the imperiled entity was addressing, but his cry for help drew both the female Q and Quinn to his side. The sad-eyed Quinn came back to the fracas reluctantly, his expression not unlike the Organians', but his Amazonian companion was all too eager to take on another foe. "There's a black hole waiting for you, too," she taunted The One, placing herself between the oncoming deity and her endangered associate. Her shield blocked bolt after bolt from The One, and she retaliated with an energy blast of her own that stopped The One in His heavenly tracks. Quinn followed her lead, protecting the third Q with his shield while firing a beam of sizzling heat from his free hand.

"Strumpet!" The One cursed, halting where He stood. "Witch!" He beat one gauntleted hand against the molded steel of His breastplate, producing a resounding clang that sounded even in the silent depths of interstellar space. The female Q's attack bounced harmlessly off His chest, while Quinn's heat ray merely caused the fringes of His beard to smoke and smolder. Even with the odds now three against one, He refused to give up, proving Himself a more dangerous and determined adversary than either Gorgan or (*). "Be thou false gods as plentiful as sands upon a beach, yet The One shall vanquish you all. None there is who can stand against The One. Great is My Glory, inescapable is My Severe and Final Judgment."

"Please," the female Q said, rolling her eyes. "Only a Q has the right to be so insufferably full of herself."

She glared at Him through narrowed eyes, her classically sculpted jaw set firmly. "Q, Q," she addressed her brothers-in-arms, "let's show this tiresome pretender what all-powerful really means."

Together, the three Q rose from behind their antique shields, uniting their wills against the common foe. The One clenched His metal gauntlets and hurled lightning from His eyes, but the jagged thunderbolts crashed uselessly against an invisible wall that left the row of grim-faced Q untouched by the tumultuous attack. Picard heard a deep, resonant hum rising from where the three Q stood side by side. Even from a distance, he could feel the power swelling between them, growing ever more indomitable as their respective energies came into synch. There was a tension building in the nonexistent atmosphere, like the hush that precedes a storm. The vacuum hummed like the engine room of the *Enterprise* right before it went into warp.

At last, even The One appeared daunted by the trinity of Q. He took an uncertain step backward, retreating from the light, while doubt blurred the rigid imperturbability of his features. "I am My Own Deliverance," he chanted, but his voice lacked the Old Testament certainty of before, "I shall not quaver in My Resolve. I am The One!"

"Oh, lighten up," the female Q said in return.

A dazzling aura enveloped the three figures, uniting them within a single shimmering nimbus of energy. The light was so bright that Picard had to look away, the unexpected blaze leaving dancing blue spots before his sight. He raised a hand before his face to protect his suddenly watery eyes from the glare.

"Pure, raw Q power," Q told Picard. "Lacking in style somewhat, but effective."

An instant later, The One's right leg disappeared. There was no beam or weapon employed, no projectile force or matter penetrated the armor and amputated the limb; it simply ceased to exist, erased bloodlessly from the Q's level of reality. The One stared down in shock at the space His leg had occupied. "No," He murmured, his vainglorious self-worship shaken, "this cannot be." But even as He spoke, His remaining leg vanished, followed by His right arm. His truncated body, encased in the remains of his armor, floated awkwardly in space. "Stop it!" He commanded. "I am The One. I am eternal!"

The Q systematically dismembered Him. They bloodlessly erased His solitary arm, then His armored torso and throat, until all that remained was His bearded head, floating disembodied in space as It screamed obscenities at the heavens.

The severed head, looking like a bust of some forgotten prophet, drifted away from the battlefield, while the cosmos echoed with the sound of His bellicose vows of vengeance. "Perhaps we should delete His tongue as well," the female Q suggested, the light about the trio dimming gradually.

"Let's not be savages," Quinn advised her. "Even the damned deserve to give voice to their torment."

"If you say so," she said, sounding none too convinced. "I think He's a frightful boor who deserves everything He gets."

"Let's just call it a win," the third Q urged, his shoulders sagging forward. "I don't know about you two, but I'm positively tapped out. A mere stellar breeze could blow me away."

He had a point. By now the luminous halo surrounding the trio had faded enough that Picard could once more look upon them directly. He wiped salty tears from his eyes as his vision cleared. All three Q were breathing hard and looked exhausted, although the female Q was doing her best to maintain her customary hauteur. Q's contemporary and chum removed his helmet and Picard saw that his blond hair was pasted to his skull by perspiration. "That was more difficult than I expected," he said. "How ever do lesser species manage to fight wars all the time?"

"I know what you mean," Quinn agreed, leaning forward with his hands upon his knees. Even in the absence of gravity, he acted like he could barely support his own weight. His helmet disappeared in a blink, horsehair crest and all. The bags beneath his eyes looked deeper than before. "Just wait until you're my age.

"This isn't over yet," the female Q chided them, despite her own evident fatigue. The last glimmer of their amplified aura quietly expired, and she strode away from them toward her future husband, still crouching amid infinity, unable to tear his aghast gaze away from the endless clash between 0 and the authoritative Q who so resembled Picard. Both par-

ties in the duel paused barely an instant to acknowledge the brutal defeat of The One.

"You are alone now," the spokesman for the Q
intoned. "Your foul creatures fled or undone." Spears
and crossbow had given way to crossed swords. 0 and
the Q fought with silver blades as everyone from
Picard to the miserable young Q looked on. The ring
of steel against steel rang paradoxically through the
vacuum as the unforgiving Q sought to subdue his foe.
An avid fencer himself, Picard saw no flaw in his
doppelgänger's technique, although 0 fought back
with an undeniably effective mixture of calculation
and ferocity. "Abandon this irrational resistance," he
demanded. "Surrender to the judgment of the Continuum."

"Never!" 0 swung his scimitar at his opponent's
head, only to be blocked by an upward parry of the
Q's shining saber. "And I'm not alone. Young Q will
come to my aid yet, you'll see!"

Surely the strangest aspect of this cosmic sword-
fight, Picard observed at once, was that the precise
nature of the duelists' blades kept changing from
second to second. As Picard studied the fight, critiqu-
ing every feint and parry, 0's curved scimitar became
a cutlass, then a broadsword, then a Klingon *Bat'leth*.
Likewise, the Q's weapon of choice transformed se-
quentially into an elegant epee, a rapier, a Scottish
claymore, and a Romulan *gladius*. Regardless of their
shape, all the blades appeared constructed of the
same indestructible material; although sparks flew
when the protean swords met each other, neither

blade broke beneath its adversary, no matter how overmatched one might seem when compared to the size or weight of the other. Both blades, after all, were not really made of tempered steel, but were in fact tangible extensions of the duelists' preternatural powers of concentration. *I wonder what this actually looks like,* Picard mused, *from a perspective of a Q.*

"Take that, you draconian dictator!" 0 said, laughing exuberantly. He thrust the point of an Italian *cinquedea* at the Q, barely missing the other's hip. "I defy your despotic Continuum and its suffocating sobriety. Q is the only one of you with any spark of talent or initiative in him. He'll see that, too, after I've destroyed the lot of you!"

There had to be a reason 0 cowed The One and the others, Picard guessed; he had to be the most puissant of them all. The captain wished he knew more about where 0 had come from originally, before Q found him in that interdimensional wasteland. What manner of being was he really? All Picard knew was that 0 was something darker and far more dangerous than the charming rogue he occasionally feigned being. That congenial façade was rapidly slipping away as he hacked and slashed at the Q with a long *katana*. "See, Q," he hollered to his hesitant protégé, "you've no need to fear the likes of these sour-faced spoilsports. Never fear! Never again!"

The female Q had a different idea. Still panting from the exertion required to dismantle The One, she reached Q's side and yanked his hands away from his ears. "Look at me!" she pleaded, throwing away her helmet so she could confront him face to face. "Look at them." She compelled him to open his eyes and behold his fellows. "You're one of us, Q, and you always will be."

Hearing her impassioned declaration, 0 scowled and risked glancing away from his intricate duel with the lead Q. If looks could kill, which in 0's case was a distinct possibility, the female Q would have been incinerated instantly. Since that didn't occur, he was forced to resort to other measures. A stray asteroid, consisting of several million tons of solid iridium, passed within his field of vision and, without missing a stroke of his swordplay, he snatched up the asteroid with his free hand, imbuing it with a lethal quantity of energy, and sent it hurling toward the female Q like an assassin's bullet.

"Watch this, Picard," the later Q advised. "You may find it of interest."

Caught up in her efforts to bring the young Q to his senses, the female Q did not notice the deadly asteroid rocketing toward her unshielded head at nearly warp speed. Her future husband spotted it, though. "Look out!" he shouted, pushing her out of the line of fire—which left the accelerated asteroid zooming toward him.

Reacting faster than light, Q ripped open the fabric of space-time, creating a gash in creation between himself and the speeding projectile. The asteroid flew into the fissure, where it traveled backward in time and space until it emerged back into reality on a collision course with the third planet of an obscure solar system countless light-years, and millions of years, away from the heart of the battle. With Q's power enhancing his perceptions, Picard had no problem recognized the blue-green orb that the asteroid slammed into with breathtaking force. *"Mon dieu,"* he gasped. "That's Earth!"

"So much for the dinosaurs," Q said, shrugging.

Picard was staggered by the implications of what he had just seen, watching in horror as a cloud of dust and ash enshrouded the entire planet, cutting it off from the warmth of the sun. "You can't be serious," he gasped. "Surely, you don't mean—"

"No use crying over spilled iridium," Q said curtly. He clapped his hands and the catastrophic collision receded from view. "As fascinating as that little sideshow must be, given your provincial roots, we mustn't neglect the main event, especially since my younger self is finally emerging from his morass of confusion, and after a mere one hundred millennia."

Numb with shock, Picard let his eyes wander back to the pitched combat between 0 and the quaestor. . . .

He almost killed Q, the young Q thought in amazement. He could scarcely imagine such a thing, let alone witness it with his own all-seeing eyes. Obliterating the Tkon was one thing; tasteless and excessive and even sadistic, true, but still only affecting one mortal population. But to threaten the immortality of a Q . . . !

And 0 appeared perfectly willing to do so again. At

this very moment, he menaced another Q with a sword in each hand, assailing the Continuum's implacable quaestor with a bayonet clenched in one and a *kukri* dagger in the other. The savage intensity of his onslaught was slowly but surely winning out over the meticulous fencing skills of the Q, who clearly lacked 0's gleeful hunger for the kill. The Q fought defensively, wielding a darting saber, but he was beaten backward by 0's vicious blows. The stranger's shape-shifting sword rang against the other's metal cuirass and greaves as he repeatedly slipped past the Q's desperate parries. "See," 0 called to the young Q, "the Continuum doesn't stand a chance. And it's all thanks to you!"

He's right, Q realized. *Q can never forgive me what I've done, none of them can.*

But maybe that wasn't the point. He had never really wanted the Continuum's approval anyway. Far from it, in fact. All he ever truly craved was the courage to follow his own instincts, no matter where they led.

Driven back by the simultaneous thrusts of a Viking broadsword and an Apache tomahawk, the quaestor tripped over a constellation. He tumbled through space, momentarily out of control, while his weapon slipped from his fingers, evaporating into the ether. 0 pounced on the opportunity; by the time the quaestor righted himself, the point of a sharpened leg bone was at this throat. "Pay close attention," 0 instructed Q, "and you'll see how to deal with opposition. This pallid entity"—he pressed the tip of his prehistoric pigsticker hard enough to spill a drop of luminous silver ichor—"will never dampen our fire again. Never!"

Q glanced about him in a panic. The other Q stood by helplessly, even his formidable girlfriend. He could sense that they were all too depleted to rescue their leader, even if they knew how to extricate him from his perilous situation. "Wait!" he asked 0 desperately, stalling for time while he tried to figure out what to do.

"What for?" 0 demanded, brandishing the primitive poniard beneath the other Q's chin. "Admit it, Q. You've wanted to do this a hundred times before."

True enough, he conceded. There had been times when he would have liked nothing better than to run the Continuum through with an ectoplasmic skewer. He recalled all those occasions in his turbulent childhood and early youth when this particular Q had disciplined and restrained him, imposing odious limits on the young Q's freewheeling imagination. All he needed to do now, Q recognized, was stand aside and let 0 deliver a killing blow that might scare off the rest of the Continuum for an eternity or two. Total freedom, unlimited anarchy, beckoned. He could do whatever he pleased. He could become just like 0. . . .

"I have a better idea," he said.

In a fraction of a second, the young Q traded places with the Q who resembled Picard. Suddenly, the tip of 0's weapon was poised at Q's throat instead, with the quaestor safely out of the way.

Now it was 0's turn to be disoriented. He blinked in

72

disbelief as his mouth fell open. The point of the sharpened bone wobbled in his grip. "I don't understand," he began. "What are you do—"

Q grabbed on to the bone with both hands and sent a powerful galvanic current rushing down the length of the filed tibia into 0's manifested form. The stranger twitched spasmodically as the shock coursed through him, and, for an instant, Q caught a glimpse of subliminal tentacles writhing in pain. His shoes blew off his feet while the ruffled sleeves of 0's linen shirt burst into flames. 0 stared at Q with a look of anguished betrayal in his bulging blue eyes. "How could you?" he gasped before his bad leg gave out and he collapsed face-first toward the empty abyss of space.

In a strange, uncomfortable sort of way, Q felt as if he had struck down a part of himself.

Chapter Five

"Handle with care the spider's net,
You can't be sure that a trap's not set. . . ."

THE YOUNG Q STOOD IN DOCK before the high tribunal
of the Continuum, along with 0 and, disturbingly,
the disembodied head of The One. Chained and
manacled, 0 crooned to himself, his mind seemingly
undone by this latest defeat. He rattled his chains in
time with his demented ditty and refused to look
at Q.

Only a few paces away, with neither arms nor legs
to fetter, nor even a torso on which to slither snakelike
upon the floor, the severed head of The One had been
confined within a sturdy metal cage resting on the
floor of the courtroom. His angry eyes, impossibly

alive, glared through the bars of the cage while he ground his teeth together impotently, reminding Picard of those rare occasions on which Data's head had been detached from his body. But Data had never looked so enraged and vengeful.

"Is this it?" Picard asked. "The end of the war?"

"Almost," Q promised. "All that remains is the disposition of the prisoners, including myself."

The female Q, still armored Amazonian-style, stood guard between the two outsiders and the young Q, ready to defend Q should either of the alien entities attempt to exact revenge on Q for his betrayal. Her hand rested on the sword at her side. The two other Q sat in the jury box, looking on with solemn expressions. They had retained their armor, but removed their plumed helmets out of respect for the court.

Picard's doppelgänger stared down at the prisoners from an elevated seat behind a high black bench. He had exchanged his armor for a Roman toga, and a crown of laurel leaves rested upon his hairless dome. Recalling the memorable instances in which the later Q had placed Picard (and the rest of humanity) on trial, the real Jean-Luc found it oddly satisfying to see the roles reversed for once.

No walls or ceiling enclosed the courtroom of the Continuum. Tipping back his head, Picard could see the entire Milky Way Galaxy spread out overhead. To think, he mused, that that shimmering spiral of stars and solar systems, a hundred thousand light-years in diameter, contained the whole of the Alpha, Beta,

Delta, and Gamma Quadrants, holding every species and civilization from the Borg to the Dominion to countless new life-forms as yet unknown. Even in his own time, Starfleet had explored only a fraction of the galaxy above. It was a humbling thought.

The quaestor brought down his gavel, calling the court to attention. "Enemies of the Q Continuum," he addressed 0 and The One in as stern a voice as Picard had ever heard. "You have been accused of malicious mischief and conduct unbecoming that of highly advanced entities."

"I reject your authority," 0 protested, breaking off from his song and shaking his adamantine chains. "You have no jurisdiction over me."

The One seconded the motion, the jaws of the disembodied head speaking loudly despite the absence of lungs or anything else below them. "All commandments flow from My Wisdom. Thou shalt have no higher laws than Mine."

The quaestor was unimpressed by the prisoners' arguments. "Your access to this plane was done at the sufferance of the Continuum, and at the instigation of one of our less prudent constituents." The magistrate fixed a cold eye upon the young Q, who gulped nervously. Having exchanged his sackcloth robe for prison stripes, Q looked as guilty as he doubtless felt. "This renders the Continuum responsible for your future activities, just as it renders you both subject to our considered rulings."

For better or for worse, Picard reflected, he and the usual Q seemed to have arrived at the tail end of the trial. Just as well, he thought; as much as he enjoyed seeing Q among the accused, he was eager for this odyssey to reach some conclusion. The sooner Q returned him to the *Enterprise,* the less anxious he would feel.

The magistrate rapped his gavel again. "The entity who quite presumptuously calls Himself The One shall be confined to the center of this galaxy until the heat death of the universe or His sincere repentance, whichever comes first. This sentence is effective immediately."

"No!" The One screamed as a glowing blue force-field surrounded His cage, lifting it from the floor and sending it rushing upward toward the very center of the sprawling starscape above. The living head rocked back and forth within His cage, smashing His forbidding visage against the bars. "Mine is the Power and the Glory and the Will. You cannot lock Me away!" His strident denials faded rapidly in volume as the cage ascended into the sky. Picard watched it rise until its tiny blue glow was lost amidst the dazzling panoply of the galactic core.

Of course, he thought, realizing at last who and what this entity truly was. James T. Kirk had reported encountering just such a malevolent force, trapped behind an energy barrier at the center of the Milky Way, during one of the historic early voyages of the *Enterprise*-A. In theory, The One was imprisoned within the core still, even in the twenty-fourth century. *Remind me to leave that particular barrier alone,* he thought, triggering yet another revelation in his mind.

Now the toga-clad magistrate turned his attention to 0 himself. Arrogant and unrepentant, the prisoner waited defiantly in the dock, singing off-key to music only he could hear. His fancy velvet coat, damask vest, and fashionable breeches were soiled and disheveled. His orange-red tresses, once neatly tied, were loose and in disarray, thatches of frizzy hair jutting wildly in all directions. Having lost his buckled shoes in his moment of defeat, he stood barefoot upon a simulated marble floor, his scarred and twisted left foot exposed to view.

"A young babe lay asleep in bed,
When a shadow passed his silken head. . . ."

"The entity known only as 0," the quaestor went on, ignoring 0's self-absorbed singing, "is banished from this galaxy, on every dimensional plane, without hope of pardon or parole."

"You bundled him in, and kissed him goodnight,
Trusting that all 'twould be well in the night. . . ."

"A barricade shall be erected around the galaxy to prevent your return, thus protecting lesser life-forms from your depraved amusements until they are advanced enough to defend themselves against you and your kind."

"But ever present, always there,
Too common t'matter, too small for a care—
Heedless of what might befall—
You neglect the spider on the wall. . . ."

It all made sense now, Picard thought, nodding. The galactic barrier did not exist to hold humanity or anyone else within the galaxy; it was intended to keep 0 out. A galactic quarantine, in effect, with a capital Q.

And a quarantine that Lem Faal's artificial wormhole could undo in a few moments, exposing the Federation and the rest of the galaxy to 0 once more. . . .

0 spat upon the courtroom floor, his spittle eating away at the marble tiles like acid. "You can't be rid of me so readily," he vowed, interrupting his sinister ditty to threaten the court directly. "I'll be back if I have to wait a million years, just wait and see." His head snapped around to glower at the young Q. The female Q started to draw her sword, but 0 only flung words at his onetime protégé. "I won't be forgetting you, Q. We'll meet again, count on it." His angry gaze swept the courtroom; Picard felt a chill pass over him as 0 looked his way, even though he knew the vengeful prisoner could not see either he or the older Q. "I hope you like games, young Q, because I know whom I'm testing next. You, Q, you." He fixed his baleful gaze on Q as he resumed his song:

"While the lad is tucked in snug,
It crawls along across the rug. . . ."

"Enough. The sentence had been pronounced." He rapped his gavel decisively. "Make it so."

"Deep in slumber, young dreams sweet,
It works its way beneath the sheet. . . ."

As with The One, an irresistible force seized 0 and propelled him upward at unimaginable speed, but this time the force aimed the prisoner at the outer limits of the galaxy. "I'll be back, Q," he shouted down at them as his raspy voice grew too fainter and fainter. "Oh, the games we'll play, games of life and death and death and death . . . ! How well can a Q die, I wonder. There's a test for you!"

"Its legs caressing dimpled chin,
It swiftly pierces tender skin. . . ."

Cast out of known space, 0 shrank to invisibility somewhere outside the galaxy, in the black abyss between galaxies. Even after he disappeared from sight, Picard could still hear 0 singing madly.

"When the spider aims his deadly spikes,
No one spies him till he strikes,
Be mindful of this when you kiss yours good-
   night,
Beware of the danger that lies in plain sight. . . ."

Then something new and different appeared. Picard watched in wonder as a thin violet cord, neon bright in intensity, stretched around the perimeter of the Milky Way, outlining the entire galaxy like a forcefield . . . or a moat.

Thus is born the galactic barrier, he realized, awestruck at the enormity of what the Q had done. That glowing cordon, the same immense wall of energy that had confronted daring starfarers since time immemorial, was the first line of defense for over one hundred billion stars, and all the planets and civilizations that orbited those stars, from Earth to the Delta Quadrant and beyond. Although it looked like the merest shimmering ribbon from his current perspective, he knew that this same barrier enclosed a spiral cloud of stars more than one hundred thousand light-years in diameter. It was a cosmic feat of engineering that made the Great Wall of China seem like a fraction of a fraction of a subatomic speck in comparison. *Astonishing,* he thought. Just to be present at this epochal moment was almost worth all the aggravation Q had inflicted on him over the years.

0 had been more than simply exiled, Picard also understood, as the full implications of the Continuum's decree sank in. Given the crippled 0's inability to travel at faster-than-light speeds, except via the Continuum, he had been effectively marooned in extragalactic space, over two million years from the nearest alternative galaxy; in essence, he'd been set adrift in a very large ocean with the only shore in sight barred from him forever. Even if 0 set out immedi-

ately for the Andromeda Galaxy, he was still going to be alone for a long, long time. Picard almost felt sorry for him; the Continuum's judgment had been unforgiving indeed.

But what of the young Q? Picard had to admit he was curious to see how his own people would deal with the errant Q. *Obviously,* he thought, *whatever they do, it won't be enough to curb his appetite for disorder and chaos.* Picard and his crew could testify to that.

"Q," the quaestor addressed the youth. His oh-so-familiar face frowned in disapproval.

"Yes, Your Honor," Q said, stepping forward. Unlike the departed defendants, no chains or cage restrained him. He was here of his own free will, proving that he had gained a little in maturity since his panicky flight from justice several millennia earlier. Picard admired the youth's willingness to face the consequences of his misdeeds.

"Would that we could dispose of you," the quaestor said mournfully, his expression growing more dour by the moment, "as swiftly and efficiently as the Continuum dealt with your unsavory associates." He sighed and shook his head. "Alas, you are a member of the Continuum and so we are obliged to undertake the daunting, and most likely unachievable, task of your rehabilitation." He nodded at the female Q, standing behind Q in the dock. "Will the bailiff please present Exhibit Forty-two B."

"Certainly," she agreed. Holding out her hands in front of her, she produced a spinning blue-green globe that lifted off from her open palms to take a position between the defendant and the quaestor, floating serenely in midair. "Do you recognize this world?" she asked Q.

He peered at the globe, then shook his head. "Should I?"

"The planet before you," the quaestor informed him, scowling, "is one of several that were damaged during the conflict required to apprehend you and your associates. This world, in particular, was injured by your careless attempt at self-defense near the end of that regrettable altercation."

Picard recalled, if the young Q did not, the diverted asteroid smashing into the Earth many million years in the past, causing death and destruction on planetary scale. *I still refuse to accept that was really Q's doing,* he thought. That an asteroid had struck Earth in the distant past, causing mass extinctions all over the globe, was a matter of archaeological record. That Q himself had caused the disaster, in a single careless moment, Picard found harder to accept. *That, at least, must be some twisted joke on Q's part.* Or so he hoped.

"Oops?" Q said weakly, wincing at the fierce glare his feeble defence elicited from the quaestor.

"The biosphere of this unfortunate world has been grievously harmed," the magistrate announced. "Your penance is to personally oversee the reconstruction of its environment and any life-forms that may develop therein. Perhaps the rehabilitation of this unassuming world can serve as a model for your own redemption."

He regarded Q dubiously. "Probably a lost cause, but who knows?"

Q did not take the quaestor's ruling as well as perhaps he should have. "You want me to baby-sit some insignificant little planet way off in the middle of nowhere? What sort of punishment is that? It's a complete waste of my abilities and talents. Can't you come up with a penance that's more, well, impressive? Twelve impossible labors maybe, or a hazardous quest that no one else would dare?" He grimaced at the floating orb, his nose wrinkling in disdain. "Nothing so tedious and mundane as . . . that."

That's more like the Q I know, Picard thought. *Supremely self-important even in defeat.*

"Do not question the judgment of this tribunal," the magistrate warned him, raising his gavel. "Be thankful that you were not stripped of all your Q-given powers and privileges, although I would not be at all surprised if it comes to that someday." The Q who looked like Picard rose from behind the imposing height of the bench and removed his laurel crown. "Don't let me see you here again, young Q."

Picard half-expected to see Q escorted out of the courtroom now that the proceedings seemed to have concluded. Instead the whole courtroom, and everyone in it, disappeared abruptly in a flash of white light, leaving the young Q alone with his new charge. His posture sagged gloomily as he inspected the spinning globe with a sour expression upon his face. Continents drifted beneath his gaze, and, from several meters away, Picard thought he spotted a landmass that might someday be France. The arctic icecap crept slowly downward, locking Earth in its glacial grip, then receded northward once more. "What a dump," Q groaned.

"Oh, that's enough!" Picard spun around to confront the older Q. He had seen all he wanted to see. "This is too much, Q. Do you truly expect me to believe that you were placed in charge of humanity— as a punishment?"

"What can I say, Jean-Luc?" Q replied, throwing up his hands. "It was a dirty job, but someone had to do it." He took Picard by the arm and led him away from the young Q and an even younger Earth. The captain glanced back over his shoulder, watching the birthplace of humanity spin beneath the sullen gaze of the young Q, but that unsettling primordial scene was soon lost in a dense, white fog that seemed to form out of nowhere, soon growing opaque enough to conceal all the stars that had surrounded the cosmic courtroom. Picard looked about quickly and realized that he and Q had returned to the same ghostly limbo from which their long journey had begun. He decided to take this as an encouraging sign that their odyssey was nearing its end.

"In any event," Q continued, "you mustn't dwell on that amusing little epilogue, no matter how intriguing. I trust that, by now, you have deduced the real reason why I have taken you on this cheery stroll down memory lane."

Picard nodded soberly. "Professor Faal's experiment. His plan to pierce the galactic barrier with an artificial wormhole." Knowing what he now did, it wasn't hard to grasp the dangers involved. "We could accidentally let 0 back into the galaxy."

"Oh, almost certainly," Q confirmed. "He's surely still out there, no doubt humming one of his obnoxious ditties while he waits for a chance to sneak back into your precious Milky Way." He looked sincerely concerned by the prospect. "I can't imagine several hundred millennia of isolation have improved his personality much."

Picard resisted the temptation to remark about blackened pots versus kettles. From what he had viewed, a legitimate case could be made that 0 was more of a threat than Q; Q had only threatened humanity with extinction on occasion, but 0 had actually carried out his genocidal plan to destroy the Tkon Empire. "Why didn't you just tell me the truth in the first place?" he asked. "You had any number of opportunities to explain why you wanted us to leave the barrier alone."

"Would you have believed me?" Q asked in return.

Probably not, Picard conceded. He'd be extremely reluctant to accept anything, even the time of day, on Q's word alone. Still, he suspected there was more to Q's earlier reticence than the conceited superbeing was now willing to admit. The *affaire de 0* was hardly one of Q's finest hours; no wonder he'd been unwilling to provide Picard with the full story until it became obvious that there was no other way to convince the captain to call off the experiment. *Given a choice,* Picard thought, *I'm sure Q would have preferred to explore my own follies and frailties rather than admit to any imperfections of his own.*

"But wouldn't the Continuum intervene again if 0 broke through?" Picard asked. The swirling white mist was growing thicker and thicker. He could barely see his own hands when he held them up before his face. "Surely the combined might of all the Q would be enough to banish him once more."

"Eventually," Q agreed, "but how soon is the question. Over the aeons, the Continuum has grown more detached and aloof from mortal affairs . . . and preoccupied with its own concerns." He guided Picard through the dense fog, although how he knew which way to go, if directions meant anything at all in this formless shadowland, Picard couldn't begin to imagine. "I alluded earlier to a civil war that recently divided the Continuum. Although peace was eventually restored, in no small part due to my own heroic efforts, rest assured that this has been a time of considerable turmoil and change for the Q Continuum, which now has other things on its collective mind than an interdimensional vandal we disposed of countless centuries ago. Still coping with the aftermath of our epochal civil war, the rest of the Q would also be decidedly unwilling to initiate another armed conflict so soon after our own internecine struggle."

Picard found the whole notion of a Q civil war intriguing and more than a little alarming. He recalled that it was this very war which supposedly caused the hairline fractures in the galactic barrier that had first attracted Lem Faal's attention. Although Q hadn't said as much, Picard would have been willing to wager a Ferengi's ransom in gold-pressed latinum that Q had been responsible for starting the war in the first place.

"To be sure," Q continued, "the Continuum would take note of 0's new depredations in a century or two, but who knows how much havoc 0 could inflict on an unsuspecting galaxy before the other Q took action? It's unlikely your vaunted Federation would still be around to see 0 get his just desserts."

"What do you care?" Picard asked suspiciously.

Q did not take offensive at the question, nor at Picard's skeptical tone. "Fatherhood has given me a greater investment in the future of the cosmos. I don't want my son to grow up in a galaxy contaminated by 0."

A valid point, Picard thought. As disruptive as the infant Q had been to the daily routines of the *Enterprise,* the captain could not begrudge Q his concern for his son. "Is that all you're concerned with?" Picard accused. "It seemed to me that 0 was dead-set on revenge against you in particular. Are you sure you're not more worried about your own safety?"

"Enlightened self-interest is one of the crucial hallmarks of a truly advanced intelligence," Q said defensively.

"Regardless of your motives," Picard stated, "you've made your point about the peril of violating the barrier. I have no intention of proceeding with the experiment at this time." He gestured at the featureless miasma that had engulfed them. "I trust this means we can return to the my ship with all deliberate speed."

"If you say so."

Abruptly, without any tangible sense of transition, Picard was back on the bridge of the *Enterprise.* To his further surprise, he found himself drifting in front of the main viewer, a few meters above the blue steel floor. "What the devil?" he exclaimed.

"Captain!" Will Riker said, lunging from the captain's chair to his feet.

It didn't take Picard long to realize that there was no gravity upon the bridge. Year of experience in Starfleet alerted him to the unique physical sensations of zero g right away; still, after spending what felt like hours in the abstract realm of the Q, where entities casually occupied deep space with a nary a care in the world, it felt strange to be subjected to such elemental principles as gravity, or rather the lack of the same, once more. *Which probably means I've returned to reality none too soon,* he reflected. "Q," he said, pointing in an irritated manner at the floor, "if you don't mind . . ."

"What?" Q said. Over by Ops, Q was enjoying a reunion with his family. Little q came to a landing within his father's waiting arms. A half-eaten glopsicle bobbed perilously near Q's ruffled brown hair. "Oh, I see what you mean."

Q snapped his fingers and gravity was restored to the bridge, dragging Picard swiftly toward the floor below. Bits and pieces of broken technology also plummeted abruptly, clattering onto the duranium floor. The captain himself landed on both feet with as much dignity as he could muster, then quickly took stock of his new surroundings.

He didn't like what he saw. Even in the alarmingly dim lighting, it was clear that the bridge of his starship had been through a costly battle. Besides the temporary absence of gravity—and Picard noticed now that Riker and the other crew members present, with the notable exception of Q and his family, were also equipped with magnetic boots—ominous signs of damage and violent destruction were evident in nearly every direction he looked. The overhead lighting had obviously gone out, so his eyes had to adjust to the resulting gloom as he glanced about the bridge. Flashing alert signals and the glowing viewscreen cast deep scarlet and magenta shadows over the scene. The aft engineering station looked completely devastated by some sort of electrical fire, while bits of ash and lightweight debris polluted the ordinarily pristine atmosphere of the bridge, gradually drifting toward the floor. "The Calamarain, I take it," he said to Riker, who approached the captain with a worried look upon his face. *How long have I been away,* Picard wondered, *and what has become of the ship in my absence?*

"You called it," Riker confirmed. His voice was tighter than usual, as if he was in some pain. He gave Q a dirty look. "Good to have you back, Captain."

"Trust me, you are no more pleased than I am, Number One," Picard said wholeheartedly. He turned around to inspect the main viewer. To his concern and puzzlement, the screen showed nothing but a constant purple glow. "Where are we?" he asked Riker, fearing he already knew the answer.

"Inside the barrier," the first officer informed him. "It was the only way to escape the Calamarain. At present, we are waiting for La Forge to complete repairs on the warp engines before attempting to leave this sector."

Picard nodded. He could get a full report later on; for now, it appeared that, while the ship was definitely in difficult straits, Commander Riker had the situation in hand. "And the wormhole experiment?" he asked with some apprehension.

"Aborted," Riker said bluntly, "after we ran into trouble with the Calamarain." He stepped aside and let Picard take his place in the captain's chair. "Protecting the ship took priority."

"You made the right choice, Number One," Picard assured him, "and a better one than you could even realize." Riker gave him a quizzical look so Picard elaborated, tipping his head toward Q. "I'll give you a complete briefing later, but let's just say that I've learned more than enough about the true nature and purpose of the barrier. Hopefully, that will be enough to satisfy Professor Faal and Starfleet Science."

Settling into his chair, Picard noted that the female Q had apparently commandeered Deanna Troi's seat; it was a bit odd to realize that this was the same woman whom he and Q had just observed several hundred thousand years in the past. He scowled when he saw that the baby Q had left sticky handprints all

Greg Cox

over the armrest of the counselor's chair, although, from the look of the rest of the bridge, he decided he should be thankful that the command area was intact at all. Taking a quick mental inventory of the bridge crew, he was surprised to see Lieutenant Barclay stationed at the secondary science station and that young Canadian officer, Ensign Berglund, manning the tactical podium. "Where is Lieutenant Leyoro?" he asked. "And Counselor Troi?"

Riker's face warned him there was worse to come. "Sickbay," he began. "The news isn't good. . . ."

92

Chapter Six

Bring down the wall. The wall is all. . . .

Gravity returned to sickbay without warning, but Lem Faal failed to notice. His mind ablaze with new concepts and sensations, he awoke suddenly, his transformed eyes snapping open, to find Beverly Crusher leaning over him, a worried frown upon her face. Surprised by his unexpected return to consciousness, she gasped and stepped backward involuntarily, bringing a hand to her chest.

Faal was disoriented by the familiar surroundings. Sickbay? How had he returned to sickbay? What had happened to him? The last thing he remembered was standing by a turbolift, trying to get to Engineering. *My experiment . . . my work . . . my destiny . . .* Then the power of the barrier had invaded his mind, bringing with it . . . something else. A renewed sense of purpose, along with the strength and the focus to overcome the endless limitations of his decaying body, or so he had thought until he woke here. *I must have collapsed,* he realized, *overcome by the power of the barrier . . . and the voice on the other side.* The voice had spoken to him for months, promising him immortality and infinite knowledge, enough to transcend the disease that was killing him, to overcome mortality entirely. *Come to me, free me, be me.* Faal had followed that voice to the very edge of the galaxy, all the while concealing his true purpose from Starfleet.

Closer now. Close, closer, closest. . . .

"Professor?" the human doctor asked urgently. "Can you hear me? How do you feel?"

He felt like a new being, but saw no reason to explain anything to the doctor. He had evolved beyond her, beyond everyone on this starship. *They must have brought me here,* he realized, just as Picard's crew had interfered with and delayed his mission ever since he first stepped aboard. *They can't see what I see, hear what I hear.* No matter. The ship was still within the barrier; Faal could sense its power all around him. He knew where he needed to be: Engineering, where the equipment necessary to his experiment waited. *My work . . . my destiny.* It was time for the final step, to remove the barrier between himself and the voice.

Bring down the wall. . . .

"Professor Faal," the doctor repeated. She glanced

anxiously from his face to the biobed monitor and back again. "Can you understand me? Do you know where you are?"

Engineering, Faal thought. *I have to go to Engineering.* He tried to sit up, but something restrained him. Lifting his head a few centimeters from the bed, he saw that translucent straps held his wrists and ankles to the bed. A longer strap stretched across his chest, further limiting his movement. *Why have they confined me?* he wondered. *Don't they realize how close I am? Close, closer, closest.* He had vague memories of an altercation with the doctor, and with Counselor Troi, but that felt like it had occurred ages ago, to another person, one very different from the being he had become.

Come. Hurry. He could still hear the voice, but now it seemed like the voice was his, almost indistinguishable from his own thoughts. *Bring down the wall. Break through.*

Dr. Crusher saw him inspecting the restraints. "I'm sorry, but it was for the best. I'm not sure you're fully responsible for your actions. It's just a precaution."

He ignored her babbling. The barrier was all that mattered, and the voice. The voice that was both inside him and waiting on the other side of the great wall. *Come. Hurry. Now.* He had to leave this place. Neither he nor the voice, if there was truly any difference left between them, could not wait any longer. *Hurry,* it pleaded and commanded. *Fast, faster, fastest.*

His shining eyes stared at the band across his

chest, concentrating his will upon the crude impediment, which began to undo itself as though possessed of a will of its own. *Simple telekinesis,* he observed. *Mind over matter. All that matters is mind.* Crusher made a surprised sound and grabbed for the strap, trying to pull it back into place, but the band resisted her. The straps holding down his wrists and ankles also came free. He didn't even need to touch them; just thinking at the straps was enough. *Release me. Release the voice.* He started to sit up and the doctor's hands pressed down upon his chest, struggling to keep him from rising. "Daniels. Lee," she called desperately. "Help me. He's getting free."

Faal dimly recognized the security officer who had originally escorted him to sickbay, what seemed like decades ago. He didn't know who the other officer was; he had never seen her before. *So many people on this starship,* he thought. *Too many.* He didn't need any of them anymore. All he needed was the voice, just as the voice needed him.

Come. Hurry. Bring down the wall. Release the All. . . .

They tried to help Crusher restrain him, but there was nothing they could do against the newfound power in his mind. With a casual glance, he sent both officers flying away from him. They were propelled backward, limbs flailing, until they crashed into the nearest obstacle. Daniels slammed into a sealed doorway, while the other crew member collided with a metal cart holding a tray covered with medical instruments. Both cart and officer fell over, sending hypo-sprays and exoscalpels sliding across the floor. On nearby biobeds, injured crew members sat up in alarm, the most able jumping onto their feet and rushing to assist the stunned officers.

"Stay away from him," Crusher warned them all, backing away from Faal as he swung his legs off the bed and onto the floor. He wondered for a second why he was wearing such cumbersome boots when the ship's artificial gravity was very obviously functioning again. He stared at the boots and they transformed instantly into more conventional footwear. *That's better,* he thought. *Better, best, bestow.* The voice had bestowed this power on him, the better to bring down the wall.

"Oh no," Crusher whispered, observing the seemingly magical metamorphosis. He could sense that she was confused and wary. *Best, better, beware.* No fool, she kept her distance as he stood still for a moment, savoring the restored strength and vitality in his limbs. The voice sang within him, filling with power and purpose. *Mind over matter. My mind renews my matter.* He had not felt so robust, so capable, in months, not since the Iverson's had begun eating away at his physical stamina. He felt the power of the voice rushing through his body, eradicating every last trace of disease. *I have defeated death,* he exulted. *I will never cease to be.*

The doctor reached for her comm badge, intending to alert Riker and the others, but Faal heard her thoughts before she had even finished thinking them. The shiny golden badge disappeared, transformed into nothingness with just a moment's thought. He glanced around the ward and, just for good measure, removed the rest of the comm badges as well. *No more interference,* he vowed. *No more small-minded rules and procedures.* The head nurse, Ogawa, came running in from another ward, no doubt attracted by the clamor of Starfleet personnel slamming into doors and objects, and he consigned her badge to oblivion. *No more delays. The wall is all. . . .*

He started toward the exit; then an apprehensive thought in the doctor's mind caught his attention. He looked past her to where his son lay unconscious upon a biobed.

Milo, he thought. The sight of the motionless boy gave him pause, although he wasn't sure why. He had attained true immortality at last; physical reproduction had become irrelevant. *But my family . . . ?* Peering deeper into the doctor's thoughts, he discovered that Kinya was also here in sickbay, resting quietly in the pediatric unit, her childish mind temporarily deactivated by the doctor's technology.

Milo. Kinya. He stood frozen between the insensate boy and the exit from sickbay. *My children.* Images from the past raced through his memory, coming from someplace other than the voice. The birth of each child, their first words and telepathic outpourings. He saw their entire family together, his wife, Shozana, still alive to share each precious moment. Milo opening a talking gift box on his tenth birthday, the sculpted face upon the ornate container urging him on. The whole family sharing a picnic lunch alongside Lake Cataria, the afternoon sun shining down on them. Little Milo, a few years younger than he was now, lifting up his baby sister for the first time while Shozana looked on, radiantly proud and happy. . . .

For a moment, his purpose wavered. *Hurry,* the voice demanded, but Faal was transfixed by his son's plight. *What will become of him?* Probing the boy's mind, he discovered a power not unlike his own growing within the sleeping child's brain. Perhaps Milo had followed him across the evolutionary threshold, attaining the same paranormal capabilities? Faal found himself both pleased and disturbed by the prospect. This had not been part of his plan; he had resolved to leave such mortal ties behind him forever. *Flesh does not matter. Matter does not matter.* The sunny recollections welling up inside him gave way to the searing image of Shozana as she disintegrated forever upon that malfunctioning transporter pad, demonstrating irrevocably the fundamental frailty and impermanence of humanoid relationships. He could never allow himself to be hurt that way again.

Milo has been gifted, too. He doen't need a father anymore. Mind is all that matters. Faal turned away from the boy's bed, confident that he was making the right decision. Milo could look after Kinya, too. He had always been good at that, especially since their mother died. Besides, there was another child that concerned him now, concerned the voice. An image came to his mind of an infant, a mere toddler, with incredible powers and an even more astounding heritage. *The child of Q and Q,* the next step in the evolution of the mind. The child of the future. His future. . . .

Goodbye, he thought to both of his children, the children of the past, and left sickbay. No one tried to stop him.

Come. Hurry. Now.

The corridors outside were blessedly free of people. All crew members were at their posts, he assumed. Red-alert signals, horizontal in orientation, still flashed upon the walls. Faal walked at an ever increasing pace toward the nearest turbolift. The last time he had trod these halls, intent on the same destination, he had been near the end of his tether, scarcely able to force his debilitated body to take another step; now he raced effortlessly upon legs that no longer ached with every movement. The closer he came to his destiny, the stronger he felt. By the time he reached the turbolift entrance, he was literally running. He waited impatiently for the door to slide open.

Close, closer, closest.

"The turbolifts are not currently available to unauthorized personnel," an automated voice informed him. "Civilian passengers should report to either sickbay or their quarters."

Of course, he remembered. The blasted red alert. The officious computer and its meaningless protocols had halted him before, but this time he would not be denied. "Open," he ordered the door, his enhanced mind adding force to his command. *No more obsta-*

cles. The bright red door slid open obligingly and he stepped inside. "Engineering," he said, receiving no further argument from the computer. The turbolift carried him nearer to his destiny. *Soon,* he promised the voice. *Soon, sooner, soonest.*

The trip to Engineering took less than a minute. Exiting the turbolift, he entered a beehive of activity. Moving with the efficiency and coordination of a finely calibrated isolinear relay, Starfleet personnel scurried about the massive multilevel engineering center, performing diagnostics and needed repairs on a variety systems. *Mere specks,* he dismissed them. *Specks inside a shiny, silver bug.* The bulk of their efforts appeared centered around the warp-engine controls, but the crew was also focused on systems as diverse as the subspace field distortion amplifiers and the structural integrity field power conduits. The master situation monitor, featuring a cutaway schematic of the *Enterprise,* highlighted malfunctions throughout the entire vessel, although one by one systems seemed to be slowly coming back on-line.

None of this matters, only the wall. The wall is all.

So intent on their repairs were the crew that no one noticed Faal's arrival at first. He went straight to the chief engineer's office, where La Forge had earlier delegated an auxiliary workstation to Faal. To his relief, no one was utilizing the station as he approached, although Ensign Sutter was hard at work nearby, using a handheld laser wielder to seal the ruptured casing of a waveguide conduit junction. He logged into the computer terminal and called up the parameters for the subspace tensor matrix necessary to create his artificial wormhole. He was surprised and pleased by how easily he could read the complicated display screens; he wasn't even farsighted anymore. *Mind over matter. The mind sees what mere matter cannot.* Providentially, proving the unstoppable inevitability of his quest, the data was still intact, despite all the damage caused by the senseless attack of the Calamarain. The quantum torpedo containing the specialized magneton pulse generator was unharmed as well, and ready to be launched into the barrier as soon as he took over the tactical controls.

Yes, he thought. Mind was all that mattered, but he still needed these machines, at least for this one last task. The voice told him so. The barrier was made of mind as well, and so could not be undone by mind alone. The minds of the Q had made it so. *Curse the Q, curse them all!* Only his wormhole, born of mortal science, could bring down the wall. *Machine against mind . . .*

First, though, he was going to need extra power to generate the subspace matrix via the *Enterprise*'s main deflector dish. With that in view, he began rerouting the preignition plasma from the impulse deck to the auxiliary intake. He and La Forge had already worked out the procedure, back before Captain Picard disappeared and his fainthearted crew lost their enthusiasm for the experiment. *Fine,* he thought, diverting the plasma as planned. *Fine, finer, finest.* This would only take a moment or two.

His efforts did not go unnoticed. Geordi La Forge came running from matter-antimatter reaction chamber, darting around the tabletop master systems display. "What the devil is going on with the plasma injectors?" he asked loudly, then slowed to a stop as his optical implants spotted the Betazoid scientist at the auxiliary station. "Professor Faal? What are you doing here?" He looked more carefully at Faal. "What's happened to your eyes?"

Says the blind man, Faal thought ungraciously. Not long ago, but before Faal's apotheosis, La Forge had banished him from main engineering after Faal tried to overrule Commander Riker's order to abort the experiment. Despite all that happened to him since, Faal had neither forgotten nor forgiven. *They are all against me. The crew, the Q, all of them.* "I'm doing what I came here to do," he said icily. "What Starfleet Command ordered you all to assist."

What the voice calls out for. . . .

La Forge smacked his palm against his comm badge. "Security to Engineering, pronto!" Then he wasted his breath trying to deter Faal by his words alone. "But we can't create the wormhole now," he said, badgering Faal with his timid, trivial objections, "not while the *Enterprise* is still in the barrier, too. We're too close to ground zero to initiate the wormhole even if we still wanted to."

The voice will protect me, he thought, knowing La Forge could never understand. *I am beyond physical danger.* "That's not my concern," he said, turning his back on the cowardly engineer. *The mind is all.* "Computer, prepare to launch modified torpedo, designation Faal-alpha-one."

Ordinarily, a quantum torpedo, modified or otherwise, could not be launched without authorization from the captain or the tactical officer, but control of this particular torpedo, containing the experimental magneton pulse generator, had already been diverted to Faal's personal controls so that he and La Forge could supervise every step of the experiment. *Not that any common computer could stand against my will now,* Faal thought. *My mind is mightier than any mere machine.* The preapproved launch authority only made his task easier.

"Acknowledged," the computer reported. "Torpedo Faal-alpha-one loaded and ready to launch on command."

"Sutter, stop him!" La Forge called out.

Caught by surprise, along with everyone else in earshot, Sutter improvised, aiming his laser wielder at Faal's exposed back like a phaser. "Step away from the controls, Professor. I don't want to use this weapon."

He never had a chance. The metal instrument vanished instantly, leaving him staring in amazement at his empty hand. La Forge was also stunned by this demonstration of Faal's new powers; the circular lenses in his state-of-the-art optical implants refocused on his fingers as he struggled to process this unexpected visual stimulus. Faal sensed the chief engineer's shocked surprise, along with a heightened sense of caution and concern. *Now do you under-stand?* he wondered. *Now do you comprehend the magnitude of what is at stake?*

To his credit, La Forge did not panic when confronted with the miraculous. "Professor Faal. Lem," he began, stepping toward the scientist slowly while making another futile try at dissuading Faal from his destiny. "Be reasonable. I know how important your work is to you, but—"

"You can't possibly dream how important this is," Faal declared, affronted by the human's presumption. "You never could." He watched in satisfaction as the monitor reported the power transfer complete. "I've been reasonable long enough, while Riker and Q and the rest of you did everything you could to obstruct my plans, keep me from my ultimate triumph and transfiguration." His impatience and irritation swelled when he recalled how Riker had ordered him physically removed from the bridge, taking advantage of his former infirmity and weakness. "No more," he vowed. *Never again, say I.* "Computer, initiate subspace tensor matrix."

A pair of security officers rushed into Engineering, phasers ready. "Stop him," La Forge instructed, pointing at Faal, "but be careful. He's more dangerous than he looks."

Nodding, both officers aimed their weapons at Faal and fired. Twin beams of crimson energy intersected between the Betazoid physicist's shoulder blades, only to be blocked by the invisible forcefield Faal willed into being. The crimson rays ricocheted off the protective shield and bounced back through Engineering, eliciting cries of alarm. The deflected beams triggered explosions of sparks and haze where they met with vulnerable conduits and circuitry.

Fools, Faal thought contemptuously. *Insignificant specks.*

The security team switched off the phasers to prevent further damage, then rushed ahead to subdue Faal physically, but his self-generated forcefield repelled the two officers as well. Psychic energy crackled noisily as their outstretched hands came into with his protective field. They yanked back their hands as if burned, then looked at each other in confusion. "Sir?" one of them asked, turning to La Forge for guidance.

Faal couldn't care less about the guards' dilemma. He watched the display panel avidly, his luminous eyes widening in anticipation as the *Enterprise* projected a stream of precisely modulated verteron particles into the densest region of the barrier, producing a subspace tensor matrix of exactly the correct configuration and intensity. Faal spared a moment to give silent thanks to Dr. Lenara Kahn, the Trill researcher whose pioneering work had laid the groundwork for what he was now about to do, the mind behind the machine. Only a Trill, he reflected, blessed with the accumulated knowledge of an immortal symbiont, could begin to understand his profound and transforming communion with the voice behind the wall, that voice that was now inside him. "Computer, launch modified torpedo. Vector 32-60-45."

"No!" La Forge shouted. He dashed to the master systems table, where he tried to manually override the launch command. His efforts showed up on Faal's monitor and he glared at La Forge in irritation. How long was he expected to endure such small-minded interference? *You have never understood, La Forge. You could never truly see my vision.* With a thought, he deactivated the implants within La Forge's eye sockets, casting the treacherous meddler into darkness. "My eyes! What have you done! I can't see!" A horrified gasp echoed through Engineering as the Starfleet officer groped for the controls with tentative hands, now as blind in reality as he had always been to the true importance of the work. A fitting fate, Faal thought, for so limited and faintehearted an imagination. *You never saw what I see.*

Smiling with cruel satisfaction, Faal tracked the trajectory of the torpedo. *Soon,* he thought. *Soon, sooner, soonest. . . .*

Now.

Chapter Seven

WATCHING CAPTAIN PICARD keep a wary eye on Q and his family, Riker experienced a distinct sense of déjà vu. As he sat beside the captain on the bridge, gratefully removing his gravity boots, he had a sudden vague recollection of meeting Q under very different circumstances, on a different ship with a different captain. Captain Janeway. *Voyager.* Some kind of trial. . . . He tried to dredge the details up from his unconscious, make the fragmentary impressions cohere, but it was as nebulous and hard to grasp as a half-remembered dream. *That's probably all it is,* he thought, *or more like a nightmare if Q was involved.* He kept his mouth shut, not about to give Q the satisfaction of knowing that he had invaded Riker's dreams.

Excited by his father's return, little q demanded attention. He bounced up and down in Q's arms, waving his half-eaten glop-on-a-stick like a magic wand.

"Good morning to you, little man," Q said sunnily, beaming at his child. Riker felt a peculiar twinge of jealously; for all his irresponsible ways, Q was obviously a more doting and affectionate father than Kyle Riker had ever been. "Or is it good evening?" Q glanced at Picard. "For the eternal life of me, I never have been able to figure out just how you people manage to tell the time of day in this stultifyingly artificial environment of yours."

"We muddle through somehow," Picard said dryly, unamused by the Q's touching family reunion. No doubt he was concerned about Baeta Leyoro and the other crew members now in sickbay; Riker had brought Picard up to speed on Leyoro's shocking collapse, wishing he could have spared the captain that news. Picard had enough problems to worry about, especially with three Q's aboard and the warp drive still down.

"You're going to spoil him," the female Q scolded, rising from Deanna's seat and stepping around the accompanying computer console. She crossed the debris-strewn bridge to where Q and q cavorted. She wiped her son's messy mouth with a monogrammed handkerchief (inscribed with a stylish "Q") that she drew from thin air. "Look, he's got organic residue and sucrose contaminants all over his face."

Gathered together, engrossed with each other, the

Q family presented a surprisingly ordinary portrait of domestic life. *Who'd have thought that Q would turn out to be such a family man?* Riker thought, not quite believing his eyes.

"Nonsense!" Q asserted. "There's no such thing as a spoiled Q." Riker saw the captain raise a skeptical eyebrow at that remark and look like he was tempted to dispute the claim. The first officer knew just how Picard felt. *The real question is,* he mused, *has there ever been a Q that wasn't spoiled by too much power and not enough accountability?* He was inclined to doubt it. "But why is it so dark in here?" Q asked, seeming to notice the faint lighting for the first time. "Trying to saving a few credits on the power bill, Riker?" He shook his head. "No, this just won't do. The place looks like a crypt."

As if on cue, the overhead lights came back on, dispelling the brooding shadows from the bridge. Faint blue tracking lights also reignited along the floor. *Thank heavens for small favors,* Riker thought, refusing to thank Q either verbally or mentally. His command console had previously informed him that gravity had been restored not just on the bridge, but throughout the entire saucer section. *Maybe we're finally starting to get things back under control.*

"Captain!" Ensign Berglund exclaimed at tactical. "According to the control panel, we've just fired a torpedo into the barrier!"

"What?" Picard blurted, spinning around in his chair to face the tactical podium. Riker was caught equally off guard, and even Q looked up in surprise from the babbling toddler in his arms, a puzzled expression on his face.

"It wasn't me," Berglund explained hastily, her pale face whiter than usual. "From the looks of it, the torpedo was launched from Engineering."

Faal, Riker realized intuitively. *The experiment.* Almost simultaneously, Geordi's voice came over the first officer's combadge. "Commander. We have a problem. Lem Faal has just launched the retooled torpedo. He's going to create the wormhole!"

What the devil? Riker thought. Faal had fled sickbay earlier, but security had returned both him and his son to Dr. Crusher in an unconscious state. They were supposed to be out cold, like Leyoro.

"Sickbay confirms that Professor Faal left sickbay after attacking several officers," Ensign Berglund reported. "They say he is armed with . . . telekinetic powers?"

"Faal can *do* things, Commander. Like a Q," La Forge said, unintentionally seconding Berglund's report. His voice sounded shaken, but under control. Riker guessed that the engineer was only giving him the most pertinent details; something else had happened in Engineering, something bad. Had the obsessed scientist harmed or killed a crew member? *First Deanna, now this.* One way or another, Riker intended to see that he was put away for a very long time, winner of the Daystrom Prize or not. First things first, however. "Riker to sickbay," he said via his combadge. "Casualties in Engineering."

"Faal has to be stopped," the captain declared, his

voice and expression grave. Riker could tell from the captain's manner that there was more at stake than just the safety of the *Enterprise*. "We cannot let the wormhole form, Number One. That is vitally important to safety of the entire galaxy." He jumped to his feet and strode toward the Q's family tableau. "Q!" he demanded harshly. "Do something. Quickly!"

Still distracted by his squirming, squealing son, Q glanced over his shoulder at the featureless glow on the main viewer. *Can he see something that the rest of us can't?* Riker wondered. "Yes, of course," Q stammered, awkwardly attempting to hand off q to his mother. The child was determined to stay where he was, though, clinging to Q's neck with *jumja*-stained arms while his happy hellos turned into an earsplitting wail of protest. "Just give me a second. . . ."

"Captain," Data reported from Ops. "I am detecting a subspace tensor matrix identical to the one required by Professor Faal's calculations. It is being generated by the *Enterprise* as we speak."

"Shut it down," Picard ordered. The wails of the fussing child added an extra, unwanted level of chaos to an already tense situation. "Do whatever you have to in order to terminate the matrix."

"I am trying, Captain," the android stated, "but the controls are not responding."

"Fire phasers," Picard directed Berglund. "Target that torpedo." If they were lucky, Riker realized, they might be able to destroy the specialized torpedo before it emitted the magneton pulse that would create the wormhole. But what if they failed?

"Captain," he pointed out, "if that wormhole does start to form, we don't want to be nearby. The gravitational flux alone could finish us. Perhaps we should put some distance between us and the torpedo, just in case."

Picard shook his head. "If we don't stop Faal from tearing a hole in the barrier, Number One, it may be too late for the entire Alpha Quadrant." He gave Riker a solemn look, letting the first officer see some of his anxiety. "There's a being on the other side of the barrier, Will. A being that we cannot allow into our galaxy again."

A being? Riker reacted. *Like Q?* While the first officer digested that chilling revelation, Ensign Berglund called out from tactical, her voice cracking. "The phasers aren't doing any good, sir. Something's protecting the torpedo. A forcefield maybe, or the barrier itself. The sensor readings are strange." She wiped the perspiration from her brow. "I've never seen anything like them."

How was Faal doing this? Why aren't Geordi and the others able to stop him? Riker wished now that he had confined the fanatical scientist to the brig the first time he raised an uproar. It was too late now; they were rapidly running out of options. Calling up the missile's trajectory on his own command console, he saw that the torpedo was only seconds from the perimeter of the barrier.

"Q," Picard exhorted his old nemesis. "You have to do something!"

113

Successfully prying q off his harried father, the female Q carried the crying child to the starboard side of the bridge, stroking and cooing q in hopes of quieting his tantrum. Free from his son's clutches, if not from the nerve-jangling noise of his shrieks and sobs, Q spun around and faced the shimmering view-screen. He stretched out his hands before him, as if reaching for the unseen torpedo. His brow knitted in concentration. His fingers flexed as a grunt of exertion slipped past his lips.

"What is it, Q?" Picard asked apprehensively. "What's happening?"

"Something is blocking me," Q admitted. Riker was surprised by the evident strain in the all-powerful being's voice, not to mention a note of genuine fear. "It's him, Picard. He's here."

"Where?" Picard asked desperately. Riker ground his teeth together, wishing he knew more about what was happening. What sort of being could spook both the Captain and Q?

"Here on your ship," Q said, the muscles beneath his face twitching as he sought to exert his considerable powers upon the intractable torpedo, "at least in part. And behind the barrier as well. He's all around us, Picard, flanking me at every turn. . . ."

Perhaps frightened by his father's obvious anxiety, or simply determined to escape his mother's confining embrace, little q teleported away in a twinkling of light. The female Q gaped at her now-empty arms with a look of distress. "Oh no!" she exclaimed and disappeared herself, doubtless in pursuit of her elusive child. Riker was not saddened to see them go, not if it meant two fewer distractions for all concerned, including Q, who seemed to have his hands full at the moment, as impossible as that sounded.

"Captain," Data announced with inhuman calm, "the magneton pulse generator within the torpedo has been activated. The pulse is reacting with the subspace matrix, exactly as Professor Faal's theory predicted." He studied the sensor readings displayed at his console. "I am detecting elevated neutrino levels, indicative of wormhole formation."

"What if we used phase conjugate graviton beams to disrupt the wormhole's spatial matrix?" Riker suggested, remembering that Starfleet had tried just such a tactic to permanently close the Bajoran wormhole near Deep Space Nine. That effort had failed, but only because of Changeling sabotage.

"You might as well throw rocks at it," Q said scornfully, dismissing Riker's plan. His shoulders sagged as his arms dropped to his sides. "It's too late, Picard. We've lost." His voice took on a doleful tone as he exchanged a worried look with Picard. "He's coming through."

"Um, who is *he* exactly?" Barclay asked nervously, voicing the unspoken question in the minds of everyone except the captain and the Q's. *Frankly, I wouldn't mind learning that myself,* Riker thought, but first there was the little matter of a wormhole to deal with.

Picard had reached the same conclusion. "Ensign Clarze," he addressed the conn, "get us out of the barrier now. Maximum impulse."

"Yes, sir!" the young Deltan said. There was no change upon the overloaded viewscreen, but Riker felt the thrum of the impulse drive beneath his feet as the *Enterprise* headed back toward the galaxy it came from. But even at maximum impulse, could they possibly escape the barrier before the birth of the artificial wormhole wrenched apart the very fabric of space-time?

"A massive quantum fluctuation is forming directly behind us," Data reported. "The subspace shock wave, registering 715.360 millicochranes, will strike the ship in approximately 2.008 seconds."

Riker couldn't vouch for the precise accuracy of the android's prediction, but he felt the shock wave almost immediately. The subspace tremor buffeted the *Enterprise,* nearly shaking the first officer from his seat. *Thank heaven for Barclay's psionically enhanced deflectors.* He'd have to commend the hapless engineer for his creativity during a crisis, if the ship didn't come apart first. "Shields buckling!" Ensign Berglund called out, holding on to the tactical podium for dear life.

More shocks jolted Riker as the intense vibrations rattled every bone in his body. His aching head felt like a warp-core breach. Sparks flared at the conn station, nearly burning Ensign Clarze, who shielded his face with his arm. Riker glanced quickly at Picard, who grabbed on to the back of Deanna's chair to keep from falling. The entire ship was quivering like a Vulcan gong right after it had been struck. *Has the captain returned to the* Enterprise, Riker wondered, *just in time to perish with the rest of us?*

"Captain! Commander Riker!" Ensign Clarze shouted over the quaking of the bridge. "The warp engines have come back on-line."

Thank you, Geordi, Riker thought. *And just in time.* "Go to warp, mister. Now!"

Fee fie fo fum, I smell freedom. Here I come. . . .
The scent of freshly liberated neutrinos wafted across the great wall, bringing with it the promise of rescue after oh so many aeons. His pawn within the shiny silver bug, abetted by a piece of his own splendiferous spirit, had done its part at last. He sensed the forbidding fire of the great wall, the same damnable dynamism that had held him back for so long, crumbling beneath the ingenious assault of the clever little beings inhabiting the silver bug. A window was opening, a window through which he would finally be able to slip over to the other side, where an infinity of diversions awaited him, not to mention revenge on the perfidious Q.

Q is for quisling, he chanted impatiently. *Q is for quarry.* He'd hunt Q, he would, enjoying every frenzied heartbeat of the chase, and, at the end of the game, he'd show just as much mercy and understanding as Q had showed him at the moment of bleakest, blackest betrayal. *Q is for quitter, whose questionable quibbles and querulous qualms quashed my quintes-*

sential quest and quickened my quiddity to queer and quiescent quarantine.

Within the barrier, reality twisted and contorted itself, creating a gap that had never before existed. So intent was he on the window that was being carved out of the unforgiving unity of the wall that he barely noticed the tiny silver insect fleeing frantically from the maelstrom it had engendered. Retracting his tendrils, compacting his entire being into a single infinitesimal point of consciousness, he watched and waited until the window opened all the way through to the other side. He felt exotic solar winds, exhaled by a billion distant suns, blow against his provoked perceptions, inciting him onward.

With nary a nanosecond of doubt or hesitation, he hurled himself into the voracious vortex, diving for deliverance from an eternity of exile and isolation. The empty void of the window was like an ice-cold pond compared with the blazing furnace of cosmic energies that composed the wall. The shock was enough to stop his breath, assuming he felt the need to breathe, but he barreled on nonetheless, eager to reach the other side—where Q would be waiting.

Once before, he recalled, his scattered memory racing backward in time even as the totality of his being rushed back into the galaxy, he had flung himself through another window, the so-called Guardian of Forever. Then, too, Q had been waiting, but to help him, not hinder, not yet. *Oh, those were the days,* he rhapsodized, *days of fire and fun and furor.* He flew past the pierced substance of the wall, the wall that could no longer deny him. *Those days will come again.*

But the window was a fragile one, doomed to dissolve within a heartbeat. Already it was shrinking, squeezing him tightly. The gap was narrowing, the accursed wall encroaching on his escape route at a redoubtable rate. Again he recalled that earlier window, whose graven Guardian had strived so relentlessly to keep him from emerging into the new reality on the other side. For a time, he had been trapped in the window, held fast halfway between one realm and another. Then only Q had been there to pull him through, only Q had saved him, only to betray him when it mattered most.

Q is for quisling. Q is for quitter.

Now he was nearly trapped again, the window narrowing so quickly that he feared he would not be able to squeeze his way through to the other side, no matter how small he made himself, no matter how swiftly he soared nor how furiously he fought against the wall pressing in on him. Now, as before, it was Q that gave him the strength to continue, his hatred of Q and his desire for vengeance that propelled him onward despite the noxious narrowing of the window.

I'm coming for you, he howled into the star-strewn galaxy ahead. *Coming for Q and Q and Q!*

The distant stars were closer now, but the scope of his view was diminishing rapidly, shrinking inward like the pupil of a cyclopean eye dilating in reverse. So close! *Close, closer, closest.* He summoned the remainder of his resources, all that he had not already entrusted to his surrogate beyond the wall, for one final spasm of speed to bring him beyond the boundary forever and ever. The wall tried to deter him, the frictional forces fighting him every inch of the way. Then, all at once, he was free of both wall and window, among the stars he had spied upon from afar. He had made it! Made it he had!

The window snapped shut behind him, shrinking into nothingness, the eternal wall regaining its seamless and sacred solidity, but he did not look back. There was nothing for him there, there never had been, only endless and immeasurable exile. His future, boundless and infinite enticing, lay ahead, like this gorgeous galaxy and its trillions upon trillions of waiting worlds. And Q, of course.

Q is for quarry, quoth I. Q will quake and quiver and quail. . . .

"Go to warp, mister. Now!

In an instant, the *Enterprise* was accelerated at warp speed out of the barrier and away from the wormhole. The bone-rattling shaking subsided and the eerie glow of the galactic barrier, which had filled the viewscreen since Picard's return to his ship, gave way to the reassuring sight of stars streaking past the prow at what looked like warp factor eight or more, faster than the subspace shock wave that had nearly destroyed the *Enterprise*. They'd had a narrow escape, but had they fled swiftly enough to escape 0 himself?

"Captain," Data reported, "according to the long-range sensors, the artificial wormhole has already collapsed. The total duration of its existence was no longer than 1.004 seconds."

"Long enough," Q said glumly, with uncharacteristic directness. "He's here. On the *Enterprise.*"

Chapter Eight

> *"Little soldiers in a row,*
> *One big puff and down you go,*
> *Bodies, bodies, on the floor,*
> *Sadly you will play no more. . . ."*

THE OMINOUS DITTY came from on high, echoing all over the bridge. Startled, Riker and the others looked up at the ceiling, searching in vain for the source of the inexplicable crooning. Picard recognized the raspy voice, as did Q, who could not repress a genuine shudder. "I never did like his singing," he said in a transparent attempt to maintain a brave front. For a moment, he reminded Picard inescapably of the in-over-his-head youth Q had once been. He could not possibly be looking forward to this reunion, not after playing such a deciding role in 0's downfall so many ages ago. *I almost feel sorry for him,* Picard thought.

He sat down in his chair and held his breath expectantly. He could not begin to imagine how 0 would manifest himself. Had the immortal entity changed at all over the last five hundred thousand years? What might all those thousands of centuries of banishment have done to him? "Be on your guard, Number One," he said tersely. "This entity is not to be trusted."

But could Q? The thought fleetingly passed through Picard's mind that maybe what he had witnessed in the distant past had been nothing more than an elaborate fiction, an illusion created by Q's vast and limitless power. *No,* he concluded, *that does not ring true.* Although he conceded that Q could certainly create just such a shadowplay if he so chose, Picard knew in his gut that all he had seen had truly happened. 0's crimes had been real, and so was the present danger.

A Q-like flash of light at the prow of the bridge heralded 0's arrival. He appeared in front of the viewscreen, facing Data and Ensign Clarze. The helmsman lurched back in his seat involuntarily while the android merely cocked his head in contemplation of the stranger's miraculous entrance and striking appearance.

"Do you still like to play games, Q?"

Picard barely recognized 0. He looked like a refuge or disaster victim, freshly rescued from some barren asteroid or moon, who had long since abandone concern over his appearance. His foppish finery had been reduced to rags and tatters, his shredded green velvet coat hanging like streamers from bony shoulders now a few sizes too small for his garments. Oily, uncombed orange hair, streaked with geriatric shocks of white, spilled over those same shoulders, joining a thick, matted beard through which cracked, yellow teeth bared a skull's unsettling grin. Callused toes, the nails curled and overgrown, protruded from beneath the overlapping strips of fraying damask wrapped around his feet, the left of which remained twisted and distorted. Ancient scars climbed up his deformed ankle, disappearing beneath the torn cuffs of his antique trousers.

The emaciated figure before Picard bore little resemblance to the charismatic ne'er-do-well who had so captivated the younger Q. The present Q stared aghast at what 0 had become. "By the Continuum!" he whispered hoarsely.

The interdimensional exile appeared to have fallen on hard times indeed. *Perhaps,* Picard hoped, *he is no longer as powerful as once he was.* Certainly there was a glint of utter insanity in the figure's gleeful blue eyes that Picard did not recall seeing there before. The wild eyes searched the bridge hungrily, taking in every detail before settling on Q. A string of saliva drooled from one corner of 0's mouth.

"Q!" he proclaimed. "And not just any Q, but my Q, the Q of all Q's!" His manic grin stretched even further, more than Picard would have thought was even possible. Was it just his imagination, or were 0's very features more fluid and mutable than he remembered, as if the crippled castaway could no longer be bothered to maintain a consistent appearance? The bones and musculature beneath his beard and sallow skin seemed to shift subtly from moment to moment. "I told you I'd be back, I did. Are you ready for our game? I know I am."

"What game is that?" Q said warily, keeping his distance. He slowly raised his palms toward 0, just as he had once attempted to fend off Guinan the first time they encountered each other upon the *Enterprise*. He looked ready to defend himself if necessary.

Glancing back at tactical, Picard saw Ensign Berglund reach for her phaser. Catching her eye, he shook his head to discourage whatever she had in mind; he was not about to risk any crew member's life on a futile attempt to take the omnipotent intruder into custody. *Let's see what happens between him and Q before we try anything rash.*

"Why, the only game that matters, Q old Q. The game of life and death, remember?" He pointed a curling yellow fingernail, at least three centimeters in length, at Q, who flinched instinctively even though no lightning bolt or metaphysical death ray leaped from the extended digit. "I'm game if you are."

"More gamy than game, I think," Q said, unable to resist the insult. He wrinkled his nose at 0's wretched and debased appearance.

"Don't put on airs with me, Q!" 0 barked

vehemently that Q stepped back in alarm. "I knew you when, don't forget." A bolt of energy leaped from his open hand, smashing through Q's defenses as if they didn't exist and knocking Q off his feet. The impact of the blast was enough to make the whole ship lurched downward, throwing everyone forward. Picard grabbed on to his armrails to keep from falling onto the floor of the command area. The inertial dampers restabilized their orientation after a moment, but it was a terrifying demonstration of the power that remained within 0's degraded shell. Picard wanted desperately to intervene, to take a stand against 0's callous disregard for the ship and the crew, but he knew better than to provoke 0 to no purpose. *This is Q's game for now. Let him play the first cards.*

0 paced back and forth before the viewscreen, dragging his mangled foot behind him. "Are your wits as sharp as your tongue, Q? I wonder. You'll need all your wits to play my game. It's time to be tested!" He fired another bolt that sent Q tumbling backward. "Sorry to keep you waiting."

"I could have waited a good deal longer," Q said weakly, climbing awkwardly to his feet. The look on his face deeply concerned Picard; Q looked genuinely surprised. *But is he shocked by 0's actions or his power?* Picard wondered. He could only hope it was the former, given that Q was their best defense against the dangerous entity. *Surely Q can put up a better fight than this?*

"No more waiting! Wait no more!" 0 cackled. "I had to wait for this shiny silver bug," 0 said, spinning around on his good leg to take in the entire bridge. "I had to wait a very long time. Long, longer, longest."

He's lost his mind altogether, Picard realized, a chill running down his spine. What was more to be dreaded, a cool and calculating 0 or a lunatic with the power of the gods? At least the intruder seemed focused exclusively on Q so far; he had yet to even acknowledge the presence of Picard and the others. *We're too far beneath him, I suppose.*

"What a fine, fast bug this is, too," 0 declared. Something wriggled beneath the tattered fabric of his oversized coat. *What in the world?* Picard thought. Peering more closely at the raving superbeing, he took note of various mysterious moving objects coiling sinuously over 0's shoulders and beneath his arms, making their way underneath his ragged clothing. With a start, Picard recalled the spectral tentacles he had sometimes glimpsed flickering about 0's human form during moments of great stress or exertion. He got the distinct impression that the consistency of that human guise had suffered as much as the rest of his appearance. He was almost afraid to guess what was lurking and flexing beneath 0's coat.

"I can use this bug, when I'm through with you, Q. I have places to go, people to free." The quivering tip of some luminous, phantasmal appendage poked from beneath 0's collar and through the unkempt cascade of hair flowing over his shoulder. It wagged back and forth next to where 0's neck presumably was, as if sampling the atmosphere of the bridge, then withdrew back into the concealing layers of hair and fabric.

From the startled gasp and nervous gulp behind him, Picard guess that both Berglund and Barclay had spotted the tendril as well.

"Careful," Q chided him, tugging at the neck of his Starfleet uniform. "You seem to have a bad case of writhing around the collar."

Was that an attempt at courage, Picard wondered, or was Q simply unable to overlook an opportunity to be snide? Knowing Q, he feared the latter.

"Don't worry, Q, I won't forget you." 0 limped across the prow of the bridge until he stood directly in front of the conn. "Just thinking ahead a bit. Remembering a Head I have to go get." He eyed the navigational controls with keen and avaricious interest. "Right," he muttered into his beard. "Ready the rudder. Ready and roaring."

He poked at the controls with a gnarled nail, keying in new coordinates with the speed and assurance of a veteran pilot, treating cutting-edge Starfleet technology like a children's toy. Picard was appalled at how quickly the deranged entity had mastered the intricacies of starship navigation.

"Wait! What are you doing?" Ensign Clarze protested as the ship began to pitch and yaw. Without thinking, he reached out and seized 0 by the wrist.

It was the last thing he ever did. Before anyone even grasped what was happening, a glowing tentacle burst from 0's chest, ripping his soiled shirt front asunder and wrapping itself around the young Deltan's throat. . . .

Chapter Nine

"DR. CRUSHER, COME QUICKLY!"

The holographic physician's entreaty drew Beverly Crusher instantly to the biobed where Lieutenant Leyoro's body rested within the protective embrace of the surgical support frame. She left Deanna Troi, freshly wakened from her cortically induced coma now that the *Enterprise* had left the barrier behind, to watch over the unconscious form of Milo Faal, while Nurse Ogawa supervised straightening up the disarray caused by Lem Faal during his telekinetic rampage. *Thank heaven no one was hurt seriously,* she thought, although the crazed and mutated scientist remained at large, and capable of most anything, or so it seemed. *It must have been the barrier,* she realized; somehow the awesome psionic energy of the galactic barrier had amplified the Betazoid's already formidable mental gifts. *Was this what he was planning all along? No wonder he resisted all my efforts to protect him from the barrier.*

Crusher pushed such speculations aside to concentrate on the patient at hand. "What is it?" she asked the EMH. Had Leyoro taken a turn for the worse? At a glance, her condition appeared unchanged.

"Look," the hologram said, pointing at the monitor above the bead. "Her neurotransmitter levels are dropping dramatically."

He was right. The activity within the unconscious officer's brain was rapidly returning to normal. It was too early to predict what sort of neurological damage, if any, had already been done by her overstimulated synapses, but this was a very hopeful sign. "Did you do anything?" she asked the computer-generated doctor.

"I wish I could take the credit," he admitted, "but I'm afraid not. I was simply monitoring her condition as you instructed." He glanced past her at the ward beyond, where Alyssa Ogawa was retrieving the last of the fallen exoscalpels from the floor. Like everyone else in sickbay, Ogawa had removed her magnetic boots now that gravity had been restored. Another nurse was handing out newly replicated comm badges. "What in the name of Starfleet medical protocols went on over there?" the EMH inquired, referring to Professor Faal's spectacular escape. "My programming did not begin to prepare me for any events of that nature."

"Join the club," Crusher murmured, preferring to focus on Leyoro's surprising recovery. What could have triggered this turnaround? The triclenidil, she wondered, or something else? Another thought occurred to her: Perhaps it was simply that the *Enterprise* had finally exited the galactic barrier? The removal of the barrier's direct influence upon Leyoro's artificially enhanced nervous system might account for the sudden diminishment of her symptoms.

"How is she doing, Beverly?" Deanna asked, joining her at Leyoro's side. Crusher noted that Ogawa had taken over the watch on Milo. *Good,* she thought. She wanted to know the minute the boy showed signs of consciousness.

"She's been through a rough time," the doctor told Deanna. Although Leyoro's brain was no longer in danger of burning itself out, the Angosian woman remained unconscious, her face immobile. "I can't say yet when or if she will recover."

Troi rested her hands gently upon the surgical support frame enclosing the stricken woman's torso. The EMH stepped aside to give her a little more room. "I can barely sense her consciousness," she said softly, "it's so faint. But she's in pain, terrible pain."

Trusting the counselor's empathic abilities implicitly, Crusher adjusted the dosage of analgesic being administered to Leyoro by infusion system in the SSF. "That's better," Deanna reported a few moments later. She gazed at Leyoro's comatose face.

"I've barely had a chance to get to know her, and now this. It's so tragic."

"She might well pull through," Crusher assured her. "I don't approve of how the Angosian military tampered with her biology, but their goal was to produce extraordinarily strong and resilient individuals. Survivors." She glanced up at the biobed display, glad to see that the patient's neurotransmitter levels were practically back to normal. She made a mental note to access the medical archives of the Angosian veterans facility on Lunar V as soon as possible, although she doubted that anything in their records bore a close resemblance to what effect the galactic barrier could have on a humanoid brain. "We shouldn't underestimate her innate stamina and recuperative powers."

"Not to mention the considerable talents and medical expertise of certain attending physicians," the EMH pointed out, leading Crusher to wonder briefly whether it was technically possible to turn down the volume on the hologram's self-esteem. He was just a little too much like the real Dr. Lewis Zimmerman, whom she'd had the dubious pleasure of meeting a few years back when she'd temporarily taken charge of Starfleet Medical; his ego had required excess stroking as well, she recalled. *I'll have to ask Data or Geordi about how to adjust the program.*

"What about Milo?" she asked Deanna. "Were you able to sense anything?" Milo Faal had not stirred since his unconscious body had been brought to sickbay by Sonya Gomez and the others, although the psionic-energy readings in his youthful brain were scarily similar to those recorded in his father before Lem Faal fled sickbay amid a flurry of telekinetic violence.

Troi shook her head. "I'm very familiar with the ordinary telepathic abilities of full Betazoids—you've met my mother—but this is something new. I've never sensed anything like it. It's like white noise. I can't even sense his emotions anymore."

Crusher frowned. This didn't sound good. She had to worry if Milo would wake with the same astonishing—and dangerous—powers his father had displayed. *Just one more thing to agonize about,* she thought; it didn't help that the eleven-year-old boy invariably reminded her of Wesley at that age.

How do I treat something like this? she wondered. *I could accidentally do more harm than good.* She was starting to wish she had never heard of the galactic barrier.

"At least his younger sister is fine," Crusher reflected. Little Kinya had come out of her artificial coma with no apparent side effects and was now napping quietly in the pediatric unit. Beverly wasn't looking forward to trying to explain to the toddler what had happened to her father and brother. Part of her was still astounded that Lem Faal could just abandon his children like this, no matter what the barrier had done to his mind. *In a way,* she thought, *that's even more unbelievable than his amazing new mental powers.*

"Why don't I check on little Kinya?" Deanna volunteered. Crusher recalled that the counselor had a Betazoid baby brother about the same age as Kinya Faal. "You have enough to keep an eye on here."

"Thank you," Crusher said, grateful for Troi's assistance during this crisis. Both children were going to need plenty of counseling now that their father had apparently lost his mind. "That would be very helpful."

Giving Leyoro one last look, Troi headed toward the emergency pediatric unit attached to the primary care ward. She had only been gone a few minutes, however, when a startled cry from Deanna electrified Crusher's senses and sent her adrenaline rushing. Crusher raced into the children's ward, Ogawa close behind her, to find Troi backed against a row of empty, child-sized biobeds, her hand over her heart. "I'm sorry, Beverly," she stammered quickly, her face flushed, "but he appeared so quickly he caught me by surprise."

Beverly didn't have to ask whom she referred to. The source of the counselor's startlement was readily apparent atop the counter beneath the pediatric supplies cupboard, his pint-sized legs dangling over the edge of the sleek metal counter. Little q was back, doubtless in search of yet another of Crusher's prescription lollipops. His cherubic face looked more anxious than she had ever seen it before.

"Scared," he confessed sheepishly, although of what the doctor couldn't guess. A pudgy little hand reached out to her. "Yum-yum?"

Then the floor tilted forward violently. . . .

* * *

At last, Faal thought. Long-range sensors reported the birth and almost immediate collapse of the wormhole he had created. The transitory nature of its existence did not disturb him; he had not expected his wormhole to last any longer than the ones previously generated by Dr. Kahn and her colleagues. However short-lived, the quantum fluctuation had lasted long enough to serve its purpose—to break through the galactic barrier to the other side. *I did it,* he thought triumphantly. *It I did.* After endless months of planning and striving, after what felt like half a million years, he had succeeded at last.

Now he could turn his expanded mind to even loftier matters. For so long, he had been forced by the limitations of his treacherous flesh to fixate exclusively on one goal, compelled to achieve genuine immortality before death by disease claimed him forever. He had seldom been able to spare one precious moment contemplating what he could do once he attained that immortality. Now, all at once, he had the freedom to find a new purpose in existence, to expand his work to a whole new level of scientific inquiry. *I have evolved beyond mere physical matter. Now my mind can explore the full potential of mind itself. . . .*

The frightened mortals surrounding him, chattering anxiously and cluttering up Engineering, could not appreciate his triumph. They were too caught up in anxiety and adrenaline generated by his takeover of Engineering, not to mention their foolish Starfleet rigmarole. Even now, Lieutenant La Forge sought to take control of the situation, despite the true blindness into which Faal had plunged him. "La Forge to bridge," he reported, holding on to the tabletop display to keep himself oriented in the dark. "We need more security. Faal is free and dangerous." He shouted a command to his engineering crew, as well as to the first security officers on the scene, whose phasers had proved useless against Faal's inexplicable new powers. "Everyone else, stay away from Professor Faal. Keep at your posts. We still have a job to do!"

Daniel Sutter, a merely competent engineer in Faal's opinion, tried to guide La Forge away. "Sir, you should be in sickbay."

"No," La Forge said passionately. "I'm not leaving Engineering in the hands of that menace. I don't need my eyes to do my duty."

Faal shook his head in bemusement. *Specks. They were nothing but specks.* Even now, the sightless engineer could not see past the petty responsibilities of his post, beyond some routine mechanical repairs. Scanning La Forge's mind in an instant, Faal saw the entire infrastructure of the *Enterprise* laid out before him, from the replicator system to the warp engines themselves. Despite Faal's historic triumph over the barrier, part of La Forge's mind was still worrying about repairing a series of sundered thermal isolation struts, and the difficulties of realigning the off-axis field controller. Faal could have done so in an instant, simply by thinking of it, but why should he bother? He had transcended such mundane chores, even if La

Forge and his equally shortsighted servitors had not. *The mind is all that matters now. My mind and the mind of one special child. . . .*

Yes, the child, a voice echoed at the back of his mind, so persuasively that he could scarcely distinguish whether it was his own thought or another's. *The child of Q and Q. The next stage in evolution, beyond the Q, beyond you. . . .*

"Beyond," he breathed softly, recalling the miraculous infant he had briefly observed in the *Enterprise*'s holographic child-care facility. Had not the female Q boasted that her offspring represented a potential advance beyond even the considerable evolutionary development of the Q Continuum? What more suitable subject could he choose for his experiments now that he had transcended his own mortality, achieving a state of being that perhaps rivaled that of the Q themselves? Only he and he alone had the predestined combination of preternatural power and bold scientific imagination to correctly study the unique phenomenon that was the Q child under controlled and rigorous experimental conditions. He had the intellect. He had the ability.

Now all he needed was the child.

He reached out with his mind, searching the entire ship for any sign of the supremely talented toddler. *Where is the child? The child of the mind.* Somehow he knew, perhaps via that voice whispering constantly at the back of his mind, that Q and his family remained aboard the vessel, pursuing their own enigmatic agendas. *The cursed Q, the meddling Q.* All that power and knowledge, he thought rancorously, wasted on frivolous antics and diversions; Q was an embarrassment to immortals everywhere. Faal was surprised at the intensity of the animosity he now felt toward Q. The bitter resentment seemed to course through his soul as surely as the metaphysical might he had absorbed within the barrier. *Damn you, Q,* he cursed, railing against an entity he had scarcely encountered before. *You don't deserve that child.*

His natural telepathy amplified more than he could have ever possibly imagined, he scoured the ship from deck to deck without stirring from his workstation in Engineering. As La Forge and his fellow mortals watched him warily from what they hoped was a safe distance, he located his target in sickbay of all places. *Where Milo and Kinya are,* he recalled, feeling a momentary pang before forcibly shoving the thought away. *Never mind those children. Mind over matter. The child of the mind was all that mattered.* Funny, how his path kept returning to sickbay. What other proof did he require that his destiny was following some mysterious preordained pattern? It was his scientific duty to take custody of the Q child, no matter who might try to oppose him.

That's right, the voice seconded his resolve. *Test the tot. Test him to the breaking point, then probe and peruse the pieces. Test him till there's nothing left of Q and Q. . .*

The Betazoid scientist strode decisively, on strong and tireless legs, toward the exit. His work in

Engineering was done. Now the future, in the unlikely form of child, awaited him in sickbay.

He didn't even notice when the floor of the corridor pitched forward beneath his feet.

Instinctively, Beverly Crusher reached for q the instant she felt the pediatric unit dip toward the bow of the ship. Granted, the toddler was probably infinitely more indestructible than she was, but years of experience as both a doctor and a mother brought with them protective impulses too compelling to be denied. She snatched the child off the metal counter, holding on to him tightly until the floor leveled out again.

"What was that?" Troi gasped, gripping a biobed to steady herself. Standing in the doorway, Alyssa Ogawa looked equally startled. Beverly assumed that the EMH and the other nurses were monitoring Leyoro and Milo.

"I wish I knew," Crusher said. Was the *Enterprise* under attack again? And if so, from whom? The Calamarain? The barrier? Professor Faal? Q? Something else altogether? There were too many possibilities, she thought grimly, at a time when sickbay was too full already.

Carrying q with her, she peered through a transparent aluminum porthole, seeing no sign of either of the luminescent cloud-beings that had besieged the *Enterprise* earlier, nor any trace of the distinctive glow of the galactic barrier. Judging from the way the stars were streaking past, though, she saw that the ship had gone into warp at some point. *That has to be a good sign,* she thought. *I hope.*

She tapped her brand-new comm badge. "Crusher to bridge. Is there an emergency?"

Lieutenant Barclay responded to her hail, indicating that both the captain and Commander Riker, not to mention ops and security, were too busy coping with the latest crisis. *At least Jean-Luc is back,* she thought, the bridge having alerted her to the captain's return. *That's something.*

"There's an intruder on the bridge," Barclay stammered, sounding badly rattled. "Another Q, I think, or something like him. I really don't know much more." She could hear him gulp even over the comm line. "Prepare for casualties, Doctor. Barclay out."

Casualties? Another Q? Crusher craved more information, however bad, but knew better than to distract the bridge crew during a battle. This wouldn't be the first time she had found herself holding the fort in sickbay while praying that Jean-Luc and the others would save them all from the Borg or the Romulans or whomever, but that didn't make the waiting any easier.

Not surprisingly, the turbulence and activity had roused Kinya Faal from her nap. The little girl sat up in one of the pediatric biobeds and started crying. Crusher didn't blame her one bit for being frightened. She was feeling more than a little apprehensive herself.

She tried to hand Q's son over to Deanna, intending to calm Kinya personally, but he started to squirm and fuss. "Okay, okay," Crusher assured him. The last thing she needed was two crying kids; Kinya would have to wait a few more moments. "I know what you want." She nodded at Troi. "Deanna, can you get me one of those replicated lollipops from the storage locker? I think he likes the uttaberry ones."

"Actually, his favorite flavor is Baldoxic vinegar," the female Q said, appearing without warning between Crusher and Troi, "but I don't suppose you're familiar with that particular taste treat."

Crusher had never heard of it before and frankly she didn't care. How in the world was she supposed to get used to people just popping in like that? Her heart went out to Jean-Luc when she realized how many times the original Q must have startled him that way; it was a miracle that the captain's blood pressure was as consistently low as it was. "I thought we had a little talk about these surprise appearances," she reminded the female Q a bit tootily.

"My apologies," the Q replied with surprisingly little argument. "Darling q just keeps me hopping, you know." She reached out for her child. "Forgive me if I don't linger to chat, but I'm afraid there's been some unpleasantness on the bridge, and I would just as soon see q safely elsewhere."

"What sort of unpleasantness?" Crusher asked quickly, desperate to learn more of what was happening on the bridge. She held on to q in hopes of delaying the female Q's departure for just a few moments. "Who is that intruder?"

"Well, it's a rather long story," the Q replied, a

pained expression upon her patrician features. In her Starfleet uniform, she stood several centimeters taller than either Crusher or Ogawa. "A few billion years long, in fact." She paused for a second, placing an elegant finger beneath her chin as she considered how best to summarize the tale. "Let's just say," she said finally, "that an unsavory acquaintance of my husband has made a most unwelcome return."

What exactly did that mean? Beverly wondered. Had the *Enterprise* ended up stuck in the middle of some petty Q feud? Stranger things had happened, especially where Q was concerned. "What sort of acquaint—" she began.

A cry from the primary ward cut off her next question. *That sounded like the EMH,* she thought, anxiously wondering what had caused the disturbance and whether it had anything to do with the "unsavory acquaintance" the female Q had just mentioned. Or maybe Milo had woken up much like his father? Ogawa hurried toward the cry, but Beverly hesitated, reluctant to leave either child alone before she knew what sort of danger might have arrived. More shouts came from outside the children's ward and Troi ran to the doorway to investigate, only to back up immediately when she saw what was coming.

An instant later, Lem Faal appeared framed in the doorway, his eyes glowing with the energy of the galactic barrier, his lean face as cold and expressionless as a Vulcan's. Crusher knew in an instant that he had not returned to sickbay to check on his dormant children.

Faal's icy composure faltered perceptibly when he spotted the female Q standing behind Crusher. "You," he said in evident displeasure. "What are you doing here?"

"I don't believe we've been introduced," the female Q said stiffly. If she remembered Faal at all from their fleeting encounter in the holodeck a few evenings ago, she gave no evidence of it.

Faal eyed her like he might a specimen on a slide. "You don't matter anymore," he told her. "You're no longer the forefront of evolution. You've been rendered obsolete." His luminous gaze shifted from the female Q to the child in Crusher's arms. "It's the child I'm after. The child of the future."

"What?" Before any of the women could react to Faal's astonishing declaration, Crusher felt a powerful force rip baby q from her arms. She struggled to hold on to the child, but it was like trying to hang on to a loose padd during explosive decompression, something Beverly had personal experience of. The toddler was gone, and clutched under Faal's arm, before she even knew what was happening. Snatched from Crusher, q started to cry, but Faal placed his free hand against q's unprotected neck. There was a flash of discharged energy and q's body drooped limply within Faal's grasp, his tiny arms and head sagging toward the floor below.

A sense of horror rushed over Crusher, and she could only imagine what the baby's mother must be feeling. Had Faal just killed q? Was that even possible? At a glance, she couldn't tell if the child was still breathing, if that meant anything at all where a Q was concerned. "What have you done?" she gasped. "What did you do to him?"

"Anesthetized the subject," he clarified, "to prepare it for further testing."

Further testing? Crusher still couldn't believe what she was hearing and seeing. Even with his unearthly new powers, how could Faal knock out a baby Q? *What in heaven's name has happened to him?* she wondered, shocked as much by his psychotic behavior as his unexpected new abilities. What had changed a noted physicist and father into a crazed stealer of children?

For the first time in Crusher's experience, the female Q's arch and haughty manner gave way to a very human emotional outburst. "My baby!" she cried out in anguish. "q!" Her eyes flashed with murderous hatred. "Give me back my son this instant!"

Faal laughed, remarkably unconcerned by the female Q's maternal fury. "That might have terrified me before, when I was a powerless corporeal being like the rest of them." He sneered in Beverly's direction. "But I'm stronger now, a transcendent being like yourself. Strong, stronger, strongest."

He keeps getting more and more disturbed and irrational, Crusher thought, remembering the soft-spoken Betazoid scientist she had met at the onset of their mission. He had seemed so sane, so normal, then. *It's like there's been a different person growing inside him.* How else to explain those dual brain

144

patterns, as well as his increasingly criminal be-havior?

The female Q was not interested in explanations. All she wanted was her child, and to strike out at the being who had harmed him. "Die!" she spat. "Die and disappear!"

She flung out her fingers—and nothing happened. Faal remained as humanoid as before, the anesthe-tized baby Q still tucked under one arm, his innocuous-looking hypospray held out before him like a weapon. Then he did the last thing Crusher ex-pected him to do. He started to sing.

> "Sweet little baby,
> Peaceful you lie,
> We'll play some games,
> And then you will die. . . ."

"Oh no," the female Q whispered, her confidence and anger replaced by an unmistakable look of alarm. Beverly could tell that more than just the sinister lyrics of the lullaby had disturbed her. She just wished she knew why.

Chapter Ten

ENSIGN CLARZE GRABBED ON TO the twisting appendage with both hands, trying to pull it away from his throat, but the inhuman limb was too strong, seeming composed of equal parts matter and energy. He opened his mouth, either to breathe or to scream, but could succeed at neither. He was being strangled to death upon the bridge of the *Enterprise,* before the horrified eyes of Jean-Luc Picard.

"Q!" the captain shouted at the other immortal, who stood dumbfounded next to ops. "Save him, blast you!"

Although more solid than the spectral limbs Picard had intermittently spied in the past, this tentacle was not made of flesh as the captain knew it. Lambent veins of azure light, the same hue as 0's wild eyes, coursed along the length of the monstrous extension. It was like a limb of pure phaser fire, or a small child's first crude attempt at a hologram, but clearly no less tangible for all that.

Q blinked in surprise, as if the importance of rescuing one insignificant crewman had not occurred to him before. "As you wish," he said, apparently too unnerved by 0's return to want to debate the issue. Ignoring the radiant tentacle, he extended an open palm at 0 himself. A blinding beam of white light fell upon 0, throwing his ragged shadow upon the viewscreen behind him.

"Ha!" 0 barked loudly. He staggered, but did not fall, before Q's broadside. The white light washed over him, bleaching his image beneath its brilliancy, yet the manic grin on his face did not change. "Not bad at all, not at all bad. Picked up a grain more gumption over the ages, I see."

"I'd hoped to disintegrate you," Q replied, lowering his hand in disappointment. The white light seeped into the folds and crevices of 0's scarecrow-like form, leaving him conspicuously unharmed. "No such luck, alas."

Data, with his superhuman reflexes, reacted next. Springing from his seat at ops, he dug his golden fingers deeply into the shining tentacle and struggled to pry it loose from Clarze's throat. Amused, 0 stepped back to let the android work, stretching the tentacle taut between his chest and the endangered ensign. No symptom of exertion showed upon Data's impassive features, but Picard knew that Data had to be using every kilogram of strength he possessed. Placed under tremendous strain, concealed servomotors within Data's arms and shoulders whirred audibly. Horribly, that didn't seem to be enough. The tentacle resisted Data's strenuous efforts while it continued to choke its victim, even as Riker hurried to assist Data.

"Security!" Picard ordered. "Phasers on full." Racing around the starboard side of the bridge, Sondra Berglund positioned herself so that Data was out of the line of fire, then unleashed her phaser upon the tentacle where it stretched between 0 and Clarze. A young security officer, Caitlin Plummer, joined Berglund, adding her own phaser to the assault. Parallel beams of crimson energy struck the tentacle, producing a crackling cascade of white-hot sparks, but the luciferous tendril did not come apart. 0 cackled raucously, insanely indifferent to whatever pain the three-pronged attack on his extremity inflicted on him. Smaller tentacles erupted from his shoulders, flailing about alongside his head.

Clarze's eyes bulged from their sockets, his tongue protruded from his wide-open mouth. "Keep firing!" Picard commanded, consumed by fury and frustration. *Couldn't anything stop this monster?* "Q!" he demanded. "You can't let him kill again!"

Q shook his head mournfully. "I'm sorry, Jean-Luc. I tried."

"Then try again, damn you!" Picard refused to give up, even as 0 laughed off the heroic efforts of four

Starfleet officers to rescue their comrade from 0's homicidal grasp. He couldn't accept that he had to sit by helplessly again while 0 murdered with impunity. The destruction of the Tkon, as tragic and horrible as it was, had been a chapter out of ancient history, long known to Picard. This was happening *now*.

"What's the matter, Q?" 0 mocked him. "Not up to your game these days? Playing the impotent bystander again? Take a good look, Q. You're next!"

Intent on Q now, 0 released Clarze and retracted his ectoplasmic tentacle back into his torso. The Deltan ensign dropped from his seat at the conn, his limp body crumpling to the floor. Berglund and Plummer switched off their phasers immediately, but, moving even faster, Data had already knelt to check the young man's condition. Picard held his breath, hoping for the best, while the android's fingers felt Clarze's throat.

Data rose without ceremony, letting Clarze's skull lie where it fell. "His neck is broken," he announced gravely. "I regret to say he is dead."

Picard stared in horror at the young helmsman's body, at the deep bruises mottling his exposed neck, the blue cyanotic tint of his lifeless face. He remembered, with bitter irony, that he had assigned the inexperienced crewman to the conn because the captain had anticipated smooth sailing on this mission and it had seemed like a valuable opportunity to give new personnel like Clarze a taste of bridge duty. Now the Deltan youth's Starfleet career had been cut prematurely short, along with any other dreams or ambitions he might have harbored. All thanks to 0.

This one death should not shock me, Picard thought numbly. After all, he had already seen 0 murder trillions, when the sadistic entity condemned the entire Tkon Empire to extinction; intellectually, Clarze's brutal slaying was just one more casualty to add to 0's age-old list of crimes. But it didn't feel that way. "How dare you?" he said, his voice choked with feeling. He rose from his chair to look 0 in the eye. "He was only a boy."

"Bye-bye, boy," 0 sang giddily. "Boy oh boy." He snapped his fingers and Clarze's body stirred unexpectedly. Picard experienced a moment surge of hope. Could Data have been mistaken? That was practically impossible, but there was Clarze moving again, clumsily climbing off the floor. Riker reached out to help the young man rise, then yanked back his hand abruptly, eyes wide with shock and disgust. Picard understood why when the figure's dead blue face turned toward him for a moment and he saw the emptiness in the fixed, blank eyes. Suddenly, he realized the full horror of what was occurring. Ensign Clarze was quite dead, in fact, but 0 had revived his lifeless body.

With awkward, jerky motions, the animated corpse of the Starfleet officer retook his former seat at the conn. Dead fingers mechanically tapped the helm controls. "There," 0 said smugly, "the boy is back where he belongs. Take us bye-bye, boy."

Even Q looked appalled by 0's latest atrocity. He

released another burst of light against his former mentor, this time to even less effect. "By the Continuum," he whispered in hushed tones, "what have you become?"

"And you!" Picard said furiously, turning on Q. "Why couldn't you stop him?"

Looking puzzled and somewhat disturbed, Q contemplated his own empty hand, then peered suspiciously at 0. "I'm not sure," he said finally, three words that Picard had never expected to hear from Q. "He's . . . different now. He's found some new source of power."

"I don't like the sound of that," Riker said, leaving the empty conn and joining Picard. He signaled Berglund and Plummer to back away from 0 slowly before they attracted his attention. Picard didn't like the idea of leaving 0's zombie at the conn, but was not willing to sacrifice another crew member by assigning one to that post.

"Captain," Barclay shouted from science II. "The warp drive is accelerating." Proving him completely accurate in his assessment, the rushing streaks of white upon the viewscreen stretched even thinner, approaching invisibility as the *Enterprise*'s velocity increased by several orders of magnitude. "Warp factor eight point five," Barclay reported.

Is this 0's doing as well? Picard confronted Q again. "What's wrong, Q? You stopped him five hundred thousand years ago. How can he be more powerful now? Explain." Before he could attempt any strategy against 0, he needed to know what was happening.

"I don't understand," Q murmured, more to himself than Picard. "Unless—" An unwanted realization rushed over his features, chilling Picard as he was forced to wonder what dire possibility Q could have possibly failed to anticipate, and whether Q would even attempt to explain. "Oh no."

Before Q could share his fears, 0 turned his back on the conn and strolled counterclockwise around the bridge to where Q waited apprehensively. "The rudder is readied," he declared, "our course is corrected. Ready to play, Q?" The smirk on his face could not conceal the ancient enmity in his eyes. "Quisling. Quitter. Quarry."

Q flinched with each epithet 0 spat at him. "I didn't have any choice," he began, "not after what you did. You went too far, or farther than I wanted to go at least." His faced darkened as he remembered all that happened millennia past, all that he had just relived with Picard. "Besides, the Tkon won! They beat you fair and square."

0's cocky grin devolved into a grimace. "Quell your quibbles, Q, or I'll quash you like the quivering, quarrelsome quadruped you are."

"I should never have let you into this multiverse in the first place," Q said defiantly. "I should have left you to freeze in that arctic limbo where I found you. Which reminds me, I never got a chance to ask: Just how many realities have you been kicked out of anyway?"

"Quack! Quadroon!" 0 clenched his fists above his

head and, spiderlike, matching pairs of energized tentacles sprung from his sides, granting him eight limbs in all. Four incandescent extremities leaped forth to ensnare Q within their grasp. Q seemed to welcome the clash, which had been so many aeons in the making; with uncharacteristic violence, he grabbed for 0's scrawny neck with his bare hands and began to throttle his onetime mentor and role model. Picard had never seen Q act so savagely.

For less than a moment, they grappled upon the bridge, 0's glowing tentacles wrapping around Q like coruscating cables, Q's fingers digging into 0's metaphorical flesh, each of them quite intent on squeezing the life out of the other. Then, in a burst of light that left Picard blinking, both figures disappeared from the bridge.

Where did they go? the captain wondered, staring at the empty space that two superbeings had occupied only a heartbeat before. Had that flash been Q's doing or 0's? They could be anywhere in time or space right now, he realized, battling for who knows how long. Was it possible that the dueling entities could keep each other occupied for all eternity, or at least a mortal lifetime or two? There were worse outcomes to imagine, even though he wasn't sure that even Q deserved to be locked in combat with his first and worst enemy until the end of time.

But what if 0 succeeded in destroying Q, as he clearly seemed to have the potential to do? Then every species and civilization could be facing mortal jeopardy. Picard found himself in the peculiar position of rooting for Q. *Better an mischievous imp like Q than the devil himself,* he thought.

In the meantime, he needed to prepare for the eventuality that either Q or 0 or both could return at any moment. He surveyed the bridge, his gaze quickly falling on the abominable sight of the murdered ensign's resurrected body still manning his former post, soulless fingers making minute course corrections to the *Enterprise*'s trajectory even as Picard watched.

No, he thought. *Not one minute more.* Until this instance, he had always thought that nothing worse could happen to a sentient being than to be assimilated by the Borg, but this obscene desecration might have disgusted even the Borg Queen. Picard could only pray that no trace of Ensign Clarze's consciousness remained within the undead revenant he had become. "Ensign Berglund," he said coldly. "Give me your phaser."

Taking the type-1 phaser from the young Canadian officer, he clicked the weapon to its highest setting, then fired it directly at all that remained of Ensign Clarze. For a split second, an intense red glow outlined the reanimated body; then the phased energy broke down the atomic bonds holding the flesh and bone and blood together, vaporizing them until not a single molecule remained intact. Picard lowered the weapon to his side, feeling his heart pound within his chest. *0 will pay for this,* he vowed.

"You did the right thing, Captain," Riker said,

standing stiffly at his side. "Request permission to take over at the conn."

"Make it so," Picard said hoarsely, grateful for Riker's offer to take the helm under such grisly circumstances.

Riker sat down at the conn, occupying the space so recently filled by Clarze's animated cadaver. "Let's hope Q and that other creature are gone for a long time." His fingertips rested atop the helm controls. "Shall I set course for Starbase 146?"

"Most definitely," Picard agreed. From the looks of it, the *Enterprise* was badly in need of maintenance. Furthermore, he wanted to warn Starfleet of the threat posed by 0 as soon as possible. Returning the phaser to Ensign Berglund, who had resumed her station at tactical, he resolved to contact Engineering next, to get a complete status report on the ship's primary systems from Geordi La Forge. Q had obligingly restored the lights and gravity upon the bridge, but what about the rest of the *Enterprise?* His hand hovered above his comm badge.

"Captain," Riker addressed him crisply. The urgent tone of the first officer's voice alerted Picard at once that there was more trouble afoot. "The conn is not responding to my commands."

Blast, Picard thought. This was 0's work, no doubt. "Switch to auxiliary controls," he suggested.

Riker shook his head. "I tried that. I'm completely locked out." His hands marched over the controls decisively, but the hairbreadth streaks rushing past them on the viewscreen revealed that the *Enterprise* was still heading straight along the course set by 0 and his zombie helmsman.

An ominous suspicion stirred within Picard's mind. "What is our heading?" he demand. "Can you deduce our ultimate destination?"

Riker consulted the navigational display at his console. "As nearly as I can tell, Captain, we're headed directly toward the very center of the galaxy."

I feared as much, Picard mused. "People to free," 0 had said in his ranting, rambling way. 0 almost certainly intended to use the *Enterprise* to liberate The One from his eternal confinement behind the Great Barrier, which surely meant that, unless Q succeeding in exterminating his ancient adversary, he and his crew had not seen the last of 0. Picard realized that he could not possibly let 0 unleash another genocidal superbeing on the cosmos, even if it meant destroying the *Enterprise*-E and everyone aboard. *Let us hope it doesn't come to that, and that 0 cannot immobilize our self-destruct procedure as easily as he took control of the conn.*

There was much he needed to explain to Riker and the others, but first Picard glanced once more at the spot where both 0 and Q had vanished from sight. *Where are you, Q,* he wondered, *and how can we stop the greatest mistake of your youth from wreaking havoc on the future of all who live?*

Chapter Eleven

"GAMETIME, Q! READY TO PLAY?"

The corridors of the *Enterprise*-E were as streamlined and antiseptic as Q had come to expect from Starfleet. To be perfectly honest, he had always been a trifle disappointed by the Federation's sense of design, and this new flagship of Picard's was no exception. He would have gone for something a good deal more baroque or rococo; not as gothic as that dreary Deep Space Nine, but certainly something with a bit more flash and style.

Picard would hate it, of course.

But how had he ended up in this hall in the first place, and where was 0's voice coming from? Only a nanosecond ago, he'd been locked in mortal combat with the deranged entity, their respective powers pitted against each on a dozen different levels simultaneously. He could only assume his involuntary transportation to this unremarkable locale meant that he had lost the first round of their contest.

How terribly galling and unexpected. Q had hoped that the age and experience he'd gained since he last clashed with 0, over half a million years ago, would have given him considerably more of an edge this time around, but, no, he had failed to anticipate how greatly 0's insanity had progressed during his long exile. *His madness gives him the advantage,* he realized, allowing 0 to distort and transform reality, even transcendental reality, in ways that Q could equal only if he was willing to sacrifice his own sanity. He wasn't quite willing to go that far . . . yet.

"I said, ready to play, Q?"

0 appeared at the far end of the corridor. Once again, Q was shocked at how radically the castaway's self-image had mutated since the old days. His torn and shredded clothing testified to millennia of neglect and disregard, while his sallow complexion and disordered hair reflected the chaotic jumble his mind had become. He was like a rabid beast now, with just enough cunning and depraved ingenuity to make him truly dangerous.

Even more alarming were the murderous weapons he brandished in each of his two hands and four tentacles. Primitive implements of death—a dagger, a phaser, a mace, a boomerang, a flintlock pistol, and a Capellan *kligat*—menaced Q, who had no doubt that 0 had made them real enough, in metaphysical terms, to inflict actual injury upon both mortals and immortals alike.

"Er, what sort of game did you have in mind?" he asked, deciding that it was not entirely prudent to ignore 0's query much longer. He tried to back away unobtrusively, only to discover that something hampered his steps. Glancing down in surprise, he saw that his legs were shackled together by a sturdy length of chain, about half a meter long. "What's this?" he asked indignantly. Try as he might, he could neither extricate himself from the shackles nor wish them away. 0's madness was too strong.

"Just a little something to even the odds. Odd, odder, oddest." 0 tapped his bad leg with his lower left tentacle. "You wouldn't want take advantage of my innocent, illustrious infirmity, or would you?" He scowled beneath his shaggy beard. "You always had a soft spot for cheaters, a tedious tolerance for treachery. There'll be no cheating this time, Q, oh no. You're playing my game now, by my rules. Rue the rules, you will, the rules you'll rue."

"What rules?" Q demanded. 0's addled mind had left him about as coherent as some atrocious Klingon opera. "What game?"

Malicious glee glinted in 0's pale blue eyes. "Hide-and-seek," he said. "You hide, I seek. I find, you shriek." He waved his grisly weapons like a multi-limbed savage. "You can go anywhere on this vast, variegated vessel, but nowhere else, nowhere at all. No Continuum, no cosmos, no craven retreat." His twisting Malay dagger whistled as it sliced through the pressurized atmosphere of the corridor. "Q is for quarry. Run, Q, run!"

"Don't you think this is something of a childish game for beings of our lofty stature?" Q suggested. He tried to transport himself directly to the Continuum, go in search of much-needed reinforcements. *I know I can make the other Q listen,* he thought, belying what he had told Picard earlier. *Never mind all the distractions of the Reconstruction. . . .* But the accursed irons upon his ankles apparently did more than simply inhibit any ambulatory motions. He was bound to this one particular time and place, for better or for worse. Mostly worse. "Perhaps we should just talk things over over a couple of steaming cups of Thasian ambrosia?"

0 responded by firing a warning shot with his flintlock that left a flattened lead pellet embedded in the ceiling above Q's head. The acrid smell of gunpowder filled the air. "No more talk!" he snarled. "Talk no more. I'll count until ten. Take your head start or I'll take your head."

A vivid picture of The One's disembodied cranium popped out of Q's memory like a monotheistic jack-in-the-box. He quickly pushed it back down again. *No more of that,* he ordered his omniscient unconscious. *The future looks bleak enough without dragging the past in as well.*

"One," 0 counted aloud, "thirteen, seven, eighty-four, *pi,* one hundred and eight . . ."

Who knows when he'll actually hit ten, Q thought. *I'd best put some distance between me and that walking arsenal.* Hide-and-seek, was it? Very well, there were lots of places to hide aboard a Sovereign-class starship, and Q knew them all.

He hobbled down the empty corridor, 0's lunatic countdown ringing in his ears.

". . . thirty-two, five, the square root of infinity . . ."

"What I don't understand," Riker said, "is why this 0 can't just blink himself over the galactic core on his own? Why does he need the *Enterprise?*"

The first officer had maintained his post at the conn, for all the good it had done them. The ship remained on course for the Great Barrier at the center of the galaxy, and nothing they had attempted so far had managed to override the coordinates that 0 had fed into the helm controls through the late Ensign's Clarze's lifeless fingers. The *Enterprise* was on automatic pilot, and Picard didn't like it one bit. Few things were more frustrating than to lose control of his ship at such a crucial juncture.

"I'm not sure I can explain, Number One, at least not fully." He had done his best to concisely update Riker and the rest of the surviving bridge crew on the nature of the foe they now face. "For reasons I don't entirely understand, no doubt relating to 0's true nature as an advanced energy being, he cannot travel past lightspeed on his own power. In the past, he used the Q Continuum as a shortcut through space, or tried to harness the early Calamarain for his personal transport. Even though he is no longer physically manifest upon the bridge, I can only deduce from our current course that he is somehow still using the *Enterprise* as a means to traverse the considerable distance between the edge of the galaxy and the core."

Riker scowled as he inspected the readout at the navigational controls. "Well, he's getting there as fast as our warp engines will take him. I don't know what he did to our engines, but we're approaching warp nine."

Data confirmed his analysis. "To be precise, we are currently traveling at warp factor eight point eight nine nine nine and climbing."

That was not encouraging news. The sooner they came within range of the Great Barrier, the sooner 0 could use Professor Faal's revolutionary technology to liberate The One from his age-old prison. *We can't allow that to happen,* Picard resolved. He had seen with his own eyes the devastation that The One and 0 could inflict on a planetary, and even a stellar, scale. Perhaps Starfleet Command could assemble a blockade to stop the *Enterprise* from reaching the Great Barrier, even though that would surely deplete Starfleet's resources at a time when the Dominion and the Borg already had the Federation's defenses stretched far too thinly. *That has to be a last resort,* he decided.

"What if we separated the saucer from the stardrive section?" Lieutenant Barclay suggested. Picard was impressed by the sometimes nervous crewman's initiative; Counselor Troi's therapy sessions seemed to have borne some fruit.

"That might work," Picard agreed, "if we could

positively determine that 0 was only aboard the saucer section, and that he couldn't simply transport himself onto the stardrive section when we attempted the separation." Besides, he considered, the bulk of the crew resided in the saucer section, not to mention Professor Faal and his children, and Picard was not inclined to leave all those souls to the tender mercies of 0, even if he thought it was at all possible to strand the insane superbeing upon the saucer. "I think we should consider other options as well," he said diplomatically, not wanting to quash Barclay's morale at a time when it was showing genuine improvement.

"First, we need to locate 0 as precisely as possible. If he *is* physically present on the *Enterprise,* as our heading suggests, I want to know where he is and what he's doing." Picard settled back into his chair, uneasy with all the vital questions that remained unanswered. "I wouldn't mind knowing where Q is, too."

His comm badge beeped, heralding a message from a unlikely but familiar voice. "Q to Picard. I hope you're listening, Jean-Luc, because this mess you've gotten us into is getting worse every minute."

The mess I *got us into?* That was a singularly Q-like take on their situation, Picard thought, but now was no time to debate who was really to blame for 0's past and present abuses of power. "Where are you, Q?" he asked crisply.

"In one of your cramped and uncomfortable Jefferies tubes, if you must know," Q said. "Who designed these things? A Horta?" A weary sigh escaped the comm badge. "Never mind that. The important thing is that I'm keeping 0 occupied so you can devise one of your typically heroic solutions to the problem at hand. But you have to hurry." Q's voice was hushed, as if he was trying hard not to be heard. "I'm not sure how much longer I can keep away from him—I mean, keep him distracted."

Picard had to wonder just how willingly Q had consented to play decoy. Was he voluntarily luring 0 away from the bridge, or was he merely putting a self-serving face on circumstances he was helpless to prevent? "What do you mean?" Picard asked. "What do you need us to do?"

"How should I know?" Q said impatiently. "You're the ones who specialize in triumphing against overwhelming odds. Have Data whip up some technobabble. Tell Counselor Troi to get in touch with her feelings. Let Riker punch someone." Exasperation gave way to desperation in his voice. "Do *something*, Jean-Luc. Don't you understand? He's going to kill me. Probably more than once."

"But why can't stop 0 yourself?" Picard wanted to know. At the conn, Riker heard enough of Q's tirade to give the golden comm badge a dirty look. "You subdued 0 before, when you were younger."

Another frustrated sigh. Picard could practically see Q roll his eyes condescendingly. "Let me try to explain this in terms your primitive intellect can grasp. He's *crazy*. Even the Q recognize a common consensual reality, a certain metaphysical bedrock or foundation that transcends even our own infinite command over time and space, energy and matter. The alternative is utter chaos, and we all understand that. So do the Organians and the Metrons and the Douwd and all of the other truly advanced intelligences. But not 0, not anymore. He's different now. He doesn't recognize any reality at all, on any level, except his own twisted perceptions, which means he's free to distort the fundamental underpinnings of the multiverse to an absolutely unthinkable degree. The observer affects the observed, Picard. Even your own quantum physicists know that. So 0's insanity grants him an insane amount of power. Does this make any sense at all to you, *mon capitaine?*"

"I'll take your word for it," Picard said. To tell the truth, he wasn't sure how much any human could truly understand the subtleties of existence as Q and 0 knew it. So one omnipotent being was more all-powerful than another omnipotent being? *Fine,* Picard thought. It wasn't intuitively obvious, but he could accept it if that was the case, which apparently it was. *I'm sure all humanoids seem equally inscrutable and unstoppable to an ant.* "Can't you offer any suggestions?" he prompted. "What about your wife."

"She has problems of her own at the moment," Q explained, not divulging the source of his information. "Protecting little q takes priority over everything else, even my own—wait, what was that?" Picard thought he heard footsteps in the background, plus a distinctive singsong chanting. *The Jefferies tubes have excellent acoustics,* he recalled. "I have to go, Picard. He's found me somehow. He's getting closer." Q sounded close to panic. "The ball is in your court, Picard. I'm counting on you."

"Q? Q?" Picard tapped his badge, but the transmission was over. Q was on the run presumably, somewhere within the labyrinthine network of access crawlways that ran throughout the entire ship. *He could be anywhere,* Picard realized.

He felt a stab of anger at Q. How dare he place the responsibility for defeating 0 on him? Not that he could have turned his back on this crisis even if Q had commanded him to, but it was typical of Q to make him feel as uncomfortable as possible. "Well, Number One," he said grimly, "it seems both 0 and Q are indeed still aboard the *Enterprise.*"

"Lucky us," Riker commented. His hands continued to manipulate the helm controls, stubbornly searching for a way to regain control of the conn. "Too bad our ship's sensors have never been able to get a handle on Q. Might make it easier to keep track of him."

"Maybe there's another way," Picard said, a thoughtful look coming over his face. "Data, I want you to carefully monitor energy demands throughout the ship. Let me know if you detect any unusual activity that might provide us with a clue as to our guests' whereabouts."

"Understood, Captain," the android acknowledged. He cocked his head in a quizzical manner. "Sir, would this constitute 'whipping up some technobabble'?"

Picard gave Data a wry smile. "I would not put too

much credence, Lieutenant Commander, in any of Q's more acerbic remarks."

"I see, Captain. Thank you." Data returned his attention to the console before him. Suddenly, he assumed a more alert posture. "Captain. Commander Riker. I am detecting a dramatic surge in tachyon collisions against the ship's hull."

Tachyons! Picard knew exactly what that foretold, and his fears were confirmed when an iridescent cloud of vapor washed across the screen of the main viewer, accompanied by a thunderous roar that set the entire ship vibrating. The gaseous mass, so very like the conglomeration of vaporous entities Picard had encountered one hundred million years in the past, blotted out the streaking stars upon the screen, even as Picard felt the *Enterprise* drop out of warp.

"It's the Calamarain," Riker stated, speaking aloud what they all understood. "They're back."

Chapter Twelve

POLLEN TICKLED THE NOSTRILS of his humanoid guise and Q fought against a compelling urge to sneeze, convinced that 0 would hear any nasal outburst from a dozen decks away. Perhaps the hydroponics bay was not such an ingenious hiding place after all.

Flora from all over the Alpha Quadrant and beyond filled the spacious nursery, growing from trays filled with a moist inert medium whose organic content Q preferred not to think about. The shallow trays were stacked one atop the other in parallel rows that permitted an individual to wander, if he was so inclined, between lush assortments of greenery that positively reeked of chlorophyll. It was Q's hope that the sheer abundance of life force would help mask his own energies from 0. He had briefly considered the ship's arboretum instead, but hiding in the woods struck him as just a little too obvious.

Q crouched behind a tray of venomous foliage ranging from the mildly toxic Borgia plant to the lethal cove palm of Ogus III; he found the deadly nature of these particular sprouts uniquely soothing and reassuring. Behind him, samples of Cyprion cactus grew beside a Folner jewel plant and a spray of blooming orange and yellow crystilia. The air was thick with the aroma of flowering vegetation.

His nose tickled again and Q was tempted to materialize a silk handkerchief, but he was afraid that even the most inconsequential use of his powers would register on 0's otherworldly senses. *One more thing to thank 0 for,* he thought resentfully; why, he had even been forced to go to the enormous physical inconvenience of actually *traveling* through the Jefferies tubes to the hydroponics bay, located quite unhelpfully on Deck 11, instead of simply willing himself there. Even though he sensed that he could still teleport within the confines of the ship, despite the burdensome fetters about his legs, there was no way he could he bypass three-dimensional distances without producing subspace ripples that would call down 0 upon him like a Vulcan *sehlat*.

How ever did Picard and his sort ever cope with the tedious necessity of physically transporting themselves from place to place? The sheer monotony of it, Q thought, would surely drive him to suicide within days.

Breaking off a ten-centimeter spine from the cactus

behind him, Q tried to use it to jimmy the lock on his leg irons. Unfortunately, he was an all-powerful superbeing, not a safecracker, and it seemed hardly likely that there were any veteran criminals aboard the *Enterprise* to whom he could turn for tips. What had been the name of that cutpurse and sneak thief with whom he had consorted three or four millennia ago? The one who stole all those cattle from Sisyphus? Now, there had been a rogue after Q's own heart; too bad he couldn't risk plucking him out of history for a quick refresher course in lock-picking.

At least he had succeeded in contacting Picard via the ship's primitive communications technology. Now it was up to the captain and his dauntless crew to snatch victory from the gaping maw of obliteration as they had so many times before. Q had tremendous faith in Picard; after all, hadn't the somewhat dour humanoid managed to surmount some of Q's most inventive puzzles? Q did feel a tad bit guilty about dumping 0 in Picard's lap, though. Despite what he had implied to Jean-Luc a few minutes before, he had to admit to some small responsibility for the present contretemps. In retrospect, he probably should have leveled with Picard earlier about the true purpose of the barrier, but he could hardly be expected to willingly divulge the imperfections of his youth, especially to so judgmental and self-righteous a lesser life-form as Jean-Luc Picard.

The tip of the cactus spine broke off in the lock, and Q tossed the remainder of the spine away in disgust.

That was no good; he would have to think of something else. *What would Jean-Luc do in a fix like this?* he wondered, slightly embarrassed to have to resort to such a demeaning comparison. *How the almighty have fallen,* he brooded, indulging in a few moments of richly deserved self-pity.

A machete slicing through stalks of *Draebidium calimus* interrupted his introspection, raining violet petals upon his head. Q scooted back on his rear, impaling his dorsal region upon the sharp spines of the cactus. He let out a shocked and indignant yowl of pain before mentally expelling the stinging barbs from his back.

"Tag, you're dead!" 0 leered at him over the decapitated flower stems in the upper tray. "Dead you are." He took aim with his phaser, which was almost certainly set to kill. "I always suspected you were nothing more than a hothouse flower, Q, unable to cope with cold, cruel choices outside the Continuum." He laughed maniacally, exposing chipped and corroded teeth. "Prepare to be pruned, petunia!"

Exposed and unarmed, Q grabbed a nearby hypoatomizer and squirted 0 in the face with concentrated bacillus spray. The madman rubbed frantically at his eyes with his upper tentacles while firing wildly with his phaser. The crimson beam went astray, disintegrating a garlanic seedling and setting a patch of Diomedian scarlet moss ablaze. Then the beam swung in an arc, incinerating some bristly *mutok* cuttings from Lwaxana Troi's private garden on

Betazed before barely missing the top of Q's head. He felt the searing heat of the beam radiate down through his scalp.

With nothing more to lose, Q teleported away from the hydroponics bay, arriving in a flash in a half-filled cargo bay on Deck 21. Molybdenum storage bins were stacked four high along the opposite wall. Clear and meticulous labeling identified their contents as, respectively, thermoconcrete, inertial dampers, driver coil assemblies, and self-sealing stem bolts. Nothing he could possibly have any use for, in other words.

He hurried toward the wide exit doors as quickly as his shackles would permit. He could not afford to linger at this site much longer; that bacillus spray was not going to detain 0 for more than a second or two, and he would surely be able to follow Q's fifth-dimensional trail to the cargo bay. Q loped down the corridor outside, scanning his new surroundings for the best possible escape route or hiding place. As he ran, he cursed the fateful moment he first heard 0's ingratiating voice singing through the snow of that frozen limbo outside reality. His close call with the phaser and the machete had shaken him more than he wanted to admit, even to himself.

Must get away, he thought, taking a sharp left at the next intersection. He passed a pair of Starfleet technicians at work repairing a power conduit behind a displaceable wall panel; they stared wide-eyed at his shackled state, but he did not waste a single breath to respond to their shouted inquiries and offers of assistance. There was nothing they could do to help him, not against O. He had no doubt that O had created the cumbersome fetters to be phaser-proof.

Find someplace to hide, he urged himself, *someplace O will never suspect.* At any moment, he expected to hear the sound of limping footsteps behind him. He trembled just imagining it. The sensation of genuine fear was not something he had ever had the opportunity to become accustomed to; he hadn't felt so vulnerable and at risk since that time the Calamarain had hunted him after he lost his Q-ish abilities. How was he supposed to concentrate on outwitting O when he had to fret about being murdered at the same time? It just wasn't fair!

His self-made comm badge beeped, and for a moment Q expected to hear Picard explaining the details of some cunning, Starfleet-style plan. Instead his immortal ichor went cold as O's raspy, singsong voice came over the communications device:

"Say, Q, O Q, whatever happened to that fine, fancy filly you were fiancéed to, once upon a time? She wouldn't happen to be aboard this sleek, shiny ship, would she? Perhaps looking out for some wondrous whelp or another?"

Q, he thought in alarm, *and little q, too . . . !* What could this unscrupulous monster want with them? *Aside from revenge on me, that is.* This was absolutely intolerable; he couldn't allow O to turn his perverse attentions to Q's family, no mattered what was required.

"Don't tell me you've stooped to picking on women

and children, 0?" Q squeezed all the scorn and sarcasm he could muster, which was quite a considerable amount, into every syllable he uttered. "What's the matter, *mon ami?* Hide-and-seek proving too much to handle? Finally find an opponent you can't cheat or bully into submission?" He tsk-tsked into the badge. "What a disappointment. Here I was looking forward to a good, challenging game, but I guess that's not to be. Pity. Why, even these insignificant humanoids have given me better competition than this."

"Run, Q, run!" 0 barked via the badge. Q prayed to the highest power he knew, himself, that his barbs had indeed hit a nerve within 0's chaotic consciousness, enough to make the insane expatriate forget all about Q and q. "You can't fool me," 0 insisted, dashing Q's hopes. "You're as transparent as Time, Q, as obvious as ozone. You think if I go chasing you-Q-you, this wily old wanderer will leave your tart and your tyke alone." A bone-chilling cackle emerged from badge. "But you're wrong, Q, wrong as Reason. I have them already, or part of me does. . . ."

0 appeared in a flash, only five meters away. The three-sided *kligat* whizzed past Q's ear, lopping off a lock of his hair. "Hide, Q, hide!" he hollered, his husky voice echoing down the corridor. "This game's not over until I say so, unless I kill you by mistake!"

Chapter Thirteen

THE STANDOFF BETWEEN LEM FAAL and the female Q had drawn a crowd. Nurse Ogawa lingered in the doorway to the pediatric unit, flanked by two security officers summoned to the scene. Their phasers were raised and ready, although they held their fire for fear of hitting the hostage q. Behind them, the EMH stood on his toes, trying to peek over the shoulders of the security personnel. "This is highly irregular," he protested. "Why won't anyone listen to me?"

This is my fault, Crusher thought, staring helplessly at the tranquilized child under Faal's arms. *I should have given q to his mother the moment she appeared, but instead I stalled her in hopes of finding out more about some trouble on the bridge.* Now she still didn't know much more about what was happening elsewhere on the ship, but an innocent child had been taken captive by an insane and potentially dangerous individual who had somehow attained enough power to keep q from his mother.

"I know you," the female Q said cryptically, glaring at Faal with anger and contempt in her eyes. "At least I recognize the part that's pulling the strings behind this pathetic puppet show. The Continuum should have annihilated you, and all your loathsome comrades, when we had the chance. Eternal exile was too good for you."

Crusher had no idea what she was talking about, nor, from the looks of him, did Lem Faal. "You're just trying to confuse me," he accused. Beverly shuddered at his eerie white eyes. "I have a duty to science to study this child, to record his development, test his abilities to the utmost."

Even as he ranted like a mad scientist from some gothic holodeck program, Faal's telekinetic abilities began to reshape the pediatric unit into a laboratory of sorts. The supply cupboards turned into visual display monitors, charting the Q equivalent of brain waves and metabolic functions. The elevated incubator at the center of the ward morphed into a transparent dome about a meter high and another meter in diameter. *Did he intend to cage q inside there?* Crusher wondered. *For how long?* Faal was acting like he intended to experiment upon the Q child for as long as q lived, which was probably forever. Her heart ached at the prospect of an innocent child, immortal or otherwise, treated like a guinea pig, while his mother watches helplessly. *There must be someway to stop Faal without endangering q, but how?*

"Deanna," she whispered to the counselor, who had retreated to the back of chamber, "take Kinya and go. I don't think he'll stop you." Crusher refused to leave the pediatric unit while the Q child was in jeopardy—this was her sickbay, after all—but there was no reason to risk either Troi or the sobbing little girl. She took care not to refer to Kinya by her full name, lest the female Q get the idea to retaliate against Faal by taking his own daughter hostage. *I hope she's not reading my mind right now,* Crusher thought. Fortunately, the mother Q only had eyes for her child while Troi scooped up the frightened girl and edged toward the exit cautiously, watching Faal with wary eyes.

As Crusher had anticipated, the scientist couldn't have cared less about Troi or even his daughter, paying no attention as the security officers stepped aside to let them pass. She exhaled a sigh of relief. That was two fewer individuals she had to worry about, at least in the short term.

Then, just to make matters worse, the ship underwent another tremendous jolt. Crusher hoped for an instant that the unexpected turbulence would cause Faal to lose his grip on baby q, but he held on to the sedated child as if that was all that mattered to him. Beverly herself had to grab for the incubator to keep from falling, only to yank her hands back as she felt the solid transparent aluminum move beneath her palms like a living thing.

Stepping back from the shapeshifting incubator, while keeping close to the female Q to offer whatever moral support she could provide, Crusher saw one of the security officers speaking hurriedly into his comm badge. *Good,* she thought. No doubt he was updating the bridge on the ongoing hostage crisis in sickbay. Crusher wasn't sure what Jean-Luc or Data could do that the female Q couldn't, but she didn't feel quite as trapped and alone anymore.

Then, to her surprise, she heard the unmistakable voice of Captain Picard responding personally to the officer's report. That was good news, no matter how dire things were here, since it suggested that the crisis on the bridge had calmed down for the moment. Had the mysterious intruder been dealt with, perhaps by Q? Beverly was surprised to find herself counting on Q of all people, but she couldn't imagine that Q would permit his own son to be threatened much longer. Between the two of them, surely Q and his mate could overpower Lem Faal, despite whatever uncanny attributes he had mysteriously acquired. *Where are you, Q?* she thought silently. *Do you even know what's happening to your child?*

"Under attack by the Calamarain," Picard's voice explained tersely, "plus an alien intruder of incredible power is loose aboard the ship. Keep on your guard, and do whatever is necessary to protect the children. Commander Riker is en route to take charge of the situation. Picard out."

Then the intruder has left the bridge and could be anywhere, Crusher realized. She knew that Jean-Luc could not possibly be referring to Lem Faal, whose identity was well known, so that meant there were now two highly dangerous individuals at large aboard the *Enterprise*. She couldn't imagine that was a coincidence. Plus the Calamarain had returned as well? Her spirits sank, taken aback by all the threats facing them. Only her faith in Jean-Luc Picard and her fellow crew members kept her hopeful that they would come through these multiplying hazards as they always had before. *We beat the Borg twice,* she remembered.

The incubator had completed its evolution into a high-tech cage. Faal nodded approvingly and his eyes flared even more brightly for an instant. Suddenly, q was no longer under Faal's arm but deposited within the transparent dome. The female Q rushed to free him, arms outstretched, but flashes of crackling purple energy repelled her eager fingers as soon as they came within a centimeter of the dome. The enclosure was obviously protected by a forcefield, Crusher realized, one capable of withstanding the female Q's maternal might. She pounded on the forcefield with her bare hands, determined to shatter the obstacles between her and her son. Her fists smashed against the forcefield, sparking more flashes of energy, whose violet hue reminded Beverly of the galactic barrier itself, yet both forcefield and dome remained intact. "My q!" the distraught mother cried out. "Give me back my child!"

Faal ignored her heart-tugging plea. "Initiate experimental log," he coolly instructed the surrounding equipment. "File: Faal/hyperevolution. Title: Preliminary Notes on the Onset of Trans-Transcendental Consciousness in the Offspring of Advanced, Multidimensional Life-Forms. . . ."

No longer shielded by the proximity of the unconscious child, he presented a tempting target to the two security officers, who immediately fired their phasers at the seemingly defenseless scientist. Twin beams converged on Faal, who just kept dictating his notes.

". . . subject remains under sedation in observation chamber. In appearance, resembles humanoid infant of Terran ancestry, approximately two years in age. Observation: The population of *Starship Enterprise* is predominately of Terran descent, suggesting that subject's current appearance is a direct response to his recent environment, perhaps even a form of protective coloration. . . ."

The crimson rays bounced off Faal, rebounding back to their points of origin. Phaser beams struck the security team squarely in their chests, dropping them to the floor. Crusher thanked standard Starfleet procedure that weapons had been set on stun; in theory, the downed officers had not been permanently injured. Showing laudable initiative, the EMH began to drag the inert bodies out of the doorway into the primary ward, assisted by Ogawa. She knew she could count on the nurse and the hologram to tend to the fallen crew members as much as was necessary.

Faal appeared oblivious of the incident and its aftermath. ". . . exact chronological age of the subject has yet to be determined," he continued. "Further

study is required. . . ." The biobeds along the port-
side wall of the children's ward started reassembling
themselves into an array of scanners and probes
whose precise functions Crusher couldn't begin to
guess at. What kind of tests could you perform on a
baby god? And could any of them actually harm little
q? Metal and synthetic polymers flowed like liquid
mercury while sophisticated electronic circuitry established new links and configurations.

The pounding and the phaser fire combined to
rouse the toddler from his drugged slumber. He sat up
slowly, rubbing his eyes, then looked around wildly as
he became aware of his surroundings. The density of
the transparent dome muffled his high-pitched wails,
but there was no mistaking the panic in his eyes as he
pounded at the interior of the cage with tiny fists.
"Out!" he shouted. "Out! Out!"

"It's all right, sweetie," his mother tried to comfort
him, placing her face so close to the forcefield that
purple traceries flickered along her profile. "Mommy
is here. Mommy's not going to leave you."

Claustrophobia must be especially terrifying to a
child who is accustomed to teleporting wherever he
wishes, Crusher thought. Her heart went out to the
mother as well, their past differences forgotten. Beverly vividly remembered how anguished she'd felt
when Wesley had been taken captive on Rubicun III.
How could she not sympathize with what the female
Q had to be going through?

Baby q spotted Lem Faal and drew back in fear.
Somehow he seemed to know that the Betazoid

scientist, with his luminous eyes and unfeeling expression, was responsible for his captivity. As small children have done throughout galactic history, q covered his eyes with his hands, evidently hoping that if he couldn't see Faal, then Faal couldn't find him. *Wesley used to do the same thing,* Crusher remembered.

The childish ploy appeared to touch some vestige of mortality within Faal. His expression softened, as if recalling similar behavior on the part of his own children. Beverly hoped desperately for a change of heart as abrupt and comprehensive as the alterations he was imposing upon the pediatric unit. But her hopes for a peaceful resolution to the crisis faded as Faal's lean face froze back into the impassive mask of a detached observer. "Subject's infantile attempt at concealment reveals perceptual errors arising from the immature nature of the developing superconsciousness. Confusion between objective/subjective criteria resembles comparable phenomena in the development of preadolescent primates and equivalent species."

That's one way of putting it, Crusher thought bitterly, both disturbed and offended by Faal's clinical description of a child in distress. Unable to watch q's torment any further, she glanced around the chamber, barely recognizing what had only minutes ago been a state-of-the-art medical facility. The mutated pediatric unit now bore little resemblance to its former self, as transformed in form and function as so much of the ship had been during the Borg occupation several months ago. Illuminated screens presented close-ups of q taken from every possible angle and in a wide variety of formats. Newly created scanners, reminiscent of the docking pylons at Deep Space Nine, loomed over the domed observation chamber like vultures intent on some dying prey. At the center of this intimidating array of technology, the trembling child in his miniature Starfleet uniform looked both out of place and vulnerable.

"Future areas of research," Faal droned on, completely unaware of how horrific the situation looked, "include physiological and behavioral responses to changes in environmental stimuli, including extremes of heat and cold, as well as conditions of absolute vacuum. Also to be explored: the long-term psychological impact of sleep and/or sensory deprivation. . . ."

Beverly couldn't believe what she was hearing. This was like some sort of inhuman medical experiment from the age of Khan Noonien Singh. Less than a meter away, the female Q looked like she wanted to personally dissect Faal himself. Crusher didn't blame her one bit.

"Dad? What are you doing?"

The voice caught them all off guard, even halting Faal's compulsive dictation. Crusher looked to the open doorway, where young Milo Faal stood unsteadily, holding on to the doorframe for support. "Dad?"

His eyes glowed just like his father's.

Interlude

SICKBAY? HOW IN BLAZES did I get to sickbay?

Lieutenant Baeta Leyoro awoke groggily upon a biobed, a surgical support frame pinning her down. Her head felt as if a Tarsian dreadnought had landed on it and her eyes throbbed like a photon grenade. She just hoped whoever zapped her felt a whole lot worse.

The last thing she remembered was being on the bridge. Her head had hurt then, because of that plasma-sucking barrier, but not as badly as it did now. Commander Riker had just ordered her to sickbay, over her vehement objections, and she had been making her way toward the turbolift about as slowly as she could without courting charges of insubordination. Then a white-hot light had exploded behind her eyes . . . and here she was, flat on her back like a damn fatality.

And this was supposed to be a peaceful scientific mission, she recalled. *Hah!* If there was one thing she had learned from a lifetime spent fighting, first for Angosia and then for Starfleet, it was that danger could strike at any moment. The rehabilitative counselors back at Lunar V would call that paranoia, she suspected, and tell her that she needed to overcome such "antisocial" tendencies, but what did any of them know about the life of a soldier? None of them ever had to worry about a Tarsian sneak attack, or be responsible for the security of a starship at the literal edge of the galaxy.

A sickeningly recognizable clap of thunder shook the sickbay, causing miniature warp-core breaches inside her aching skull. *The Calamarain,* she realized, feeling a savage sense of vindication through the pain, which now seemed to extend all the way down to her toes. *I knew we hadn't seen the last of those BOVs,* she thought, using a bit of Angosian army slang. Better Off Vaporized, it meant, although that had proved maddeningly redundant where the gaseous Calamarain were concerned. Still, barrier or no barrier, it was obvious the *Enterprise* was under attack once more.

I need to get back to the bridge. Never mind the pain, she wasn't about to slack off in a med ward while the ship was under enemy fire. Duty called, and she had a responsibility to defend the *Enterprise* to the best of her abilities. *Now, if I can just sit up without my skull exploding . . .*

Her first try went badly. She had barely lifted her head from the padded cushion of the biobed when a sharp, jabbing pain stabbed through the back of her head like a Nausicaan bayonet. Gasping, she let her skull drop back onto the cushion, shutting her eyes against the too-bright lighting overhead. She considered calling for a doctor or nurse, but knew that any medical personnel would just try to talk her into staying put. Probably just as well that nobody seemed to have noticed her return to consciousness yet; she hoped that didn't mean that Dr. Crusher and her staff with too many other casualties to pay attention to her.

Let's try this again, she thought, gritting her teeth. She began to shove the surgical support frame off her, noticing for the first time that she no longer had any feeling in her fingertips. *I don't even want to know what that means.* The exertion caused her head to throb faster and harder, but she eventually succeeded in sliding the SSF up and away from her body. Then came the hard part: sitting up and putting her feet on the floor. The imaginary bayonet jabbed her again, but this time she was ready for it, letting the pain course through her even as she willed her muscles to keep on moving regardless.

Easy does it, she told herself as she slipped off the bed and onto the floor. At first, sickbay swirled around her like a gravitational vortex and she felt her stomach roll over queasily. The dizziness passed, though, and she took a moment to orient herself.

Where are all the medics? she wondered as no one rushed to her side. There seemed to be something going on at the other end of the ward, perhaps in the pediatric unit, but her eyes were too blurry to make out the details. *Doesn't matter,* she thought. The bridge was where she was needed most, directing the fight against the Calamarain.

Despite the disruptor blasts behind her eyes, and the creeping numbness in her limbs, a familiar exhilaration crept over her, giving her the strength to keep one foot marching in front of the other, right through the door out of sickbay. Forget what all those pill-pushers and head-shrinkers back on Angosia said. *"Reintegration into civilized society"* ... *hah!* This was where she belonged, on the front lines again, doing what she knew best. Fighting to survive.

These Calamarain were a different kind of adversary, to be sure, but they must have their weaknesses, points of vulnerability that the crew could discover and take advantage of. Another thing she'd learned over the course of her career: No enemy was unbeatable. The trick was staying alive long enough to see your victory.

Once she thought she heard a voice calling after her, urging her to return to sickbay, but she didn't look back. She just kept walking.

Easy does it. . . .

Chapter Fourteen

"Tag!"

0 appeared sans fanfare atop the bar, kicking aside a row of freshly replicated glass goblets. They crashed onto the carpeted floor of the officer's lounge, shattering to pieces and showering Q with tiny glass slivers that might have stung him inordinately had he not had the wit and the wherewithal to transform them into harmless bits of soft-cooked rice first.

With the ship on alert status, the lounge was deserted except for a single Bolian bartender, who was currently hiding at the far end of the bar. The sky-blue upper hemisphere of his round head peeked over the rim of a bin of fresh ice, gawking wide-eyed at the ragged, scarecrow-like figure who had just materialized upon the bar. *I suppose it really is too much to hope,* Q thought, *that such a timorous specimen will have the fortitude to enforce the dress code around here.*

"Where's this?" 0 asked exuberantly, looking around the empty lounge. "This is where?" He hopped off the bar, his remnant-wrapped feet scattering the grains of rice further. Q could not resist staring in morbid fascination at the scarred and ruined remains of the madman's mangled left foot. "A well-stocked watering hole for wayward wanderers? An excellent choice, Q. I could do with a swallow of spirits. Hunting a heinous hound like yourself is thirsty work, or my name isn't—" He hesitated, his eyes glazing over as if he couldn't quite place his own appellation. "Faal? Q?" He smacked the side of his head and Q thought he heard neurons rattling. His madness would have been amusing if it weren't so unnerving. "0! Now I remember. You're Q and I'm 0 and you have to die. Devils and demiurges, do I need a drink!"

His upper right tentacle snatched a clear, cylindrical decanter from the bar counter. From the bilious green hue of the beverage sloshing within, Q identified it, with a revolted grimace, as Sluggo Cola, the most popular soft drink throughout the Ferengi Alliance. 0 pried open the bottle with his yellow teeth and spit the cap onto the floor. Q watched in amazement as 0 drained off half the bottle. *I thought only Ferengi could drink that dreck,* he thought, *or would want to.* "Ah, that hits the spot it hits." He thrust the bottle at Q. The viscous green brew fizzed when exposed to the air, sending a spray of tiny bubbles out the open neck. "Here, have a quaff on me, Q. Make it last because that's what it is, your last."

"Er, no thanks," Q demurred. If he absolutely had to choose a last drink, he'd prefer something more along the lines of a fine Saurian brandy, vintage 2247, say. "It's all yours," he insisted, pulling back his hands to reject the vile libation. Out of the corner of his eye, he glimpsed the Bolian bartender creep out the closest exit. *That's it,* Q thought, piqued by the mixologist's cowardly desertion. *He's definitely not getting a tip.*

"Drink!" 0 demanded, pointing both a phaser and an antique derringer at Q's head. "You weren't too proud to share a bottle of elixir the first time we met, or so I recall. Drink, Q, drink."

If you'd been drinking this loathsome concoction then, Q thought, reluctantly accepting the bottle, *I might have left you where I found you.* He discreetly wiped the neck of the bottle on his sleeve, eyed the spuming contents doubtfully, then closed his eyes and took a hasty gulp.

It was even worse than he had imagined, both slimy and sickeningly oversweet; he couldn't decide what was most unappetizing, the texture or the taste. Taken together, they made Klingon bloodwine taste like Chateau Picard in comparison. It took all his omnipotence not to gag on the repellent slop. Instead he forced himself to finish off the bottle. *If ever I had any doubts that 0 was a total sadist at heart, this clinches it.*

At least that insufferable Guinan creature was not

around to witness his humiliation. Praise the Continuum for small favors! He wondered if Picard had finally had the good sense to dispense with her dubious services and, more important, if he would live long enough to congratulate Jean-Luc on his great good fortune if this were indeed the case.

Despite the truly awful nature of the Ferengi soda, he dragged out the last swallow for as long as he could, uncertain what 0 would do once this celebratory drink was concluded. He peered down the length of the bottle at the firearms poised to extinguish his immortal existence. Could he blink away faster than 0 could spray him with phaser fire and/or hot lead? Probably, but he didn't want to chance it. *I need a foolproof distraction,* he mused.

"Fast, faster, fastest," 0 ordered impatiently. His lower lateral tentacles yanked the bottle out of Q's hands so quickly that a mouthful of Sluggo Cola spilled onto the pristine carpet beneath their feet. "That's enough," he said, cocking the derringer and upping the setting on the phaser. "Say goodbye, Q. Don't worry, I'll take good care of that talented tot of yours, see if I don't."

"Watch out!" Q shouted desperately, pointing at the bar. "Behind you!"

0 frowned, giving Q a look of utter contempt. "Oh, now I'm disappointed, Q. Doubly and duly disappointed. That trick was old, old, old before I ever set foot in this great, glittering galaxy." He shook his head while keeping his guns aimed steadily at his onetime protégé. "A bad note to bow out on, boy oh

191

boy. Good thing there was no one to see it but you and me."

Just then, the Calamarain returned with a vengeance. A dense, scintillating fog spread past the wide, panoramic windows of the lounge while a violent shudder shook the hijacked starship from prow to stern. "Smoke!" 0 exclaimed in surprise, taking his eyes off Q for only a fraction of a second. "That stinking, sulphurous, sanctimonious smoke!"

A split second was all Q needed. Humorless and vindictive the Calamarain might be, and sanctimonious, too, but he certainly couldn't fault their timing. By the time, 0 looked back at his quarry, Q was already somewhere else. Transporter Room Three, to be exact.

A single crewman was stationed at the transporter controls. A Caldonian, from the look of his bony forehead. "Halt! Who are you?" he demanded, with admirable presence of mind, when Q materialized without warning upon the transporter platform. He reached for his phaser, but Q had no time to waste with Starfleet security procedure so he simply relocated the Caldonian recruit to the first place that came to mind, namely the bridge. *Maybe Jean-Luc can use an extra pair of hands,* he thought.

Racing the clock, knowing that 0 would be following close behind him, Q hastily reset the transporter controls from about two meters away, programming the console to erase the coordinates as soon as it completed the transfer. With any luck, using the *Enterprise*'s own primitive matter-transmission technology would throw 0 off the trail for a time, at least long enough to give Q a chance to regroup and reevaluate the situation.

But where exactly to beam to? Q hesitated, momentarily stumped. He had already tried the hydroponics bay, the environmental science lab, stellar cartography, a shuttlebay, a torpedo tube, an empty escape pod, Picard's private quarters, the matter-antimatter reaction chamber, the gymnasium, the lounge, and inside Data's cat, but 0 had found him every time and he was running out of ideas. The *Enterprise*-E was larger than the last one, but it wasn't *that* much bigger.

Where next? The arboretum? Sickbay? The deflector dish? Suddenly, the perfect hiding place popped into his mind. And none too soon; even as he programmed the appropriate coordinates into the transporter controls, 0 appeared upon the platform less than a meter away, brandishing his bloodthirsty arsenal. "There you are there!" he cackled. "And no thanks to that fulminating fog that saved you the last time. Smoke and mirrors, that's all it is. Smoke and mirrors, I say!"

They're no friends of mine, Q thought, having no doubt that the Calamarain would be perfectly happy to see both him and 0 destroyed forever; after all, hadn't the gaseous beings been nursing the same grudge for over a million years? Granted, Q was forced to concede, there was something nauseatingly appropriate about their appearance on this occasion. The Calamarain, back when they'd been the Coulalakritous, had been there at the beginning of his escapades with 0, and they had never forgiven him for his own small part in that unfortunate episode, so it was only fitting (in a thuddingly hamhanded and moralistic kind of way) that they be here at the end . . . if the end this be. That their unexpected return had actually worked to his benefit at first he chalked up to pure coincidence, possibly the only force in the universe that was beyond even the control of the Q.

He did not explain any of this to 0. Why bother? Instead he said three little words that Picard and his predecessors had practically worn out over the last century or so. "Beam me up."

Q dissolved into a pillar of silver sparks. . . .

Chapter Fifteen

"And thou, all-shaking thunder, strike flat the thick rotundity of the world!"

Lear's immortal words came back to Picard as the Calamarain subjected the *Enterprise* to their tumultuous animosity. The ship pitched and yawed beneath their assault. He gripped the armrests of his chair tightly even as his spine slammed into the cushion padding the back of the seat. Coruscating bolts of lightning arced across the viewscreen, igniting flashes of sky-blue Cerenkov radiation wherever the electrical bursts intersected with the ship's deflector shields.

"Shields down to forty-four percent," Ensign Berglund reported from tactical. Given the destructive barrage directed at the *Enterprise,* Picard thought it was a minor miracle that the shields were holding up as well as they were.

"The extra energy we absorbed from the galactic barrier, and diverted to the deflectors, is fading the farther we get from the barrier, Captain," Lieutenant Barclay confirmed from his own station. "And the standard field generators were badly damaged earlier. Engineering is still conducting repairs."

"I see," Picard said gravely. According to Riker, before he left the bridge to cope with the crisis in sickbay, the *Enterprise* had already endured several hours of such abuse while Picard was away, before the first officer took the ship into the barrier to elude the Calamarain. What's worse, Riker also reported that none of the *Enterprise*'s offensive capabilities had demonstrated any lasting effect upon the living plasma storm, making retaliation all but impossible.

Perhaps that's a blessing in disguise. Knowing what he now did, Picard could hardly blame the Calamarain for their fury against 0 and Q and anyone else who might seem to be associated with them. When last he saw the Calamarain—mere hours ago by his reckoning, a million years past by the rest of the universe's—the sentient cloud of ionized plasma, or perhaps only their ancestors, had been frozen into an inert block of solid matter by 0's unearthly powers, with Q as his unwilling accomplice. The older Q had told him that 0's victims had remained frozen so for thousands of years. If the Calamarain of the present truly believed that the *Enterprise* had deliberately liberated 0, as it must have appeared to them, small wonder that they were so determined to exact revenge. *Guilt by association,* he thought, *the hardest kind to refute.*

Riker had attempted diplomacy as well, and to no avail, but Picard believed it had to be worth another try. No matter how damning the evidence against them, which had only grown worse thanks to Lem Faal's unsanctioned breach of the barrier, he had to convince the Calamarain that they shared a mutual foe in 0. *That we protected Q from their wrath years ago cannot help our case,* he acknowledged reluctantly. "Data," he instructed, "initiate a tachyon transmission to the Calamarain."

The Calamarain communicated via faster-than-light particles, not speech as humanoids knew it. When last Picard had encountered them, Q's special brand of magic had permitted him to comprehend their inhuman language. Now, in the absence of Q and his miraculous abilities, he was forced to rely on a translation program newly devised by Lieutenant Commander Data, a program that Riker had warned still had some rough edges. *It will have to do,* he resolved.

Before he could began to formulate his address, however, he was surprised by the unheralded appearance of a shocked-looking crew member, who appeared suddenly in front of the main viewer. Picard recognized Lieutenant Royel, a junior-grade officer assigned to transporter operations. "Captain? Lieutenant Commander Data?" The Caldonian crewman glanced around the bridge, clearly befuddled by his abrupt arrival. "I don't understand. I was just in Transporter Room Three a second ago, then this strange man appeared out of nowhere. He had a Starfleet uniform, but I didn't recognize him."

"Understood," Picard said, suspecting that he had a better idea of what had occurred than the displaced lieutenant. Picard took this as confirmation that 0 had not yet caught up with Q, and thus an encouraging sign. "I believe you ran afoul of the entity called Q." Royel's eyes widened in recognition of the name; Picard envied the lieutenant his prior lack of personal contact with Q, who had doubtless moved on by now. "You may return to your post."

"Yes, sir." Royel still looked a bit dazed, but ready and willing to do his duty. He headed briskly toward the starboard turbolift.

What did Q want with the transporters? Picard had to wonder. He felt like he was fighting a war on three fronts. The Calamarain without, 0 within, and Lem Faal raising havoc in sickbay as well. The Calamarain presented the most immediate threat to the overall safety of the ship, he decided, so that took priority at the moment. Q would have to keep 0 occupied for the time being, while Riker dealt with the problem of Lem Faal. "Is the translation program still on-line?" he asked Data.

"Affirmative, Captain. You may speak normally."

Picard took a moment to survey the bridge. With the priceless exception of Data, the bridge was uncomfortably devoid of senior officers. Leyoro, Troi, La Forge, Riker . . . all were injured or occupied elsewhere on the ship. At the captain's direction, Lieutenant Jim Yang had taken on the rather thankless job of manning the frozen conn, leaving Ensign Berglund at tactical. Picard had total faith in the young officers, who had all graduated at the top of their classes at the Academy, but, deep down inside, he had to admit to being slightly troubled by the fact that the most experienced officer on the bridge, aside from he and Data, was none other than Reginald Barclay. *At times like this,* Picard thought, *I rather regret that both Worf and Chief O'Brien transferred to DS9.*

Still, there was nothing to be done about it now. "Attention, people of the Calamarain. This is Captain Jean-Luc Picard of the *Starship Enterprise.* Please call off your attack on this vessel. Like yourself, we seek to contain the entity known as 0, whom we recognize that you have a legitimate grievance with. Let us discuss this problem and arrive at a solution of benefit to us all."

The storm continued to rage outside, and Picard feared that the Calamarain would not deign to respond to his diplomatic overture. Then, coming over the comm system, an inhuman voice, flat and genderless, spoke for the gaseous life-forms laying siege to the *Enterprise:*

"We/singular am/are the Calamarain. Woe/vengeance to *Enterprise* for bridging moat/restoring chaos. Woe/tragedy to vastness/life entire. Crime/atrocity/madness. Shall not forget/forgive *Enterprise.* Dissipate/scatter/extinguish."

Riker had not overstated matters, Picard noted, when he said that Data's translation program still had some bugs to be worked out. This cryptic and expressionless communication bore little resemblance to the passionate discussions and debate that Picard had eavesdropped upon when he and Q observed the Calamarain in the distant past. Then the Calamarain had struck him as an immense symposium or university, devoted to the life of the mind and engrossed in an endless exploration of the cosmos, values quite in keeping with the highest ideals of Starfleet and the Federation. He heard little such common ground in the cold and somewhat garbled vocalizations emerging from the computer.

Still, the gist of the message was clear enough. The Calamarain blamed the *Enterprise* for releasing 0 back into the galaxy and were determined to exact revenge. How could he convince them otherwise, especially since the accusation was more or less true? He needed to persuade them that defeating 0 here and now was more important than assigning blame for the mistakes of the past. But how to do so, after Riker had done his best and yet failed at the same task?

I have an advantage Will did not, Picard realized. *I know who the Calamarain are and where they came from.* "Hear me," he said. "I speak not of the Calamarain, but of the Coulalakritous. I remember their suffering and understand their anger."

There was a pause, longer than before. Then the artificial voice spoke again, sounding as though it was coming from very far away:

"Who/how calls we/singular by oldest/sacred/hidden name? Who/how/why/where? Explain/illuminate now."

Well, at least I got their attention, Picard mused. The tricky part was going to be using this minor breakthrough to turn their attitude around before they did irreparable harm to the *Enterprise* and all aboard. "I have traveled to the past," he began, deciding that it might be more politic not to mention Q's involvement in that expedition, at least for now, "and I saw with my own eyes what 0 did to the Coulalakritous. It was an appalling crime and he deserved to be punished. But it is even more important that not he not be allowed to commit further crimes. Save your strength for the true enemy. Help us against 0 now."

Was it just wishful thinking, or had the thunder and lightning outside subsided to a degree over the last few minutes? Perhaps he was getting through to the Calamarain after all. He prayed that was so.

"Shields down to thirty-seven percent," Berglund updated him, adding yet more urgency to the Picard's efforts.

"Why bridge moat/succor chaos?" the Calamarain asked atonally. "*Enterprise* rescue/restore chaos then. Wherefore/how fear chaos now?"

That the Calamarain were seeking to understand the *Enterprise* at all, no matter how suspiciously, Picard took as a very positive development. He only wished he had a better answer. "We were deceived," he said simply. In truth, even now he did not fully understand what connection might exist between Faal and O, although the Betazoid scientist's bizarre behavior and inexplicable new powers strongly suggested that Lem Faal must have had a secret agenda all along. *Deanna warned me,* he recalled, *that there was something not quite right about Faal.* But who could have guessed he was working to let loose an ancient evil from the dawn of time?

"No/negative. *Enterprise* cannot be believed/trusted. Chaos-haven yesterday/today/tomorrow. We/singular cannot be misled/deterred."

The Calamarain punctuated their unambiguous refutation of Picard's claims with a resounding clap of thunder that set the captain's ears ringing and shook the bridge like a raft adrift upon a surging sea. "Captain," Data stated with admirable composure, "external sensors report increased tachyon radiation against our deflector shields, approximately 69.584 rems along the berthold scale and rising."

"Thank you, Mr. Data," Picard acknowledged, scowling. The Calamarain did not emit tachyons solely to communicate, he knew; they employed the faster-than-light particles as weapons as well, effective against both organic and inorganic matter. Only the ship's crumbling shields protected the crew and the *Enterprise* from the deadly emissions, but for how much longer?

He glanced back over his shoulder at the lighted schematic of the *Enterprise*-E mounted on the wall directly behind him. Blinking amber lights indicated malfunctions on practically every one of the ship's twenty-four decks. If only the cutaway diagram could show him where Q and 0 were . . . !

Orange and yellow sparks cascaded from the secondary aft science station. "Not again!" Barclay yelped, backing off from the console in a hurry. He cast a frustrated glance at the engineering station a few posts away, its surface already charred and melted from a previous conflagration. "Science Two inoperative," he reported dutifully.

"Take over at environment," Picard instructed briskly, filling the position left vacant when Lieutenant Yang took the conn. Obviously, he needed to end this pointless conflict with the Calamarain soon, while there was a bridge left from which to run the *Enterprise.*

It's that old business with Q, Picard realized, silently signaling Data to deactivate the translator for a moment. *The Calamarain don't believe us because we appeared to take Q's side when they came after him nearly a decade ago.* He didn't regret saving Q from a summary execution on that occasion—at least not entirely—but it didn't make winning the cloud beings' trust any easier. *Some kind of gesture of good faith is required,* Picard thought. *The burden of proof is upon the* Enterprise. *We need to trust them before they can trust us.*

"Ensign Berglund, prepare to lower shields at my command."

"Lower?" Her face blanched, but she quickly composed herself. "I mean, yes, sir."

"Captain," Data inquired evenly. Years of service

under Picard made him more comfortable addressing Picard than the ensign was. "Are you sure that is wise, sir?"

"It may be our only chance, Mr. Data," Picard said. Out of habit, he tugged his jacket into place before signaling Data to resume the transmission. "Captain Picard to the Calamarain, in memory of the Coulalakritous." The ancient name had made an impact upon the Calamarain before; it couldn't hurt to invoke it again. "To prove that we mean you no harm, and that we sincerely seek peaceful cooperation with your people during the present crisis, I am prepared to lower our defenses. Please accept this gesture in the spirit in which it is intended, and refrain from taking violent action against us until we have had the opportunity to speak further."

Do the Calamarain even comprehend the concept of a truce? The Coulalakritous that Picard observed in the past had impressed him as a peaceful people, not a warlike or predatory species, although who knew how much their culture and psychology might have changed over the course of a million years? *I guess we're about to find out,* he thought. "Ensign Berglund, lower shields."

"Yes, sir," she said with a gulp. For a moment, he was almost relieved that Lieutenant Leyoro was confined to sickbay. The Angosian security chief would have surely objected strenuously to this particular tactic. *And she might well have been right,* he conceded.

Picard held his breath, his body as tense as an

engaged warp coil, as Berglund carried out his command. The first evidence of its effects came when the brilliant blue flashes of the stressed shields vanished from the turbulent display of churning clouds and jagged thunderbolts upon the main viewer. He braced himself for everything from a catastrophic hull breach to the searing pain of radiation burns, but all that greeted his expectant senses was the muted rumbling of the storm as it seemed to hold back the full force of its fury. *Yes,* he thought, elated. The Calamarain were honoring the truce!

"Captain, look!" Ensign Berglund called out. She pointed at the ceiling above the command area, where a glowing mist was phasing through the solid duranium over Picard's head. He rose from his chair, his neck craned back, watching in wonder as what appeared to be an actual portion of the Calamarain entered the confines of the bridge. "Er, is this what you were expecting, Captain?" Berglund asked.

"Not exactly," Picard admitted, although this physical manifestation was not entirely without precedent. Ten years ago, during their previous encounter with the Calamarain, a segment of the gaseous mass had infiltrated the *Enterprise* in search of Q. *Welcome aboard,* he thought wryly.

The shimmering cloud, roughly the size of an adult Horta, descended from the ceiling and began to circulate around the bridge, inspecting its surroundings with evident purpose and curiosity. Lieutenant Barclay and the other officers were quick to make way for the traveling cloud, being careful to give it a wide berth, although the security officer stationed between the port and starboard turbolifts, Ensign Plummer, looked to Picard for guidance. "Shall I attempt to apprehend the intruder, Captain?"

Picard shook his head. He wasn't even sure how to approach the amorphous entity, let alone take it prisoner. "I believe we should think of this as more of an envoy than an intruder," he declared. The cloud completed its circuit of the bridge, then began to hover over the mangled engineering station, emitting a steady hum that reminded Picard of the honeybees in his father's vineyards. "Data, can we communicate with the entity at this proximity?"

"Just a moment, Captain," the android replied. His fingers moved across the operations panel faster than Picard's eyes could follow. "There," he announced less than five seconds later. "The revised algorithms, along with a directive to detect and produce low-intensity tachyon bursts via the inertial dampers, has been downloaded into the primary translation system linked to your comm badge. That should suffice, sir, within a 94.659 percent range of accuracy." He shrugged sheepishly. "My apologies, Captain. It was the best I could accomplish under such rigorous time constraints."

Give Data a couple more hours, Picard, *and he could probably compose sonnets in Calamarain.* "This will do, Mr. Data. Thank you." He approached the iridescent cloud, being careful not to make any movements, sudden or otherwise, that might be construed as hostile. He felt a tingling sensation, like static electricity, upon his hands and face as he neared the representative from the Calamarain. *Do they have individual names,* he wondered, *or even a singular noun?*

"Greetings," he said. "Welcome to the *Enterprise*. I am Captain Jean-Luc Picard." Ordinarily, he would offer a hand in friendship but that hardly seemed appropriate given the complete absence of anything resembling an appendage. The vaporous substance of the entity appeared completely undifferentiated; he couldn't begin to tell where its head was, if that term had any meaning at all to the Calamarain. *Hard to imagine,* he thought, *that Q and I actually assumed the form of the Coulalakritous during our voyage through the past.* Already, the experience seemed like a half-remembered dream; his human brain had never been meant to retain the experience of existing as an intelligent gas.

"I am/are of the Calamarain." The voice emerged from Picard's comm badge, sounding identical to the inflectionless tones the Calamarain as a whole had employed. "State/propose your intentions/desires."

Small talk was not on the itinerary, it seemed. "The entity called 0, who injured the Coulalakritous in the past, is aboard this vessel," Picard explained. "Can you help us subdue him before he does more harm?"

The cloud hummed to itself for several seconds before replying: "Negative/never. Chaos is too ascendant/hazardous. Condemned/congealed the Coulalakritous. I/we cannot oppose again/ever."

Picard thought he was starting to get a feel for the

Calamarain's bizarre syntax, but he didn't like what he believed he was hearing. Although perfectly willing to defend the galactic barrier or punish the *Enterprise* for its perceived transgressions, it appeared the cloud entities were not willing to confront 0 directly. Were they merely made fearful by ancestral memories of their defeat and persecution in the distant past, or was 0 truly that much more powerful than the Calamarain? If so, then all their struggles might be in vain.

"Captain," Data spoke up. "Forgive me for interrupting, but I believe I may have located a clue to the location of either Q or 0."

"Yes?" Picard asked. He recalled that he had asked Data to monitor power consumption throughout the ship in hopes of keeping track of 0's pursuit of Q. He considered deactivating the Universal Translator for this discussion, but reconsidered. *Let the Calamarain see and hear what we are doing to cope with the danger.* Perhaps it would inspire them to action of their own. *I might even settle for a useful suggestion or two,* he thought.

"The EPS power grid indicates that Holodeck Seven is in use," Data reported. He turned from his display console to face Picard. "I find this unusual during a state of red alert."

So did Picard. *That must be Q and 0,* he felt convinced. Who else would be playing games in a holodeck in the middle of a galactic emergency? "Excellent work, Mr. Data. I think you may be on to something." He spun around to face the envoy from the Calamarain, a strategy for survival coming together in his mind. It would take all his diplomatic skills to pull it off, but maybe there was a way to put 0 back in the bottle again, before he could enlist The One to his cause once more.

"Listen to me," he told the swirling cloud of ionized plasma, standing so close to the radiant entity that the minuscule hairs on the back of his hands stood at attention. "I know that 0 hurt you badly long ago, but maybe you don't have to fight him alone. . . ."

Chapter Sixteen

"DAD?"

Milo hoped that he was dreaming, that he hadn't really woken up yet, but knew in his heart that this nightmare was all too real. That really was his father, his eyes glowing like a Tholian, getting ready to perform some kind of experiment on a baby in a transparent bubble. Looking more closely, he recognized the baby as that weird Q kid who had popped into the holodeck during their first night aboard the *Enterprise*. A barely healed scab on his soul tore open again as he remembered how impressed his father had been by the Q baby, even as he ignored both him and Kinya. *Figures,* he thought. Even with all that had happened—cloud monsters and the barrier and everything—*that* hadn't changed. Their father still cared about everything except his own children.

"Milo, please come away from there," a voice said behind him. "It's not safe." Counselor Troi placed her hands gently upon his shoulders and tried to pull him away from the doorway. He was very relieved to see that his father hadn't killed her after all, but he didn't want to be shuffled off to some holographic daycare center again. His father had gone crazy, it looked like, and Milo had to find out what was going to happen next, no matter what. "Please, Milo." The counselor tugged insistently. "Come with me."

"No," he said emphatically and, to his surprise, her hands sprang away from him as if burned. *Did I do that?* he thought, astounded. It sort of felt like he did; right when she let go of him he sensed something flow out of him. Like telepathy, but stronger. He *pushed* her away, using a muscle in his head he hadn't even known was there before.

Funny thing, though. Counselor Troi didn't look half as surprised as he was. Scared, yes, worried, sure, but not surprised. He looked into her mind to find out why and, sure enough, there it was. *The barrier.* The galactic barrier had given him amazing new powers, just like it had his father.

Does this mean Dad's not dying anymore? he wondered. He didn't like the image of himself he saw in the counselor's thoughts, with the creepy glowing eyes and all, but maybe it would be okay if this meant that his father had been cured of Iverson's disease. Maybe their family could finally get back to normal, sort of.

The way his father was acting, though, that didn't seem likely. He had glanced in Milo's direction when he first showed up, and for a second Milo had thought he saw a trace of real live interest, and maybe even a glint of approval, in his father's spooky new eyes, but then he went right back to staring at the Q baby like it was the Sacred Chalice of Rixx or something. "Beginning environmental testing," he droned aloud, more boring science stuff like always. "Introducing concentrated zenite gas into observation chamber. . . ."

Zenite? Milo didn't get it. That stuff caused brain damage, didn't it? He watched in horrified fascination as a gray mist began to fill the transparent dome containing the Q baby. What was the point of this? Milo had read all his father's scientific treatises, about the barrier and wormholes and such, and he didn't remember anything about testing zenite gas on alien babies. He felt faintly sick to his stomach.

The baby's mother, whom Milo spotted on the other side of the dome, looked more than nauseated; she looked positively crazed with fear. Tears ran down her cheeks and her eyes were wild. From out of nowhere, she somehow produced the largest phaser rifle Milo had ever seen and fired it directly at his father.

"No!" Milo cried out, but his father just looked annoyed. With a wave of his hand, he created a vortex in the air that absorbed the phaser beam before it reached him. Milo's panicked shout attracted his father's attention, though. He looked away from the Q baby to peer at his own son with new eyes. *In more ways than one,* Milo thought.

Meanwhile, the gray fumes reached the baby's nostrils. He wrinkled his nose and made a face. Then he stomped his feet and the toxic smoke turned into a miniature rainbow that dissolved into a hundred prismatic floating crystals before vanishing entirely. "Oh, good boy, q!" his mother gasped in relief, while stubbornly trying to shoot past the vortex protecting Milo's father. She fired high and low and even attempted a ricochet or two, but his father managed to keep the vortex between himself and the business end of the crimson phaser beam. "That's a very good boy!"

"Interesting," his father noted, talking to himself. "Subject responds to negative environmental stimuli through metamorphic substitution. To compensate for subject's paranormal behavioral strategies, future tests must—" The oncoming phaser beam attempted to bypass Faal's vortex by branching into two separate streams. Faal barely managed to summon a second vortex in time, blocking both forks of the phaser attack, but the effort broke his train of thought. He glared at the mother Q with a look that Milo knew too well: the leave-me-alone-I'm-working look.

"Milo," he called out unexpectedly. "I need your help, son. Use your new powers to keep that interfering woman away from me. Use your mind. Mind is all that matters."

Milo was stunned and excited. His father needed

him? For the first time in months, since his mother died really, Dad was paying attention to him again, including him in his life. And all it took was these strange new powers. This was almost too good to be true.

"No, Milo!" Counselor Troi urged him. "You have to get away from here. Your father's . . . not well."

But he's still my father, Milo thought, shoving the counselor away more forcefully, all the way out into the adult ward. The more he used his new powers, the more natural they felt. *I can't let him down now, not when we finally have a chance to be together again.*

"Leave my father alone!" he shouted at the baby's mother. He felt kind of bad about it, since she just seemed to want her baby back, but his father knew what he was doing, didn't he? Maybe the baby wasn't really a baby, but some sort of the shapechanging alien in disguise. Like a Changeling or an allasomorph.

Whatever she really was, the distraught woman paid no attention to Milo, but just kept firing wildly at his father. By now the single beam had diverged into over a dozen separate forks, attacking his father from every conceivable direction. His father had been forced to transform his defensive vortex into a protective bubble that covered him from head to toe. "Please, Milo," he called. "I can't work under these conditions."

There had been a time, Milo recalled, before everything went wrong, that his father had sometimes taken Milo into his lab and let him help out with the experiments. Dad had given him simple tasks to perform, like replicating fresh isolinear chips or entering gravitational statistics into the wormhole simulations, and called him his "best lab assistant." Milo felt an ache at the back of his throat; he hadn't realized until now how much he'd missed that.

The ruby-red phaser beams hemming his father in, crisscrossing each other in their attempts to sneak past his defenses, reminded Milo of the Tholian webs in his favorite computer game, the same one he'd been playing the night he first met the baby Q and his mother. *Well, two can play at that game,* he thought.

With a thought, a pair of miniature Tholian warships popped into existence and flew straight for the woman (if that's what she really was) firing at his father. The diamond-shaped, prismatic ships began to enclose the woman within an intricate energy field consisting of overlapping rays of red-gold light.

At first, the woman looked more irritated than concerned by the web, sweeping the first few strands away from with the muzzle of her rifle, but Milo closed his eyes and concentrated harder. To his surprise, he discovered he could still see the entire room even with his eyes shut. He clenched his fists and the severed strands snapped back into place.

Behind him, Counselor Troi pounded uselessly on the soundproof forcefield he had erected in the doorway of the children's ward. Commander Riker stood beside her, scanning the door with a tricorder and shaking his head. The invisible wall swallowed her words, but he could still hear her thoughts in his mind. *Stop it, Milo. This is wrong. Your father is wrong. You'll just make things worse.*

"Please, Milo, don't do this," Dr. Crusher pleaded, echoing the counselor. He had barely noticed the doctor before, standing behind the baby's mother, safely out of the line of fire. Now she eased away from the other woman, seeking safety from the glittering Tholian vessels. "You're making a mistake."

No, he thought desperately. Tears stung his eyes. *You're wrong. You have to be.* Both the doctor and the counselor had argued with his father before. They had insisted that the barrier would harm Milo and his father, might even kill them, but it hadn't hurt them after all; it had made them stronger instead, maybe even cured his father of the Iverson's, which everyone said was impossible. His father had been right then. He had to be right now, too.

Didn't he?

Moving as fast as Milo's racing thoughts, the tiny Tholian ships completed the web around the mother Q, enclosing her completely within a lattice of gold and red strands. "Very good, Milo," his father approved. Milo couldn't remember the last time his dad had actually praised him for anything. "I'm proud of you, son. Proud, prouder, proudest."

Lem Faal added his own strength to the web, so that Milo could feel his father's thoughts pulsing alongside his as they worked together, father and son united at last. There was a strange sort of shadowy tinge to his father's thoughts, like a tone in his voice that Milo had never heard before, but he didn't care, not as long as they were a family again.

The web contracted swiftly, limiting the woman's range of motion. She tried to sweep the strands away again, yet only succeeded in tangling the muzzle of her weapon in the unyielding strings of energy. She finally managed to yank the rifle free, only there was no longer any room to point it anywhere but straight up. The phaser beam shot through a gap in the lattice, ricocheting off the ceiling to continue its Hydra-like assault on Milo's father. "What is this . . . ?" she snarled, frustrated and angry.

Come with me, Counselor Troi begged him telepathically. *Your sister is safe. Let me take you to her. She needs you, Milo.*

Milo's eyes snapped open. *That's no fair!* Milo thought. How could she ask him to choose between his sister and his father? It's wasn't fair at all! He looked over his shoulder at the exit to the children's ward. Where was Kinya anyway? And how would she fit in, now that he and his father had been brought together by the magic of the barrier? They couldn't just leave her alone. They were all she had, and she was just a little girl.

"It's all right, baby," the woman sobbed to her child, her fingers reaching out through the gaps in the web. The anguish on her face tore at Milo's conscience. "Mommy won't leave you."

Milo couldn't help thinking that the baby's mother seemed more worried about her little boy than his father was about Kinya. *Or about me,* he admitted, *before I got these powers.*

"Good work, Milo," his father encouraged him as the web continued to contract upon the hostile woman. She could scarcely poke her weapon through the constricting strands anymore. The multiheaded beam emanating from the phaser rifle dwindled to a single narrow beam as she had to concentrate more of her energy to keep the netting away from her face and body. "Crush her son. Mind over mother. Crush Crusher, too. Crush her. Crusher."

What? Milo blinked in confusion. He saw a look of fear appear on Dr. Crusher's face as she heard what his father said. Milo didn't understand. What had the doctor done, except try to help them? She's wasn't a shapechanging alien monster or anything. Why hurt her?

"Son?" the mother Q said. For the first time, the ensnared woman looked away from Faal and her baby to truly focus on Milo. He was suddenly very scared by the cold intensity of her regard. Nobody (except his father maybe) had ever stared at him with so little feeling or compassion. His mouth went dry and he started to tremble, especially after a crafty smile lifted the corners of the woman's lips. *Please, Dad,* he thought. *Don't let her do anything to me.*

Too late. In a flash, he suddenly found himself inside the web, held tight against the woman, whose right hand was clenched around his neck like a magnetic vise. Her phaser rifle had vanished, and she had her other arm around his waist, even as his own web held him fast as well, the glowing strands of energy digging into his skin like taut optical fibers. *How did this happen?* he wondered in despair. *Nobody told me she could do this!*

"You!" she snapped at his father. "You and the creature inside you. I have a painfully simple proposition for you. You have my son. I have yours. Give me back my baby or I will exterminate your unfortunate offspring posthaste."

To make her point clear, she squeezed Milo's neck until he whimpered. *Help me, Dad,* he thought. He wanted to be brave, but his heart was pounding in his chest and his skin had gone cold all over. He tried to push her away with his mind, the way he had Counselor Troi, but she was too strong for that. Between the netting and her iron grip, he couldn't move a millimeter. *Don't let her hurt me, Dad,* he pleaded.

"No!" Dr. Crusher exclaimed, hurrying up to the woman as close as the patrolling Tholian vessels would allow. "I know you want to get your baby back, but you can't hurt this boy. He's not to blame for his father's madness. He's just a child."

"Don't tell me that," the woman said sharply. She sounded furious enough to kill entire worlds if necessary. "Tell his father. It's his choice to make. A child for a child. A son for a son."

Milo bit down on his lower lip, trying not to cry. *Please, Dad, give her want she wants. Give her back her baby.* Maybe the woman would go away then. He and his father could start all over again, and Kinya, too. He still wasn't sure what his father wanted with the Q baby in the first place, but he didn't want to die for it. *We don't have any choice, Dad. Let her have the baby!*

To his dismay, his father had to think about it. "Milo?" he murmured, and for a second he sounded like the father Milo remembered, even with the weird white eyes. "My son?" Then all the emotion drained from his face and, his neck turning stiffly like a badly programmed hologram, he looked down at the baby in the bubble instead. "No," he said mechanically. "This is the child. The child of Q and Q. The child of the future of the evolution of the mind. . . ." A padd materialized in his hand, and he began tapping out notes, as if neither Milo nor the baby's mother were even there anymore. "Appendix: Some Thoughts on the Relationship Between Advanced Consciousness and Corporeal Manifestation. To be completed following eventual dissection of subject. Compare and contrast to Vulcan concept of *katra* and synaptic pattern displacement in postsomatic organisms. . . ."

Milo's jaw dropped open as a pain as large as Betazed itself crushed his heart. This was the ultimate betrayal. Just when it looked like his father had finally started caring about him again, just when Milo had let himself hope that the bad times and the loneliness were over, Lem Faal chose the Q baby—and some stupid experiment—over the life of his own son! Milo slumped against the woman behind him, held up by the Tholian webbing stretched tightly against him. As he gave up on his father, the web Milo had created, with the help and encouragement of that same false father, began to fade away, as did the two tiny Tholian ships. Despite the absence of the web, Milo didn't even try to break away from the woman's grip. *Go ahead and kill me,* he thought bitterly. *I don't care anymore.*

Instead she shoved him away without a second's thought. "Go," she said brusquely, like she had no more use for him. Milo stumbled across the floor, dazed and uncertain. His legs felt hollow and limp, and he had to grab on to the edge of a tripod-mounted scanner several centimeters taller than he was. Dr. Crusher hurried around the back of the laboratory to throw an arm around him and guide him toward the door. The doctor's efforts barely registered on him; Milo was too numb to notice. *Now what do I do?* he thought, hurt and relieved and bewildered all at the same time.

The baby's mother had no answers from him. Freed from the scale-model Tholian web, she had gone straight to the transparent dome imprisoning her son. "Hang on, little q," she cooed, trying to reassure the anxious toddler. Her voice cracked as she spoke. "Everything will be okay. Mommy will get you out of there somehow."

"Come along, Milo," Dr. Crusher whispered in his ear. "You don't have to stay here any longer."

Milo dragged his feet, unable to look away from the heartbreaking spectacle going on only a few steps away.

The Q baby bounced up and down inside the bubble, reaching out for his mother, his tiny hands pressed against the inner surface of the dome. He looked confused and frightened, mystified by the unyielding barrier between his and his mother. "Mommy?" he cried. "Mommy?"

A new pang stabbed Milo's battered emotions. At least the Q baby, whatever it was and why ever his father wanted it, knew that his parent loved him and wanted to protect him, which was more than Milo could say. He couldn't bear to watch them anymore. *I don't care if they're not what they appear,* he decided. *A baby deserves a mother who cares about him.*

"I'll help you," he blurted.

The doctor tugged on his arm gently. "Milo, I don't think this is a good idea. Just come with me."

Milo wasn't listening. Shaking off her arm, he ran up to the woman who had, only moments ago, threatened to kill him. "Let me help you. You and me. Two against one. Against *him.*" The aching pain in his chest turned into anger and determination. He couldn't let his dad wreck *another* family. "Let's get your baby out of there."

The woman looked down at him, anxiety and fear giving way to hope in her eyes. She scrutinized Milo from top to bottom, weighing his sincerity, then nodded her head. "Yes," she said hoarsely. "I'll try anything."

His father was still tapping notes onto his padd, muttering to himself in what Milo's mother used to call "academese." He inspected the readout on one of the mounted display screens, then keyed the data into his notes. "The subspace dimensions of the subject are highly variable, with little apparent correlation to dimensions of humanoid manifestation. Disparate suggests further lines of inquiry along fourth-dimensional axis. . . ."

"Stop it, Dad!" Milo shouted as loud as he could, using his mouth as well as his mind. No matter what happened next, he was going to let his father ignore him anymore. "It's over now. All of it."

Lem Faal looked up in surprise from his padd. "Milo?" He spotted the baby's mother standing beside Milo. "What is that irrelevant Q doing free again? I thought I told you to keep her under control."

Don't tell me what to do, Milo thought. *You don't have the right.* The anger poured out of Milo then. He couldn't have held it back if he tried. Months of pain and resentment and crushed feelings hit Lem Faal like the cloud monsters had hit the *Enterprise* before, over and over again. Lem Faal staggered backward, the padd with his ever-so-important notes crashing to the floor. The mother Q added her anger to Milo's, and it felt cleaner, purer than his father's contaminated thoughts had been. Between the mother's relentless need to rescue her child, and Milo's own resolve to end his father's madness, the power they wielded had become an irresistible force. Lem Faal tried to defend himself, vortexes and forcefields and flickering energy pulses springing into existence only to be blown away like cobwebs in a hurricane. He was driven back into a wall of monitors, the manifestations of his power evaporating like mirages. "Mind over matter," he babbled incoherently. "Mind over . . . Milo?"

All at once, the alien glow in his father's eyes was

gone. He looked confused and disoriented, clutching his chest as he gasped for breath, which whistled plaintively through lungs that sounded weak and clotted. "Where is your mother, Milo?" he asked. "Where's Shozana?"

He sagged to his knees, then collapsed face-first onto the floor. "About time," the mother Q said without a trace of compassion, "although I doubt that was all of him. That was just a little piece of 0 that found a bit of power to nest in." She spun around and reached out for the transparent dome. This time no forcefield deterred her and the dome crumbled to dust at her slightest touch. Within a second, she had her baby clutched to her chest, stroking his head while she cooed in its ear. "My poor little q! My poor, brave little q!"

Now that it was over, his father crumpled upon the floor, Milo felt thoroughly drained. *At least it's finally over,* he thought. *At last.* He felt like he had lost his real father months ago, the same time he lost his mother. The rest was just a bad emptiness that went on much too long. A little piece of zero, like the mother Q said. A living, breathing hole where a father should have been. He dissolved the forcefield over the entrance and Commander Riker and Counselor Troi rushed into the children's ward. Phaser in hand, the commander knelt to check on his father while Counselor Troi squeezed Milo's hand in hers. "Let's go see your sister, Milo," she said softly, and this time he didn't push her away.

* * *

"You really scared me there for a moment or two," Crusher said to the female Q, who continued to stroke and comfort her child. The doctor felt thankful things had turned out as well as they had, thanks to young Milo. "When you threatened to kill Faal's son, I wasn't sure you were bluffing. Remind me not to invite you to our weekly poker game."

"Actually, I prefer contract bridge," the female Q replied, regaining some of her previous hauteur now that the worse was over. She beamed at her smiling child, wiping away the tearstains on his cheeks. Crusher thought q looked none the worse for his captivity. *Never underestimate the natural resilience of children,* she thought. *Especially a Q child.* "Forgive me if I don't stay to tidy up," the Q continued, looking around at the biomedical chamber of horrors that Faal had transformed the pediatric unit into, "but I have a rather important errand to run."

"What about him?" Riker asked gruffly, calling the Q's attention to the prone figure upon the floor. "Are you quite sure he's powerless now?"

"A good point," the Q conceded. Her eyes narrowed as she gave the problem of Faal a moment's thought. Then a very Q-like smirk appeared on her face, preceding a white flash that lit up the ward for a single heartbeat.

When the light faded, the containment chamber had been restored, but now it was Lem Faal, curled into a fetal position, who was confined within the clear dome. "That should hold him for the time being," the female Q declared. "Do feel free to run any tests you choose on him. The more painful the better."

And then both she and q were gone, leaving Riker and Crusher alone in the pediatric unit. Beverly hoped that Jean-Luc and the other were faring as well with the Calamarain and that unknown intruder. One more thing puzzled her as well.

What kind of errand does the female Q have in mind?

Chapter Seventeen

"UGH. WHAT A REVOLTING SENSATION."

Q's skin still itched from his emergency beam-out; he'd forgotten just how crudely *tactile* primitive matter transporters could be. Still, it beat working up a sweat, he supposed. If he never saw another starship corridor or Jefferies tube for another hundred million years, it would still be too soon.

Nevertheless, here he was. Holodeck 7. Hundreds of alternative environments, and potential hiding places, available at his command. The next thing best thing to using his Q powers. *Quite ingenious,* he congratulated himself. 0 may have forced Q into this deadly game, but Q wasn't about to make it easy for him.

At the moment, of course, the holodeck was just a

big, empty room waiting to be filled with three-dimensional illusions. A stark yellow grid pattern was laid out on the walls, floor, and ceiling, which were a singularly uninteresting shade of black. A pair of red double doors, surrounded by a stream-lined archway that looked evocatively like a the-atrical proscenium, marked the entrance of the holo-deck for those who actually cared to enter via their feet. *Easier said than done,* Q thought ruefully, contemplating the unwieldy shackles about his ankle. He had hoped the transporter would leave the leg irons behind, but 0 had made them more stubborn than that. *I should have expected as much, but who'd expect a lunatic to pay such attention to detail?*

In its bare simplicity, the default version of the holodeck was about the least promising hiding place one could imagine. *But just give a few moments at those controls,* Q gloated, *and it will be a different story.*

"All right then," he addressed the archway, "show me the specialties of the house."

The holodeck controls, which had been pro-grammed to respond to a wide variety of verbal commands, complied by displaying a menu of avail-able programs on a lighted monitor embedded in right side of the proscenium. He scrolled through the various options, not quite certain what he was looking for, but confident that he would know it when he saw it.

Aikido. *Too strenuous,* he decided.

Altonian Brain Teaser. Meditation was not exactly what he had in mind.

Ancient West. *Too rustic, not to mention conducive to shoot-outs.*

Ballroom Dancing. *Crusher's favorite, no doubt.*

Bat'leth Practice. *Left behind by the redoubtable Worf?*

Barclay 1-75. *Too numerous to choose from.*

Bridge Officer Examination. *Please!*

Champs Élysées. *Too French.*

Camp Khitomer. *Too Klingon.*

Christmas Carol, A. He'd spent quite enough time haunting the shadows of the past, thank you very much!

Q scrolled through the menu faster, glancing nervously over his shoulder. As brilliant as it was, his transporter trick wasn't going to throw 0 off the trail indefinitely. He might be crazy as a chronal conundrum, but his former mentor had an undeniable talent for showing up precisely where he was least wanted. He raced through the vast array of selections at a feverish clip, examining and discarding options as fast as the display could produce them. **Denubian Alps.** No. **Fly Fishing.** No. ***Henry V.*** No. **Klingon Calisthenics.** God, no. **Lake Cataria.** . . . .

What about that delightfully seedy waterfront dive? he wondered. *With all that cheap hired muscle to throw at 0?* No, wait, that was on Janeway's ship. Would he ever have a chance to drop by *Voyager* again? Only if Picard came through, as was devoutly to be wished.

Moonlight on the Beach. No. **Orient Express.** No. **Rock Climbing.** No. **Romulan Firefalls.** No. **Tactical Simulation.** No.

Q was running out of time and hope when finally, near the end of the alphabetical listing, he spotted something that might suit his present purposes.

The Tempest. From Picard's beloved Bard, no less. Magic, trickery, and deferred revenge, plus an entire enchanted isle on which to elude 0. It was as close to perfect as he was going to find, particularly under the circumstances. Now if he could just call up the program before 0 arrived on the scene . . . !

The sound of a heavy object whistling through the air alerted Q only seconds before a spiked mace would have collided with his skull. Ducking just in time, he pivoted around to see 0 just a few paces away, his archaic pistol aimed at Q once more. "You can't trick a trickster, Q. Tricky, trickier, trickiest. A trick in a nick gives a bit of a kick."

His maniacal blue eyes searched their surroundings. "What's this, Q? This is what? Some kind of aboriginal game room? Very fitting. Fit, fitter, fittest. Good of you to get into the spirit of the thing; too bad the game's almost gone." He grabbed Q's arm to keep him from teleporting away, then cocked his revolver. Fingernails as long as knives dug into Q's wrist. "Any last words, Q? Better make them good ones."

"Yes," Q answered. "Begin program. Act One, Scene One."

The quiet of the holodeck became at once a scene of

utter chaos. Q and 0 stood upon the rolling deck of a ship at sea, caught in the fury of a sudden squall. Sheets of cold rain pelted both ship and passenger alike. Sailors and civilians, the latter clad in drenched royal finery, ran about the deck in a frenzy of activity, shouting commands and warnings and heated imprecations at each other. The sky was dark with stormy clouds, not unlike the Calamarain, and the crash of white-capped waves competed with the howl of the wind and the rumble of thunder to drown out pages' worth of theatrical dialogue. Jagged tines of lightning stabbed at the mast and mainsails, threatening to set the tempest-tossed vessel ablaze. "Hang, cur!" a villainous-looking boatswain managed to bellow above the din, directing his tirade at one of the bedraggled noblemen. "Hang, you whoreson, insolent noisemaker!"

I couldn't have put it better myself, Q thought. As anticipated, the abrupt change in venue, not to mention the general tumult, distracted 0 sufficiently that Q was able to yank his arm free from an ectoplasmic tentacle and rush across the pitching, rain-soaked deck to put a sturdy holographic mast between himself and 0's primed firearm. *Thank you, Willie,* he thought, *for an effectively over-the-top opening.* Searching the horizon in every direction, using the electrical glare of a thunderbolt to dispel the worst of the gloom, Q spotted, right on schedule, a verdant island less than a kilometer away, its leafy greenery offering both sanctuary and, more importantly, seclusion. From 0, as opposed to the storm.

"Q! Tricky, tricky Q!" 0 limped after Q, his mangled foot equitably slowing the vengeful madman as much as Q's fetters impeded his escape. He fired his revolver, taking a chip out of the wooden rail beside Q. "Take your tricks to a watery grave, Q!"

Exit, stage right, Q decided, tossing himself over the rail into the surging, frothing sea. For a simulacrum created by shaped forcefields and holographic images, the water was convincingly cold and wet. Almost too convincing, in fact; Q swallowed several mouthfuls of holographic brine before he managed to kick his way to the surface, his head emerging amid a flurry of waves and wind. His heavy leg irons hardly helped him keep afloat, but he trusted that Prospero's magic (and the dictates of the plot) would carry him safely to shore.

Another gunshot, splashing into the water only centimeters from his head, convinced him to give the program a hand by striking out for the island as quickly as a modified breast stroke would carry him. He was sorely tempted to turn himself into a dolphin or a Markoffian sea lizard, but he might just as well fire off signal flares announcing his precise location to his pursuer. There was nothing to be done except paddle along in a humanoid form rendered unfit for this pseudo-environment by several million years of terrestrial evolution. *I tried to tell them that leaving the ocean for the land was a huge mistake, but did they listen to me? Of course not.*

It took longer than he would have preferred, and his arms would have ached had he been genuinely mortal, but time and tide eventually deposited him on a sandy beach unmarred by any trace of human habitation. Climbing to his feet, he brushed the wet sand from the front of his soggy uniform, while a chill slurry of sand and seawater streamed from his hair, running down the back of his neck. *Brrr!* Looking out over the sea, he saw the last vestiges of the squall driving the abandoned ship to a waiting harbor; in theory, the rest of the dramatis personae would be washing ashore anytime now.

Best to get going, he realized. Having not instructed the computer to cast him in any particular role, he remained an extraneous element in this *Tempest,* unobliged to take part in the actual narrative. Still, there was no reason 0 couldn't race ahead of the plot as well, once his scattered mind came to grips with the radically revised playing field. Q wanted to be safely lost in the jungle before 0 set foot on the island.

Facing the sea, across a perilously exposed expanse of sand, the jungle awaited. A thick growth of towering mangrove and banyan trees offered shelter and shadows in which to hide, preceded by hedges of high grass and leafy ferns. He bolted for the overgrown foliage, wishing there were time to erase the sandy footprints he was inevitably leaving in his wake. *I could really use a bushy tail right now,* he thought.

"Q!" a demented voice cried out behind him. "All ashore who's dying ashore!" Q peeked back over his shoulder to see 0 striding out of the surf, his stringy hair plastered to his skull. He looked as though he had walked across the sea bottom all the way from the stormswept brigantine. *Why didn't I think of that?* Q thought, snapping his fingers. *Because it didn't follow the logic of the play?*

Another instance where 0's lunacy, and propensity for cheating, gave him the advantage. *I'm going to have to think a lot crazier if I'm going to beat him at his own game.*

A flag upon a golden pole materialized at the end of 0's upper right tentacle, which jabbed the bottom of the pole into the sand. "I claim this isle in the name of 0 the First!" he proclaimed grandly. The emblem on the flag was a numeral zero that looked like it had been scrawled in crayon, or maybe blood, by either a hyperactive three-year-old or a fugitive from an asylum. Q leaned strongly toward the latter.

"What shall I name this serene and sandy shore?" Q asked aloud. "Q's End? Q-Fall? Q's Just Deserts?" He laughed raucously. "Too bad this isn't a *deserts* island!"

I still have a chance, Q thought. The outer fringe of the jungle was only a few meters away. With little to lose, he used his power to add wings to his feet. Literally. Two pairs of feathered pinions, chafing slightly at edges of his shackles, propelled him into the sylvan sanctuary at hummingbird speed. A razor-edged boomerang chased him into the trees, slicing off the tip of an emerald frond before returning to 0's waiting tentacle. "Cheater!" 0 shouted angrily. "Cheat and charlatan! Cheat, cheating, cheater!"

Now there's the singularity calling the neutron star black, Q thought as he lost himself in the beckoning wilderness. He leaped over gnarled roots and trickling streams, heading ever deeper into the lush holographic scenery. He couldn't slow down to get some bearings because he could hear 0 crashing through the underbrush behind him, hacking at hanging vines and branches with machete in each hand and swinging tentacle. "Run, Q, run!" he hollered. "Rotting bones in the jungle are as good as a burial at sea any day. Any day!"

Not exactly Shakespeare, Q thought critically, but the intent was clear enough.

The atmosphere within the tropical forest was hot, humid, and redolent of jungle violets. A dense, green canopy stretched overhead, letting through only shreds of artificial sunlight. Banyan and mangrove, mahogany and teak formed an arboreal maze through which Q ducked and weaved, changing course at random while trying to avoid running into any low-hanging boughs. Thankfully, this unnatural simulation of nature had been designed for relatively easy navigation by culture-seeking Starfleet drones already wrestling with the pitfalls and perplexities of iambic pentameter, so it was not nearly as clotted with underbrush and difficult to traverse as a real jungle would be. Thus, Q was able to make fairly good time, even hobbled by his increasingly aggravating leg irons; alas, the same applied to 0, although Q hoped that the deranged entity was having so much fun hacking and slashing his way through defenseless foliage that he might not realize such strenuous exertions were not entirely necessary. *This is a fantastical romance,* he thought caustically, deriving some small pleasure from his opponent's inferior knowledge of earthly literature, *not a quest for King Solomon's Mines!*

They were not entirely alone within this fictional forest. Monkeys chattered in the treetops while small animals of undetermined nature rustled through knee-deep ferns and creepers. Sometimes he heard the whispered conversation of unseen fairies and spirits, or ran to the lilting music of invisible pipes and drums. *"The isle is full of noises,"* indeed, Q thought. Once he even glimpsed a misshapen humanoid figure, shaggy of hide and webbed of hand and foot, who loped sullenly through the jungle, muttering to himself in verse. Caught up in his own predestined plotline, Caliban remained unaware of Q's uncanonical presence.

It was rather charming, in a lowbrow human sort of way. Q found it encouraging that Jean-Luc Picard, he of the somber disposition and rigid decorum, could find value in something so thoroughly fanciful, and regretted that he was too busy fleeing for his life to fully soak up the atmosphere. *Maybe some other time.*

"I can smell you!" 0 cried gleefully. To Q's distress, he sounded much closer than before. "Smell you I can!" Footsteps behind him silenced the chittering pixies. The ethereal melody wafting through the trees took on a more ominous tone, the rhythm of the drumming keeping pace with the narrowing distance between Q and his foe. *As if his singsong chanting wasn't bad enough,* Q groused silently, *now he has his own musical score!* "Here we go a-Q'ing, a-Q'ing we will go!"

Maybe *The Tempest* wasn't so ideal a setting after all. What he had hoped would be a refuge had turned into a hunting ground, with himself as the live game. *It's these infernal fetters,* he complained silently, chagrined at the cosmic injustice of it all. How could he, the epitome of the unexpected, whose expansive imagination and ever-restless energy had carried him to every corner and cubbyhole in creation, be reduced to shambling through a computer-generated facsimile of a nonexistent fairyland tucked into a single compartment of a dust mote of a starship light-years away from anything resembling true civilization. *This is no way for a Q to die!*

"I can see you, Q!" 0 sounded so close now that Q was afraid to turn around for fear of spying the deranged, multilimbed monster practically on top of him. "See, soon, saw . . . saw you in half, I will! See if I don't!"

With the sickening force of an inescapable cliche, Q saw his life pass before his eyes. Not the whole thing, of course—0 would be able to kill him a hundred times over and still have time to have the Federation for dessert before Q could relive his entire immortal existence—but faces and places from his wild and wayward past flashed upon the viewscreen of his memory, like a kaleidoscopic slide show from the life and times of Q:

The antimatter universe. The heart of a sun. The cliffs of Tagus III. The Guardian of Forever. The

Coulalakritous. Gorgan, (*), and The One. The Tkon
Empress. The War. The barrier. The dawn of the New
Era. Guinan. Farpoint Station. Picard. The Borg. The
Calamarain. Sherwood Forest. Vash. Amanda Rogers.
Deep Space Nine. Sisko. *Voyager*. Quinn. Janeway.
The Civil War. Q. Little q. . . .

The only face he didn't see, the one face he couldn't
bring himself to look upon, even in his mind's eye,
was the face following close on his winged heels. The
face of his greatest folly.

The face that, in a flash, suddenly appeared in his
path. A smile like a skull's stretched across 0's weath-
ered features. His ice-blue eyes shone as bright as the
supernova that destroyed the Tkon. Snakelike veins
wriggled beneath the sallow flesh of his brow, threatening to erupt at any minute. Holographic seawater
still dripped from his beard. "Surprise!" he crowed in
manic delight. "Now you don't see me, now you do!"

Q's headlong momentum was such that he almost
ran straight into 0's outflung tentacles. At the last
second he threw himself backward, tripping over the
knotted root of a sky-high mangrove. He tried to
scuttle away, crablike, only to find that the chain
linking his legs iron was caught on that very same
root, which wasn't even a real root at all, but a
confounded concoction of forcefields and projected
images. *Hung up on a holograph, of all things! Talk
about adding insult to (mortal) injury.*

"A good game, Q," 0 congratulated him. "Was it
good for you?" He turned a machete into an iron
spike, which he used to pin the chain to the exposed

root, effectively nailing Q to the spot. "But after the best of tests, you end up like the rest. No matter the game, the end's always the same." He yanked a reddish hair from his own bristly beard, then sliced it down the middle with a long silver blade. "But you know that already, don't you? You figured that out a long time ago. Long, longer, longest."

No, Q thought defiantly. *For once, one of your cruel, childish games is not going end the way you planned. I'm changing the rules even if it kills me.* With his shackles pinned in place, Q could not blink away, so he did the one thing he could do. "Computer, restart program."

They were back on the boat. Thunder pealed in the heavens as the outmatched brigantine yawed hard to port, tossing 0 to one side. His bad left leg could not support the sudden shift in weight, and he fell to the deck like a scarecrow knocked down by the wind. "Hang, cur!" the boatswain cursed the impertinent Sebastian. "Hang, you whoreson, insolent noise-maker!"

With the intrusive root dispatched to the same computer bank as the rest of Prospero's island, the iron spike was wedged into nothing at all. The spike toppled over and rolled away down the deck, freeing Q, who leaped to his feet. He savored the sight of 0, unable to regain his footing, floundering upon the storm-soaked deck, while holographic sailors and noblemen stepped over and on top of him. "Give it up, 0," he gloated, looking down at his sprawling adversary. "You must see by now that I'm hardly the naive young Q you so easily misled before. That was a half a million years ago, and while you've grown crazier, I've grown craftier. A *lot* craftier. You might as well quit now."

"Quit?" 0 sputtered angrily. He crawled across the deck on his hands and knee and tentacles, dragging his twisted leg behind him like a serpent's tail. "Q is for quitting, not 0. Never 0!" His mask of jubilant insanity slipped away, revealing the millennia-old hatred and bitterness underneath. The sheer intensity of his malignant fervor was enough to silence any thought Q might have had of gloating further. He had not seen 0 so angry since the stranger, an exile from realms unknown even to the Q, had stood against the collective judgment of the Continuum. "Enough," 0 spat. "Enough! Enough! Enough!" He slammed his fist down on the wet, wooden deck, so hard that the timbers cracked. "No more tricks!"

In a heartbeat, they went from *Tempest* to tundra. The simulated storm at sea vanished, taking with it all the theatrical noise and tumult that had twice thrown 0 off balance. Nor was there even an enchanted island on the horizon, let alone a sea to swim to safety in. Instead he was alone with 0 in the center of a desolate, frozen wasteland that seemed to stretch on forever.

"How's your memory, Q?" 0 challenged, his breath misting before him. Now that the surface beneath him—once a wooden deck, now a sheet of snow-covered ice—had ceased to roll upon frenzied waves, he levitated off the ice in defiance of gravity, then landed on both feet opposite Q. "This ring a bell? Ring-a-ding, ring-a-ding?"

"How could I forget?" Q replied. A biting winter wind blew flecks of snow against his face while his regulation Starfleet footwear sank into the icy crust. Cold and distant stars shone in the dark sky far above the endless, rime-covered plain, providing only the faintest of starlight. A single burning torch, held aloft in 0's right hand, yielded most of what illumination there was, casting lambent scarlet shadows upon the frosty tundra. Q needed no prompting to recall the bleak, inhospitable icescape where he had first encountered the being who introduced himself as 0. He knew instinctively that this was no hologram. 0 himself had created this arctic limbo from his own obsessed and spiteful remembrances.

Just the same, he couldn't resist trying again. "Computer, restart *Tempest* program. Act One, Scene One."

Nothing changed. The wintry Siberian wasteland remained, appropriately, frozen in place. *I thought as much,* Q admitted with a sigh. Picard's clever little toy had been superseded by a creator of far more dangerous games and amusements: 0.

Q shivered involuntarily. Just from the temperature, of course. He was unquestionably underdressed for this irksome Ice Age environment. That 0 could just stand there, enduring the frigid conditions while wearing nothing more than tatters and rags, was yet more proof of his insanity. *As if any more were needed.* Q indulged himself by summoning a little extra insulation from the ether. *There,* he thought, as the fabric draped upon his frame thickened. *That's better.*

A profound impatience with 0's sadistic notion of fun and games swept over him, dispelling most of his sense of self-preservation, never one of his strongest suits to begin with. Wasn't it 0 who taught him that there was more to immortality to playing it safe? He wouldn't run again. At least not yet.

"No more hide-and-seek," Q said. "How far are you going to go, 0? What form of insane restitution do you require?"

"Listen to you!" 0 snarled. "You sound just like that haughty, humorless Continuum that used to make your life miserable." He spat upon the hoarfrost, which sizzled as energetically as had the metaphorical marble tiles in the courtroom of the Continuum. "I should have known you'd turn out to be just another cowardly, craven, cringing conformist after all. Q is for quitter," he chanted. "Quitter is you, Q!"

A harpoon appeared within his free hand and, ranting all the while, he hurled it at Q. It struck home with brutal force, spearing Q in the leg. His left leg, naturally, now as useless as 0's.

After dodging missile after missile since 0's return, evading blade after boomerang after bullet by the slimmest of margins, Q had been just a nanosecond too slow this time. He dropped, overcome by shock and agony, onto the cold, boreal plain, his falling body carving a deep trench into the snow. *Serves me right,* he thought, clutching his impaled leg and rocking in pain. A stream of his immortal essence leaked out of the wound onto the frozen crust. It looked strikingly like blood. *The big problem with omnipotence is that it leads so easily to overconfidence. . . .*

He felt sure that Picard would agree.

"Always a spear to spare. Never spare the spear, say I." Limping closer to his wounded prey, 0 chuckled and leaned over Q until his smirking face was less than a finger's length from Q, his hot breath fogging the air between them. "Game's over, Q," he said with surprising lucidity. "You lose."

Chapter Eighteen

"LIEUTENANT LEYORO, REPORTING for duty, Commander."

The Angosian security officer stepped out of the turbolift onto the bridge. Her eyes widened as she spotted Picard standing in front of a dense cloud of radiant plasma, hovering about a meter above the floor. Picard saw Leyoro reach for her phaser, only to discover it was missing from her side. It was hard to say, he thought, what had surprised her more: his return to the *Enterprise* or the presence of the alien entity upon the bridge.

"At ease, Lieutenant," he assured her. "We've reached an understanding with the Calamarain, whose representative this is. Unfortunately, the real challenge lies ahead. At the moment, the true threat is engaged with Q in Holodeck Seven. I was just about to beam directly there, along with the Calamarain."

"Permission to accompany you, sir?"

Picard considered her request. Some manner of security presence was in order, yet he was reluctant to introduce too many potential casualties to the conflict ahead. Ultimately, if his plan succeeded, the decisive role would be played by Q; there was only so much mere mortals could do to turn the tide in a battle between gods. *But that's just what I'm attempting to do,* he acknowledged privately.

"Excuse me, Captain," Ensign Berglund reported from tactical, "Commander Riker reports that the crisis in sickbay has been resolved with only one casualty: Professor Faal." She looked sheepishly at Leyoro, whose post she had assumed. "The Commander also reports that Lieutenant Leyoro has, um, gone missing."

Picard nodded. "Tell the commander and Dr. Crusher that we've located their missing patient." He gave the security chief a concerned inspection. Although hardly at death's door, as she'd been reported to be, she looked distinctly worse for wear. Dark circles hung beneath her eyes, which were shot with streaks of red. "Are you quite sure you're up to this, Lieutenant?"

"Yes, Captain," she said crisply. She walked over to the tactical podium and commandeered Ensign Berglund's phaser. "As head of security, it is my duty to see this conflict through to the end, sir."

Picard recalled the extraordinary physical feats that

her fellow Angosian veteran Roga Danar had performed during his stay on the *Enterprise*-D. The man had actually broken free from a transporter beam, a feat Picard had never seen duplicated, before or since.

"Very well, Lieutenant," he said. "I commend your devotion to duty." He quickly brought Leyoro up to speed on his plan, then turned toward Ops. "Mr. Data, is the holodeck still in use?"

The android stared at his console with a quizzical expression on his face. "I believe so, Captain, although present readings are unusual." He sounded as though he could not entirely accept what he was reporting. "As nearly as I can tell, it is *snowing* in the holodeck."

If that doesn't prove that Q is on hand, nothing does. Picard decided to move promptly before either Q or 0 could relocate. "Mr. Data, you have the bridge. Three to beam to Holodeck Seven."

"Yes, Captain," Data affirmed, directing transporter operations from Ops. "Good luck, sir."

We're going to need it, he thought, as the transporter effect washed over him, enveloping Leyoro and the Calamarain as well, *since even if my admittedly improvised plan can be put into effect, the outcome is by no means certain.* There were too many unknown factors, including the daunting question of whether he, or anyone, could get Q to put aside his ego and behave rationally. *That would be a first,* Picard thought dubiously.

He recognized what the holodeck had become the

moment his molecules reintegrated at the site. The windblown snow. The endless glacial emptiness. Even the faint gray stars high above. This was a flawless re-creation of that same polar purgatory where the young Q had been unlucky enough to make the acquaintance of 0. The cold, dry air stung his face and hands. A few steps away, her phaser drawn, Leyoro felt the cold, too, the icy wind turning her cheeks red. "Snow, all right," she said tersely, fog issuing from her lips. "Must be the place."

The Calamarain seemed unaffected by the cold. Picard recalled that the vaporous entities had to generate their own internal heat, and in significant quantities, in order to remain gaseous in the extreme cold of deep space. If anything, this environment was probably much warmer than the vacuum-dwelling life-form was accustomed to. *Perhaps someday,* he mused, *if and when the menace of 0 is contained, the Calamarain will permit themselves to be studied by Starfleet.* There was so much that could be learned from so unique a species, just as the Calamarain might benefit from being exposed to the mysteries of humanoid existence.

"Captain," Leyoro said, pointing to the eastern horizon of vast icefield, "over there."

Obviously, the Angosian government had augmented her eyesight along with everything else. Picard peered into the distance, blinking against the gusts of ice crystals in the air, but all he could discern was perhaps a faint red ember. "What do you see?"

"Two figures," she reported, "humanoid in appearance. They could be Q and that other entity you spoke of. They're confronting each other. . . . Captain, I think we'd better hurry."

Picard paused only long enough to make certain that the Calamarain understood his intentions. "We believe your enemy is nearby, with the other of his kind. Are you with us?"

The voice of the Calamarain, nearly as cold and lifeless as their current setting, spoke via his comm badge. "We/singular comprehend/corroborate. Chaos/plural imminent. Approach/caution/imperative."

Was that a warning, Picard wondered, *or a statement of intent?* It troubled him that the entity still declined to draw a distinction between 0 and Q, apparently referring to both as "chaos." That spoke poorly for the only strategy he could devise that might have a chance of succeeding against 0. *I'll have to cross that bridge when I come to it, which shouldn't be much longer.* "Let's go," he said.

Distances could be deceptive in a holodeck, where a generous panoply of illusory techniques were employed to create the appearance of entire worlds within a single chamber. Picard found it difficult to estimate how much ground they had to cover or even how far they had gone. The lack of any landmarks, not to mention the inherent difficulty of trudging through the deeply packed snow, frustrated him. He had to hope that any sort of contest between two ageless immortals would not reach its climax before they had a chance to arrive on the scene.

The Calamarain, who presumably could travel faster through the air than he and Leyoro could on foot, lagged behind them instead. *Perhaps that's what it meant by "approach/caution/imperative,"* Picard speculated. It was becoming increasingly clear that the Calamarain, collectively and individually, did not intend to lead any charge against the forces of chaos, but preferred to let Picard present the first target to their foe. *Rather like negotiating with the Romulans,* he concluded. *Look how long it took their empire to enter the war against the Dominion.* He just prayed it wouldn't take a martyr or two to bring humanity and the Calamarain together.

As they fought their way through the snow and wind, Leyoro took stock of the simulation in which they were immersed. "Rura Penthe?" she guessed, citing the infamous frozen prison asteroid where the Klingons once exiled their political prisoners.

"Same idea, different dimension," he informed her, reminded, as he had been the first time he beheld this forlorn wasteland, of Cocytus, the ninth and final circle of Dante's Inferno, where the greatest traitors in history were buried in ice forever. *That's undoubtedly where 0 considers that Q belongs. . . .*

Soon, no more than ten minutes at most, the red glow that he could now identify as a handheld torch exposed both Q and 0, facing each other amid the arctic desolation, just as they had over a million years ago, but in far less convivial a fashion. Picard watched in disbelief as the debased and demented tatterdemalion that 0 had become flung what looked like a harpoon into Q's upper leg, physically injuring Q in a way that Picard would not have thought possible only days before. Yanking the spear free of Q's metaphysical flesh, 0 raised it high above the wounded superbeing's chest, preparing to deliver the killing blow, as he had to the dying sun of the Tkon Empire. "Stop him!" Picard ordered, his voice carrying through the frigid air.

Leyoro fired her phaser at the harpoon, which stubbornly refused to disintegrate. The energy beam caught 0's attention, though, halting him in mid-stroke.

"Eh?" 0 contemplated the new arrivals with bemused indifference. "Specks and smoke. Smoke and specks." His gaze swung from the humans to the Calamarain and back again. "Come to pay your last respects?"

"I'm not dead yet, you rhyming monstrosity," Q protested, wincing as he spoke. He looked past Picard and his pained expression turned into one of shock and bewilderment as he spied the Calamarain, following Picard and Leyoro's sunken footprints across the snow. "Have you gone insane, Picard?" he accused, aghast. "One revenge-crazed arch-foe wasn't enough for me, you had to invite in this unforgiving fog as well? Have you forgotten that they want to kill me?"

"Take a number. Stand in line," 0 chanted, his

fingers wrapped around the shaft of the harpoon, "nobody kills Q until I get mine." He let go of the spear and stepped back, but the weapon remained suspended in the air, poised to impale Q. He winked at Picard and the others. "Want to watch? Watch to want? Watch away!"

The point of the spear descended inexorably toward where Q's heart would be if he had mimicked human anatomy as meticulously as he had created his counterfeit uniform. Sweat broke out on his brow as he used his remaining strength to telekinetically hold back the harpoon, which hung like the Sword of Damocles over Q's chest. Picard saw the weapon vibrate from the force of two conflicting wills, but knew that Q, injured as he was, could not hold out against 0's madness indefinitely.

"What is it, Picard?" Q cried out in righteous indignation, while his eyes stared at the harpoon as if it would cost him his life to look away for an instant. His voice held enormous reservoirs of self-pity. "You couldn't turn down a chance to get rid of me once and for all, now matter the cost to creation? Thrown in your lot with the Calamarain and 0 and all the rest who want me dead and buried? I never dreamed you could be so petty. *Et tu*, Jean-Luc?"

"Shut up and listen to me, Q!" Picard barked. "You have to join your forces with the Calamarain. It's our only choice. Neither of you has the raw power to oppose 0 individually, but together you might be able to subdue him. You have to try!"

Q laughed bitterly as the spear inched closer to his breastbone. "Always searching for the diplomatic solution . . . you're consistent, I'll give you that, Picard. But you're as stark raving mad as he is if you think that the Calamarain and I can make peace after a million years of vaporous vendetta. Have you forgotten what I did to them? What they tried to do to me?"

"Chaos/plural/not singular," the Calamarain stated flatly. "Indistinguishable/unacceptable. Cannot forget/forgive." The iridescent cloud ascended to the ceiling concealed by the illusion of an open sky. "Retreat/preserve/remember."

Grunting with effort, Q managed to press back the spearpoint for a centimeter or two, but what small respite he gained began to slip away within seconds, millimeter by millimeter. "See, Picard," he chided, seizing the chance for one last I-told-you-so, "the Calamarain can't even be bothered to tell 0 and I apart."

Picard felt his hopes soar away with the departing Calamarain. Nonetheless, he grabbed on to the spearshaft with both hands and added his own human strength to the telekinetic dual between 0 and Q. The iron harpoon was freezing to the touch, and his fingers had already gone numb from the cold, but he struggled against what felt like twice standard gravity. His arms were aching after only a moment. His palms and the pads of his fingers felt like they were welded to the freezing metal. He couldn't pull them away now if he tried. And the worst part was, he didn't even know if he was making the slightest difference.

"You might as well spare yourself a dislocated arm or two," Q suggested, spitting out the words from a face contorted by the herculean mental effort required to keep the spear a bay. "0's both gifted and truly insane. An unbeatable combination."

"Sounds like someone I know," Picard grunted. The iron javelin slipped downward suddenly, tearing at the skin of his palms. He held on despite the stinging pain, renewing his hold on the shaft.

"Flattery will get you nowhere, *mon captaine.*" The harpoon's point dug into the padded insulation of Q's modified Starfleet uniform. "I'm not nearly unhinged enough to derail his maniacal momentum. That would take real craziness!"

"And what could be crazier," Picard persisted, "than you and the Calamarain, of all people, saving the *Enterprise?*" Certainly, the entire venture, his last hope for saving the galaxy from the ravages of both 0 and The One, was looking more like a lunatic's fancy with each passing heartbeat. *Who is more insane?* he wondered. *0, or me, for thinking I could stop him?*

0 paid no attention to the insignificant efforts of Picard, distracted by the ascension of the Calamarain. "Smoke and snow. Snow and smoke. Choke, smoke, choke!" His cracked lips curled downward as he recalled, possibly, the way the Coulalakritous had forcibly expelled him from their collective being a million years ago. He clenched his fist at the fleeing

Calamarain, then began to squeeze. "Smoke into snow . . ."

Baeta Leyoro had seen a lot of ugly things in her career, but this 0 character took the grand prize. He looked like a half-mad Tarsian POW crossed with a bioluminescent squid from the pitch-black bottom of some alien sea. This was the creature that had killed poor Ensign Clarze, and brought the hostile Calamarain down upon the ship? She was willing to believe it.

But what was he doing now?

His fist was clenched so tightly that his elongated fingernails were digging mercilessly into his own flesh. It was as if he already had the Calamarain in his grasp and were squeezing them into submission.

And maybe he was. The plasma cloud's airborne retreat slowed, then began to reverse itself. The Calamarain dropped toward the snow-blanketed plain, losing altitude dramatically. The cloud appeared smaller, too, and more densely opaque. *He's compressing it,* she realized, hitting on the truth intuitively; somehow 0 was concentrating the free-floating plasma into a smaller and smaller space. She wondered urgently how much longer the Calamarain would be able to maintain a gaseous state under that crushing pressure.

Not long at all, as it turned out. Before her biochemically enhanced eyes, the Calamarain liquefied in midair, raining down upon the icescape like phosphorescent sleet. Leyoro ran to get out from beneath the bizarre precipitation, then twisted around to watch the shower of living liquid crash to earth less than four meters away. But were the Calamarain still alive, she wondered. Could they survive in such a fundamentally different state?

0 was not taking any chances. "Hah!" he hooted, enjoying his triumph. "Smoke to slush! Crush the slush! Crush!" Greenish blood leaked out between his clenched fingers as he continued to squeeze whatever remained of the Calamarain.

Leyoro raced to where the transformed cloud came to ground. She found the Calamarain pooled in a shallow depression in the icy crust. Prismatic reflections on the surface of the puddle made it resemble an oil slick upon the snow, seeping slowly into the frost below. But 0 wasn't finished with the Calamarain yet; as Leyoro watched, the glowing liquid grew thicker and more viscous. Its innate radiance slowly faded as it began to crystalize, freezing solid in a matter of seconds. Its amorphous boundaries congealed, becoming fixed and immobile. Leyoro didn't know a lot about the nature and needs of the Calamarain, but she had to assume that the once-gaseous entity had been locked into a state of suspended animation at the very least, which pretty much sent Captain Picard's longshot plan straight down the gravity well.

"Smoke to slush to solid," 0 gloated. "Atmosphere to ichor to ice. The smoke never learns. Never learns does the smoke!"

Leyoro got the distinct impression that the ranting monster had done this to the Calamarain before, which might mean that the frozen life-form could still be revived. An idea occurred to her: Once, during the war back home, after her scoutship had been shot down over the south pole of Tarsus, she had used her disruptor to melt the permafrost into drinking water. She had even warmed herself over the steam. Maybe that was the way to go.

She fired her phaser at the Calamarain, not to hurt, but to heal. At first it didn't seem to do any good, but then the hard crystalline edges of the cloud creature's remains began to deliquesce. The paralyzed alien seemed to absorb the heat from her phaser as fast as she could fire the energy into it. Her weapon, which was no longer a weapon, broke down the crystal lattice into which the Calamarain had been crammed. The solid sheet of plasma residue spread out as it melted, beginning to shine once more with a radiance of its own.

Her rescue efforts did not go unnoticed. 0 glared at her murderously, flinging his torch away in disgust. It landed upon the snow several paces away, sputtering fitfully. "Cheat!" he accused her. "Cheaters, all of you! Cheat, cheated, cheating!"

He didn't charge at her. He didn't need to. Without warning or cause, the phaser in her hand emitted a high-pitched whine that stabbed at Leyoro's ears and filled her heart with dread. *It's overloading,* she realized. *He's doing it somehow.* From the sound of it, she had less than a minute before the phaser exploded in her hand.

She stared desperately at the Calamarain. It had melted almost entirely now, but had not yet attained its original gaseous state. The simmering, shimmering puddle was just starting to come to a boil, barely beginning to evaporate. *I can't stop now,* she thought, urging the process on with the intensity of her gaze. *It still needs a few more seconds.* Bubbles churned upon the reflective surface of the ionized liquid that was the Calamarain, coming to a froth as the heat of the phaser sped up the molecules composing the fluid, sending them further and further apart. Incandescent fumes rose from the shallow pool, encouraging Leyoro even as the ear-piercing shriek of the malfunctioning phaser forced her to cover one ear with her free hand. *Almost there,* she thought, so close to success that nothing short of a quantum torpedo could make her stop now; if there was one thing she had learned about the Calamarain over the last several hours, it was that they really were Better Off Vaporized. . . .

The keening phaser erupted in a deafening explosion of searing heat and concussive force that sent her flying backward, landing flat on her back in a snowdrift several meters away from the Calamarain. Embedded in the ice, her face and front scorched and smoking, she felt like she was burning and freezing to death at the same time. The pain was excruciating; it was a wonder that she could even see it all after the blinding flash. *Let's hear it for Angosian medical know-how,* she thought, coughing up blood.

She didn't need a medical tricorder to know how extensive her injuries were. She didn't have a chance. *Funny,* she thought, as her vision blurred and began to go black, *I always thought I couldn't live without an enemy. Never thought I'd end up dying to save one.*

The last thing she saw was the reborn Calamarain rising like a immaterial phoenix from the ice, glittering with all the colors of the rainbow. . . .

> *"Handle with care the spider's net,*
> *You can't be sure that a trap's not set. . . ."*

While 0 sang exuberantly, mocking Q's approaching demise, the harpoon seemed to have a life and strength of its own, pressing toward Q's heart and dragging Picard's frostbitten hands with it. The exhausted captain felt the strain of resisting the spear in his back and shoulders and, most painfully, his arms. *It's ironic,* he thought. *After all the byzantine puzzles and brain-twisting trials that Q has put me through over the years, I end up standing in the snow, breaking my back to keep him from dying at the point of a primitive spear.*

Even the light seemed to be fading with his hopes, as 0's burning brand sputtered and died somewhere upon the barren plain. The miserly stars provided scant illumination, so that the perpetual night leached all the color from the scene, reducing the world to shades of black and gray. Would he even be able to see when the sharpened tip of the harpoon penetrated Q's ribs, or would he hear Q cry out first?

"Heedless of what might befall—
You neglect the spider on the wall. . . ."

Then a light broke through the darkness, shining
down on he and Q from directly above. He looked up
in surprise and saw the Calamarain, scintillating
against the bleak arctic sky like the aurora borealis.
But had the cloud entity come to aid them at last, or
to witness the long-awaited demise of the hated Q?

"Sacrifice/deliverance. Testimony/trust/gratitude.
Sacrifice/obligation."

Sacrifice? Picard heard but did not understand.
What did the Calamarain mean? That Q must be
sacrificed to win their trust and gratitude? "No," he
stated firmly. "We do not make bargains in the blood
of others. I will not be party to Q's death."

The Calamarain cast their resplendent light, quite
unlike the blood-red glow of 0's torch, upon Picard's
upturned face. "Misunderstanding/confusion. We/
plural grateful/obliged. Sacrifice/deliverance."

"I don't understand," Picard pleaded. He felt that
he and Q and the Calamarain were on the verge of a
breakthrough that could save them all, if only he
could find a better way to communicate. What did the
Calamarain want? Who was obliged to whom? What
was the sacrifice?

Or who?

Perhaps in answer, the cloud of living plasma
plunged toward Q's anguished face, oozing its way
past his flaring nostrils and clenched white teeth,

disappearing into his agonized body like a genie returning to a bottle. Q fought against the invasive vapor, twisting his head back and forth in a fruitless attempt to evade the iridescent mist that flowed into him against his will. Then his eyes seemed to widen in understanding and he stopped resisting and took a deep breath. As Picard watched, perplexed and anxious, Q *inhaled* the substance of the Calamarain, absorbing the alien entity entirely into himself. The whites of his eyes took on the opalescent luster of the living plasma.

> *"When the spider aims his deadly spikes,*
> *No one sees him till he stri—"*

0's insidious chorus was cut off in midverse when the possessed harpoon suddenly when spinning off through the air, coming to rest in a bank of snow far from Q, who sprang to his feet, his wound healed, his vitality restored. 0 gawked at him, dumbfounded, understanding little more than Picard. "What the devil?" he asked.

"We/plural/Q are ready/prepared for another game/contest/competition," the revived figure declared. The syntax resembled that of the Calamarain, the voice and the inflections were pure Q. "Do you/singular still like/enjoy games/contests/competitions?"

This was more than Picard had imagined when he first suggested that Q and the Calamarain join forces.

Taking him literally, they had merged into a single being, with the power and potential of both. Even 0, crazed as he was, appeared intimidated by the prospect. "No," he muttered into his scraggly beard, "one is two is one is two is one. . . ."

All the colors of the Calamarain glistened in Q's eyes as he raised his hand and released a bolt of lightning from his fingertips that crashed into the snow and ice in front of 0's rag-wrapped feet. "Tag/gotcha/checkmate!"

Unable to face what Q and the Calamarain had become, 0 tried to escape, taking off across the snow away from Picard and the Q/Calamarain. At first, he ran on two human legs, but when his crippled foot slowed him down, he fell forward onto his four lateral tentacles and scuttled over the packed snow like a spider. Picard stared in wonder and disgust, until his eyes fell upon a charred and motionless body lying askew upon the ice not ten meters away.

Dear God, no, he thought, feeling a chill that had nothing to do with the wind or the weather. *The sacrifice. . . .*

Unlike Picard, the Q/Calamarain did not pause to grieve. His/their lightning chased after 0, halting his frantic flight with a white-hot thunderbolt that left him sprawled upon the ground. More lightning rained down on him, and as 0 shuddered spasmodically beneath their impact, Picard heard an awe-inducing rumble of thunder that came from outside the holodeck, perhaps even outside the hull of the *Enterprise,* penetrating the created world of 0's polar limbo with its inescapable reality. *The rest of the Calamarain,* he guessed, *surrounding the ship.* Could it be that the fragment of the Calamarain now residing within Q was channeling the collective might of the entire gaseous community, adding the full strength of all the Calamarain to the power of Q?

It was hard to imagine, but how else to explain the undeniable shift in the balance of power that had occurred when the Calamarain merged with Q? As he had hoped, the sum of two infinite powers had indeed proved more infinite than infinity. Conventional mathematics said otherwise, but, as Picard knew full well, there was nothing conventional about the Calamarain or, especially, Q.

Beneath the barrage of transcendental thunderbolts, 0's human guise began to slip away once and for all. Flesh and hair and teeth and eyes crumpled away like powder, until all Picard could see was a writhing mass of otherworldly tentacles that flailed about in agony, churning the packed ice and snow into a swirling haze that thankfully obscured the horrific vision. Then the besieged extradimensional entity began to physically shrink in size, its tendrils retracting and diminishing until all that was left was a tiny wriggling creature about the size of a small jellyfish.

Or a spider.

The Q/Calamarain strode across the tundra, leaving deep tracks in the snow, until it towered over the pathetic specimen. The little multilegged monster tried to scurry away, but it could not outrun the shadow of the Q/Calamarain's upraised foot. The sole of his/their boot hovered over the creature for one ominous moment, and Picard thought he heard an almost inaudible squeal of fear. Then the shoe descended, squashing 0 flat. A single thin tendril, no larger than a hair, stuck out from beneath the shoe, quivering weakly. The Q/Calamarain smiled with obvious satisfaction.

"Game/competition over. We/plural/Q win."

Chapter Nineteen

"WELL, IT'S A NASTY CASE of frostbite, but nothing modern medicine can't take care of."

Beverly finished wrapping Picard's frozen fingers in thermal conduction strips, then stepped aside to allow him to stand up and step away from the biobed. His fingertips still felt slightly numb but the doctor's treatment had gone a long way toward restoring their circulation. *If only Lieutenant Leyoro and Ensign Clarze could be restored as well,* he mused sadly. No matter how many times he lost one of his crew, the pain never got easier. He could only note in his log that they had perished in the performance of their duty; he could think of no better epitaph.

Geordi La Forge approached him from the other side of the primary ward, where Nurse Ogawa had just finished a test on his optical implants. "Well, Captain," he said, "I must say you're a sight for sore eyes." Picard was glad to hear that Geordi's implants had not been permanently damaged by Lem Faal's telekinetic rampage. *In the end,* he reflected, *Lem Faal's most lasting victim may well have been himself.*

A broken man, his frightening powers long gone, the celebrated Betazoid scientist, and apparent pawn of 0, now occupied his own biobed not far away. He sat upright, his spine supported by Starfleet cushions, as he stared vacantly before him with eyes that no longer held the lustrous gleam of the galactic barrier. Listening to the man's labored breathing, and observing the feeble life signs reported on the overhead monitor, Picard could not imagine that Faal had much longer to live. *A tragedy,* the captain thought, *but not nearly as terrible as the consequences of his misguided pursuit of immortality.*

Young Milo Faal sat beside the bed, holding his father's trembling hand and speaking to him softly. "It will be all right, Dad. We're going home now, where we belong. You don't need to worry. I'll take care of you."

A curious role reversal, Picard observed. The boy had indeed become more of parent to his father than a son. He admired the youth's maturity and compassion, especially after all he had heard of the shameful way Faal had neglected and abused his children. Picard could not help holding Faal's various crimes against him; still, given the sorry state to which the scientist had been reduced, he felt certain the man had been punished enough. *He's a lucky man to have a son like Milo.*

Perhaps aware of Picard's thoughts, the Betazoid boy turned to look in the captain's direction. A chill ran through Picard when he saw those unearthly white eyes directed at him. *There's a problem I wish I had a solution for.* The boy had not deigned to use his new powers since subduing his father in the pediatric ward, but Counselor Troi had confirmed that some residue of the barrier's unnatural power, derived from the Q themselves, still dwelt within the mind of this child. *How can I be sure that those powers will not pose a danger to Milo or others?*

A flash of light burst between Picard and Milo, and, for one tense moment, Picard feared that the youth's amazing abilities had been heard from again. Instead, he was surprised and relieved (and surprised to be relieved) that the light had merely heralded the arrival of the entire Q family, all three of them. *Who would have ever thought,* he wondered, bemused, *that I would ever greet the appearance of Q with anything less than dismay?*

As it was, he did experience a degree of apprehension. "What brings you here, Q?"

"Oh, nothing much," Q replied brightly. He patted the head of baby q, happily draped over his mother's shoulder, and strolled over to Picard. "Odds and ends, really. For instance, I thought you might be interested to know that my good wife here has called the recent contretemps to the attention of the Continuum and persuaded them, fractious as they are these days, to undertake an immediate project to shore up both barriers and repair all those worrisome fractures, which have proven to be just too tempting to impetuous and irresponsible species such as yourself."

We're irresponsible? Picard thought, not sure whether to be amused or appalled by Q's gall. Still, if Q wanted to shift the blame for the 0 crisis to humanity, Picard had neither the energy nor the inclination to argue the point. At the moment, that is. "And what of 0?" he asked, addressing the only point that truly mattered.

"Back where he belongs," Q assured him. "If I were you, Picard, I'd persuade your superiors at Starfleet to leave the barrier alone from now on. Even putting aside the problem of 0, the Federation, as well as your assorted allies and rivals, are simply not ready to venture out of the galaxy just yet."

"We may surprise you," Picard said, unwilling to impose an absolute limit on the future of space exploration. That was Starfleet's decision, not the Continuum's. On that point, at least, he remained steadfast. "Still, it is always best to be fully aware of the dangers involved."

"Oh, there are dangers you haven't even conceived of yet," Q promised, a mischievous twinkle in his eye. "Perhap I'll introduce you to them someday."

Don't trouble yourself on my account, Picard thought. He watched with growing uneasiness as the female Q, babe in arms, wandered away. Although Q did not seem to up to any particular deviltry on this occasion, he saw no reason to encourage their stay. "Is that all?" he asked.

"Actually, there is one more little matter," the female Q said, although she seemed less interested in Picard than in young Milo Faal. She joined the boy at his father's bedside, and spoke to him with unexpected gentleness. "Milo, I think you know you still have a piece of the Q inside. I'm afraid I have to ask for it back."

"That's all right," Milo said. He looked sadly at the wreckage of his father, perhaps considered all the anxiety and unhappiness that Lem Faal had caused in his thirst for that same power. "I don't want it."

The female Q smiled approvingly and laid her hand upon Milo's inattentively combed hair. Picard saw a soft purple glow sparkle between the woman's outstretched fingers before fading away. More important, he also watched with relief as the eerie white sheen in Milo's eyes faded as well, leaving behind eyes as big and brown and recognizably Betazoid as Deanna Troi's. "Thank you," the woman said. "You're a very well behaved boy. For a mortal."

And with that, she vanished without further ado, taking her own preternaturally precocious child with her. "Well, I suppose I'll be heading on, too," Q commented. "I'm overdue for an rendezvous in the Delta Quadrant."

"Before you go," Picard delayed him, knowing he would probably regret it, but discovering there was one final question that he could not resist posing. "After all we've been through these last few days, both in the past and the present, could it be that, perhaps, you have finally learned your lesson about the evils of testing other sentient beings?"

Q smiled impishly, looking altogether incorrigible and unrepentant. "But, Jean-Luc, how do you know that this entire odyssey hasn't been a particularly ingenious test?"

And then he was gone, leaving Picard with even more questions than before. Questions with a capital Q.

Epilogue

BEGIN AGAIN. Again, begin and begin. . . .

Behind the wall once more, he howled in frustration. For one brief interval, not more than a tormenting twinkling in the endless expanse of eternity, the galaxy had been his again. Worlds without end had awaited his wicked wiles and wild, wayward will. But then Q had taken it all away. Q!

Ever again. Forever again.

He scratched and clawed and snapped at the wall, which refused to yield to his frenzied need to strike back at Q. The wall was as permanent and punishing as it had ever been, any minute cracks and crevices healed and sealed, leaving him not even a sliver of a window into the great, glittering galaxy he might never see again. A galaxy of smoke and specks and Q and Q and Q. . . .

Forever and ever. Ever and forever. Forever and never.

The voice on the other side, the voice that had come at his call, bringing with it a fleeting fraction of freedom, had gone silent, leaving him alone in the dark and the cold and the eternal emptiness. Had he ever really been free at all? He couldn't be sure anymore. His mind rebelled at the very thought of what had occurred—and what lay ahead. Space was vast and time was long, and all he had now was space and time, forever and ever and ever. It was enough to drive him sane.

A new beginning had ended. His new ending had only begun. . . .

Look for STAR TREK Fiction from Pocket Books

Star Trek®: The Original Series

Star Trek: The Motion Picture • Gene Roddenberry
Star Trek II: The Wrath of Khan • Vonda N. McIntyre
Star Trek III: The Search for Spock • Vonda N. McIntyre
Star Trek IV: The Voyage Home • Vonda N. McIntyre
Star Trek V: The Final Frontier • J. M. Dillard
Star Trek VI: The Undiscovered Country • J. M. Dillard
Star Trek VII: Generations • J. M. Dillard
Enterprise: The First Adventure • Vonda N. McIntyre
Final Frontier • Diane Carey
Strangers from the Sky • Margaret Wander Bonanno
Spock's World • Diane Duane
The Lost Years • J. M. Dillard
Probe • Margaret Wander Bonanno
Prime Directive • Judith and Garfield Reeves-Stevens
Best Destiny • Diane Carey
Shadows on the Sun • Michael Jan Friedman
Sarek • A. C. Crispin
Federation • Judith and Garfield Reeves-Stevens
The Ashes of Eden • William Shatner & Judith and Garfield
   Reeves-Stevens
The Return • William Shatner & Judith and Garfield Reeves-
   Stevens
Star Trek: Starfleet Academy • Diane Carey
Vulcan's Forge • Josepha Sherman and Susan Shwartz
Avenger • William Shatner & Judith and Garfield Reeves-Stevens

#1 *Star Trek: The Motion Picture* • Gene Roddenberry
#2 *The Entropy Effect* • Vonda N. McIntyre
#3 *The Klingon Gambit* • Robert E. Vardeman
#4 *The Covenant of the Crown* • Howard Weinstein
#5 *The Prometheus Design* • Sondra Marshak & Myrna
   Culbreath
#6 *The Abode of Life* • Lee Correy
#7 *Star Trek II: The Wrath of Khan* • Vonda N. McIntyre
#8 *Black Fire* • Sonni Cooper
#9 *Triangle* • Sondra Marshak & Myrna Culbreath

Star Trek: The Next Generation®

Encounter at Farpoint • David Gerrold
Unification • Jeri Taylor
Relics • Michael Jan Friedman
Descent • Diane Carey
All Good Things • Michael Jan Friedman
Star Trek: Klingon • Dean W. Smith & Kristine K. Rusch
Star Trek VII: Generations • J. M. Dillard
Metamorphosis • Jean Lorrah
Vendetta • Peter David
Reunion • Michael Jan Friedman
Imzadi • Peter David
The Devil's Heart • Carmen Carter
Dark Mirror • Diane Duane
Q-Squared • Peter David
Crossover • Michael Jan Friedman
Kahless • Michael Jan Friedman
Star Trek: First Contact • J. M. Dillard
The Best and the Brightest • Susan Wright
Planet X • Michael Jan Friedman

#1 *Ghost Ship* • Diane Carey
#2 *The Peacekeepers* • Gene DeWeese
#3 *The Children of Hamlin* • Carmen Carter
#4 *Survivors* • Jean Lorrah
#5 *Strike Zone* • Peter David
#6 *Power Hungry* • Howard Weinstein
#7 *Masks* • John Vornholt
#8 *The Captains' Honor* • David and Daniel Dvorkin
#9 *A Call to Darkness* • Michael Jan Friedman
#10 *A Rock and a Hard Place* • Peter David
#11 *Gulliver's Fugitives* • Keith Sharee
#12 *Doomsday World* • David, Carter, Friedman & Greenberg
#13 *The Eyes of the Beholders* • A. C. Crispin
#14 *Exiles* • Howard Weinstein
#15 *Fortune's Light* • Michael Jan Friedman
#16 *Contamination* • John Vornholt
#17 *Boogeymen* • Mel Gilden
#18 *Q-in-Law* • Peter David

Star Trek: Deep Space Nine®

Star Trek®: Voyager™

Flashback • Diane Carey
Mosaic • Jeri Taylor

Star Trek®: New Frontier

Star Trek®: Day of Honor

Star Trek®: The Captain's Table

Book One: *War Dragons* • L. A. Graf
Book Two: *Dujonian's Hoard* • Michael Jan Friedman
Book Three: *The Mist* • Dean W. Smith & Kristine K. Rusch
Book Four: *Fire Ship* • Diane Carey